WASP

UNCOMMON ENEMIES: PANTHER FORCE
(BOOK ONE)

FIONA QUINN

WASP

Panther Force

Uncommon Enemies

By

Fiona Quinn

THE WORLD OF INIQUUS

Ubicumque, Quoties. Quidquid

Iniquus - /i'ni/kwus/ our strength is uncqualled, our tactics unfair – we stretch the law to its breaking point. We do whatever is necessary to bring the enemy down.

THE LYNX SERIES

Weakest Lynx

Missing Lynx

Chain Lynx

Cuff Lynx

Gulf Lynx

Hyper Lynx

STRIKE FORCE

In Too DEEP

JACK Be Quick

InstiGATOR

UNCOMMON ENEMIES

Wasp

Relic

Deadlock

Thorn

FBI JOINT TASK FORCE

Open Secret

Cold Red

Even Odds

KATE HAMILTON MYSTERIES

Mine

Yours

Ours

CERBERUS TACTICAL K9 TEAM ALPHA

Survival Instinct

Protective Instinct

Defender's Instinct

DELTA FORCE ECHO

Danger Signs

Danger Zone

Danger Close

This list was created in 2021. For an up-to-date list, please visit FionaQuinnBooks.com

If you prefer to read the Iniquus World in chronological order you will find a full list at the end

of this book.

.

This book is dedicated to Ciara
A wise owl.
My teacher.

And to all those who pursue science with a strong ethic for the greater good.

1

ZOE

DABBUR ZANN ALA KHARAB ESSHOH

The buzzing of the wasp brought ruin to its nest

— EGYPTIAN PROVERB

ZOE TWISTED her body into a new position under her blankets. Tugging the covers up under her chin, she desperately wished for sleep to overtake her anxious, over-caffeinated mind. She squinted at the clock readout glowing from her bedside table, calculating. It had been forty-two hours since she'd last closed her eyes. And even that had been a nightmare-driven sleep, leaving her worse off than when she'd gone to bed.

That night, her flip-flopping and moaning had propelled Gage from her side. He'd stomped across her room, pulled on his pants, and headed home to "actually get a little shut-eye." She hadn't heard from him since. Zoe rolled over to punch at her pillow, trying to find a restful position to curl her body.

He didn't answer my text.

Her friends had warned Zoe about seeing a new guy just as she'd signed contracts to start a lab project, especially one this big and this time-sensitive. But first off, Zoe didn't like to be told what to do. And second? Gage was a Marine Raider, an elite special operator, with a highly capable warrior's body. Why shouldn't she have a little indulgent pleasure to balance out the stresses of her day? Days. She hadn't slept for days.

Metal on metal, a scrape sounded at Zoe's front door, followed by the slow moan of unoiled hinges. A smile curved her lips as she imagined Gage sauntering into her apartment to answer her request for some stress relief.

Good. This is precisely what I need.

She sat up, regretting having pulled on Gage's sweats to wear to bed. She flipped her covers to the side. It would be nicer if he found her in something lacy…or maybe nothing at all. Zoe gathered the hem of the black hoodie to tug it off, but whispers from the living room stilled her hands. More than one set of heavily booted footsteps stole over the wooden floor, followed by the scratch of a drawer sliding open.

Zoe froze. Her mind was on fast forward, but the joints of her body held tight, as if rusted and ineffectual. Her brain screamed at her arms and legs to move, to grab a weapon, to hide. Something. *Anything.*

As she cowered there, her ears worked to dissect the moth-like movements down the hall. She registered the sound of each leaf of paper as it was lifted and rejected. She had a good idea of why someone had broken into her condo. Her liaison, Colonel Guthrie from DARPA—the Defense Advanced Research Projects Agency, the R and D arm of the US military—had warned her to take extra security precautions, but she had scoffed at the idea. Few people actually knew what Zoe did for a living, and as long as she was tight-lipped, she thought she was safe. She was foolish, was more like it.

This could be an ordinary breaking and entering, she tried to reason. But her gut refused to be that naïve. Everyday robberies didn't happen on the twentieth floor in a secured high-rise. When the intruders were done sifting through her desk, surely they'd come and wrench answers from her. Zoe couldn't handle pain. She wasn't a hero. She'd tell them everything.

Straining against her fear-paralysis, Zoe slid off the bed. First her toes, then her knees found the rug. As she pushed and forced herself into action, her brain whirled, feeding her information. She knew that her limbic system was working hard to keep her alive. Though letting off the brake on her body's movements would go a far distance in helping her. Ironic that the system meant to save her was probably going to expose her instead. Her mind whirled with odd tidbits of information that she knew couldn't be random. Her brain was sifting through data it had accumulated in its twenty-eight years of life and thrust specific stories forward—survival strategies.

The loudest message came from a book she had read about Nazi Germany. The Jews, in hiding, would gather all of their bed linens and turn the mattresses over so the Gestapo wouldn't feel the warmth from where their bodies had lain. Zoe eyed the crumpled linens on her queen-sized bed. She forced her arm to smooth the covers into place and shake the pillow, so it looked like a sloppily made bed. She snagged her phone from the nightstand as she pulled her arm back to her side. The effort left her panting.

Her unyielding lungs had lost their elasticity. In the ninth grade, her friend, Hope McBride, stood in front of the class to give a speech and stopped breathing until she turned red, then blue, then passed out on the floor. That's how Zoe had learned the phrase *anxiety-induced syncope*. The idea of passing out with intruders in her apartment was even scarier than her current panic, so Zoe worked to suck more air up her nostrils.

Hide. She had to hide. Zoe let gravity pull her the rest of the way to the floor. The sheepskin rug muffled the sound of her collapse. She rolled, tugging her body past the green dust ruffle until she lay under her bed. It was hide-and-seek 101—the very first place anyone would search. Her body iced at the thought.

Light waves, her brain whispered. That was how the intruders would become aware of her. Her body mass would stop the light from hitting the rear wall. *Move. Move now!* The best she could do was to swivel and align her hips with the far corner of the bed, letting her legs extend out the length of the wall; her torso stretched across the headboard. She glanced down at the phone, clenched in her fingers, and drew a blank on whom she should call for help. Someone from DARPA? The Pentagon? Zoe was learning to hate adrenaline. Thoughts refused to crystalize. Pulling up her recent calls, hoping for inspiration, she saw FBI Special Agent Damion Prescott's name and tapped out a text that read: **SOS**. She pressed send, then quickly squeezed the button to silence the ringer.

Zoe listened past her panting. The guest bedroom door scraped open. Then the bathroom. They were getting closer. Zoe toed the elastic at the ankle of Gage's sweat pants over her feet. She turtled her head and hands into the perspiration-soaked hoodie to hide her skin. The number 9-1-1 suddenly surfaced and floated to the top of her swirling thoughts. She dialed.

"9-1-1. Where is your emergency?"

Zoe wanted to jump through the phone and throttle the man for answering so loudly. "Shh. Listen." She managed to say just as her bedroom door snicked open. Zoe pushed the phone into the front pocket of the hoodie, hoping the dark fabric would hide the screen light. Her body was traitorously loud. Her pulse swished rhythmically in her ears. Her heart rate galloped. Her breath came in ragged gulps. Zoe knew they would hear her. And if they didn't hear her, they would surely smell her as her adrenal glands forced fear stench through her pores. The intruders would drag her out from under her bed. Then they would…

Before Zoe's brain formulated a prediction, a loose floorboard squeaked as someone moved into her room. The bedroom light clicked on. Exasperated voices conferred. She heard someone move toward her closet and the whoosh of hangers being thrust aside. Zoe stopped breathing. A hand shot under her bed. Fingers splayed wide, it swished through the air before it pulled back out again.

As foreign words in deep male voices jumbled their syllables together, Zoe tried to pick out what language the men were speaking. There was a pause in the men's discussion, then in heavily accented English, "She isn't here. Her bed hasn't been slept in." He was on his cell phone. "Yes, okay… Be there in five."

The front door whined on its hinges. "Hey, Zoe. I'm here." The sexy grin in Gage's voice pried open Zoe's jaw and dragged a horrified scream up her throat.

2

GAGE

G AGE'S REACTION WAS INSTANTANEOUS. S UDDENLY THROWN back to his days in the Middle East when he'd be laughing in the streets with his buddies then shot at from behind, his survival instincts didn't need priming. He was on the starting block, ready to jet into action. Gage raced down the hall.

A man in tactical gear with black face paint distorting his features filled Zoe's bedroom door. A long blade glinted in his hand. Without breaking stride, Gage's heel shot out to catch the guy's knee, forcing it backward. The intruder's arms flew up for balance. Gage slammed his fist into the tango's throat, crushing his windpipe.

As the hostile collapsed, Gage caught movement in the bedroom's far corner. An unsub, identically suited up, sprang toward the fight. Gage leaped over the dying man to get his feet clear of obstruction. The second tango depressed the button on his stun gun. Sparks crackled as he descended on Gage. Gage blocked the man's arm, twisting his body inward and exploding out in a back fist that broke the man's nose. Gage's boot settled on the man's stomach as he push-kicked him out of reach, driving the man into the highboy. The intruder's head whipped back with his momentum, cracking against the sharp edge of the wooden lip. Gage hurled himself forward, wrapped his fingers around the man's trachea, and squeezed until the threat had been neutralized.

Gage pushed back, winded by the exertion. He scanned the room, then shot through the condo, scouring the place for any other intruders.

Returning to the bedroom, he reached under the bed and dragged Zoe out into the open. Her body was slack, her skin gray. He held shaking fingers to Zoe's carotid artery, muttering a prayer under his breath that he'd find a pulse. In the field, he never felt fear when he killed the enemy or saved a victim—the fear came when Gage thought he'd lost someone from his team, his family.

With the steady thrum of her heartbeat under his fingertips, Gage sucked a lungful of air through his nostrils and sent a cloud of stress back out past his lips. He slapped his fingers lightly against Zoe's cheek. "Zoe? Hey there, Zoe. Open your eyes."

Her mahogany hair shifted back and forth, the long strands tangling in her eyelashes as she roused from her faint. Suddenly, Zoe's lids opened wide with shock. She scrambled to her knees, fists raised protectively. "Gage?" she whispered, as if not trusting what was in front of her.

"It's me, Zoe. You're safe." His heart beat furiously against his ribs, pumping blood to his muscles, held at the ready. His face was contorted into the brutal scowl he wore into battles. He worked to relax his stance and take the violence out of his eyes, so Zoe could feel secure.

Zoe's gaze shifted to the intruders in their heaps of wayward body parts. Gage watched her eyes lose their focus and roll back in her head. Her body seemed to melt. Clapping iron hands onto her arms, he lowered her onto the rug. "Zoe, it's going to be okay. You're safe." He put conviction into the words he hoped would bolster her, but his warning antennae buzzed. He didn't really know if she was safe or not. "Stay with me, Zoe. Come on. Deep breaths."

She nodded and sucked in a lungful of air. Gage focused on her body, sprawled limply in front of him. His hands swept methodically over every inch of her as he looked for blood or other signs of trauma. "Did they hurt you, Zoe? Did they touch you?" His mind tried to grasp why two armed men were in Zoe's condo.

"No, I hid." Her words rattled between chattering teeth.

Gage pushed to standing. He kicked the black military-issue bag lying near the bureau. Zip-ties, a prison hood, and a neatly folded field stretcher scattered across her floor. He kicked the bag again to reveal a plastic bag with syringes and a vial of transparent liquid. In one stride, he towered over the second man he had killed. He pulled his phone from his pocket and took a picture of the tango's face, then one of his profile. Gage scrolled through his apps list and pulled up his finger-print display. Using the hem of his shirt to cover the man's hand, Gage rolled the guy's thumb and index finger onto the screen.

"They were here to kidnap you?" Gage stooped to gather the same identification info from the guy lying in her doorway. "Why would they want to do that?" Gage dipped his head as he checked the guy's pulse, to be doubly sure that there was none.

"Kidnap?" Zoe tried to jump up but fell forward onto all-fours, her stomach heaving.

Gage shoved his phone back in his pocket and wrapped his arm under her hips. He half-carried, half-dragged Zoe to the bathroom. As she hunkered over the toilet, sirens sounded in the distance. Zoe pulled her phone from her pocket and whispered, "Thank you. I can hear them coming."

Gage read the numbers 9-1-1 on the screen before she tapped the red dot to disconnect, leaning with a moan back over the toilet bowl.

"It's going to be all right." Gage smoothed a hand over her hair and gathered the strands into a makeshift ponytail away from the bile Zoe was gagging out. "I've got you. You're safe."

Funny, but as many times as he'd said that out loud, his words held zero conviction. He had been through enough crap on his special ops missions that he'd learned to trust his instincts. And right now, every cell in his body said this was just the prelude.

Zoe tilted her head to the side and swiped the back of her wrist across her mouth. Her skin, which was usually sun-kissed tan, a gift of her Hawaiian ancestry, was still pale and clammy. Gage pulled off his jacket and tucked it around her. She plopped onto her bottom and pulled his jacket tightly about her shivering frame as she squirmed backward and hunkered against the bathroom wall like a hurt animal.

A fist hammered against her front door. "Police. Open up."

Gage put a steadying hand on Zoe to make sure she wasn't going to keel over and smack her head into the tub, then made his way to the front door.

"Hands. *Hands*!" The officer shouted with his finger twitching near the trigger of his holstered gun. Gage laced his fingers, planted his hands on the top of his head, then took two slow paces back to give the officers space to move into the condo. Gage followed the gaze of the cop in front as it landed on the contorted leg of the dead man at the end of the hall. The cop rolled Gage and slammed him up against the wall. Gage's hands flew out and smacked against the drywall to stop his nose from being crushed. A forearm pressed into his back. His feet were kicked to widen his stance. Nervous hands patted him down, yanking his knife from his waistband.

"Special Agent Damion Prescott, FBI." Gage heard at the door. He wished he could turn his head to see, but the officer's hand splayed across Gage's scalp, fastening him in place with what felt like the officer's full weight.

FBI? Gage's mind went to the reasons why tonight could have possibly played out like it had, and all he could come up with was that the Zoe he thought he knew was not the real Zoe. She must be involved in some pretty deep shit. As the officers introduced themselves as responding to a 9-1-1 call for help, Gage let those thoughts float around in his head. Testing them out. He couldn't believe for a second that Zoe would do anything outside of the law. Nope. He wasn't buying it.

Prescott, judging from his institutional-looking suit, moved past him to stick his head around the bathroom door. He swung his focus toward Gage. "Is she hurt?"

"She's in shock." Gage didn't move from his wide-legged stance, his cheek crushed against the wall. "She needs an ambulance." He heard one of the officers in the front room call for a paramedic.

Prescott pushed farther into the apartment to stand in front of Zoe's room. "The apartment was searched and secured? Only two?"

"Yes, sir," Gage responded.

"Would you let him off the wall already?" Prescott asked the police.

When the officer released him, Gage gave himself a shake.

Prescott looked past him toward the officers, who had tripled in number since Gage had opened the door. "This is a case of national security. The Bureau will be along for the ride."

3

GAGE STOOD WITH HIS BACK AGAINST THE COLD SURFACE OF THE fridge, his arms crossed over his broad chest. He was squeezed into the tiny kitchen with DCPD Detective Adamson and Special Agent Prescott. Both of them asked questions and scribbled notes, even though their tape recorders sat on the counter beside him, digitally capturing every word out of his mouth.

"What can I say? I don't know what's going on. I got a text from Zoe saying she wanted me to come over. I finished up with work—"

"At Quantico? Is that your base?"

"Quantico, for now, my unit is based out of Lejeune." Gage scrubbed a hand down his face. "I grabbed a quick shower and drove up here to spend the night. When I walked through the door, Zoe was screaming her head off, and some knife-wielding ops guy was lunging at me."

"Ops? How do you know that?" Prescott asked.

"He was combat trained. It was his stance. His eyes. The way he held his weapon. The knife was held backward in his hand.

Once you've been face to face with the real deal, it's not hard to spot someone with advanced training."

Prescott nodded.

"The only reason I prevailed was that I shocked the hell out of them when I walked through the door." He nodded his head in the direction of the dead men. "They came ready to restrain a sleeping female, give her a shot, and wait the twenty minutes or so for efficacy to do whatever the hell they were sent to do. From their gear, I'd guess a snatch and drag."

"Sent?" Adamson asked.

"It sure looked like a mission. Someone outside must have been running them."

"Do you think they were US military?" Prescott asked.

Gage sent him a scowl. "We weren't exactly exchanging phone numbers to hook up for a beer later. They didn't say anything from the time I arrived on scene until they were neutralized."

"So, Zoe screamed. You see two guys. You assumed they were there for criminal reasons, so you killed them." Adamson skimmed a finger down his notes as he listed off the sequence, then looked up at Gage with raised eyebrows.

Gage closed his eyes then opened them in disbelief. "Serious?" he asked.

"They could have been playacting some kinky scene." He tipped his head. "Is Zoe into that kind of thing?"

"She's Ms. Kealoha to you," Gage snarled as he pushed Adamson back against the counter and pinned him with a hard bone from his forearm against the detective's windpipe. "Are you fucking kidding me right now?" he growled through clenched teeth.

Prescott stepped forward to lay a hand on Gage's shoulder.

"Hey, hey, hey. I apologize for the detective. Let's cool the temperature down a bit."

An EMT walked into view as he pulled a stretcher down the hall. When Gage moved toward Zoe, he heard Adamson snarl, "Don't you *ever* apologize for me."

"He just killed two men with his bare hands to save his girlfriend's life. Do you really want to wrestle with that tiger while he's in combat mode?"

Gage reached for Zoe's hand and entwined his fingers with hers. She looked up at him, her beautiful obsidian eyes shining with horror. "I'm so sorry. I'm sorry," she stuttered out.

Gage kissed the back of her hand. "I'm glad I was here for you. You're safe now." He tried to soothe her with the calm tone of his voice. He still didn't believe this was the end, but those were the words that sprang from his lips. It physically hurt to see her so vulnerable. She shook violently under a space blanket that wrapped her body, keeping her shocked system from further collapse.

"We've got to get her to the hospital now, sir," the EMT said.

Gage bent to brush a light kiss onto her cheek and released her hand. "I'm going to help the police, then I'll come to be with you." He looked at the EMT as they headed out the door. "Which hospital?"

"Inova Alexandria."

"As soon as I can, Zoe, okay?"

THE FORENSIC PHOTOGRAPHER had been in to document every inch of the crime scene. The medical examiner had collected the bodies and taken them to the morgue for identification. The police were finishing up, and Gage was given permission to pack a bag to take to Zoe.

As he moved to the bathroom, Gage kept his ears open for any stray intel being passed back and forth between the PD and the FBI. Just outside the door, he heard Prescott cornering Adamson.

"Hey, if anyone from the media asks, it would be great if you all could seed some misinformation about the victim dying in the attack—keep the bad guys off her trail until she can be taken to a safe house for debriefing."

Prescott thought Zoe was in danger too. Enough that she warranted a safe house. His intuition wasn't off.

"You want me to lie?" Adamson asked.

"Lie? No. That would be hard to backtrack. Just plant a seed. Say something like you need to contact the family, with a look of sorrow in your eyes."

"Sorrow?"

"Yeah, dust off your acting skills."

Both men moved, and Gage pulled a travel case from the bottom drawer of the cabinet. He filled it with Zoe's toiletries and makeup, eyeliner and mascara, some tinted gloss. She liked the natural look. To him, she was effortlessly beautiful. And honestly, Gage couldn't imagine that she cared enough about what others thought of her to go to any extensive effort.

He bent down to pick up her phone from where it lay on the bathmat, then pulled her purse forward to tuck it in the front pocket. A lanyard with two work identification badges lay exposed on the corner of her vanity. He lifted them to inspect the picture of Zoe in her lab coat. He'd never seen her dressed for work. It was a DARPA issued SCI biometric badge. His brows drew together. "Sensitive Compartmented Information, Zoe? *Dr. Zoe Kealoha?*" He flipped to the second ID, a tag for Montrim

Industries. He examined her photo. Same gentle curve of her lips, same intelligent eyes framed with black plastic geek-girl glasses, same pristine white lab coat, hanging from her slender frame, same Dr. Zoe Kealoha printed beneath. "What the hell?"

Prescott leaned a shoulder against the bathroom door jamb. His gaze moved from the lanyard in Gage's hand to look him squarely in the eye. "What are you thinking?"

Gage shoved the IDs into the purse and zipped it shut. "She needs her glasses." Gage crowded past Prescott, moving to Zoe's bedroom to retrieve her glasses from the top of the alarm clock, where she always put them while she slept.

"Do you know what Dr. Kealoha does for our government?"

They were alone in her room. The techs were in the hall, snapping their cases shut. Gage focused over on him. "Not a fucking clue. She told me she was a lab tech."

"Yeah, well it's more like 'she does tech in a lab.'"

"Do you know what she's working on?" Gage had tried for nonchalance, but he knew his voice was colored a deep shade of pissed off. Six months together, and he had no clue, she held a doctorate or worked for the military. What else was she keeping from him?

"I know one of the projects she developed because I'm field testing the prototype. But what she's doing now? I'd say knowing that would give us some pretty big clues as to why someone wanted to take her for a ride tonight. I'd really like to find that out."

You and me both, buddy.

THE LAST LAW enforcement showed themselves out the front door, encouraging Gage to lock it behind them. Gage checked his phone for the time; it was nearing zero one hundred hours. The hospital probably wouldn't let him slip in to see Zoe in the middle of the night. He rubbed his index finger back and forth over his chin. Surely, she would have called him if she'd been released. He did a quick search for the hospital number and dialed. He had little hope of gathering any information because of HIPAA restrictions. But the nurse who answered said that he was listed on Zoe's advanced directives form on file. While he waited to talk to Zoe's nurse, he wondered when Zoe had filled out those forms. How long had she thought that he was one of the people she could rely on to make a health decision if she was incapable? That thought just about winded him. If any other woman he had dated had been so presumptuous, without even a discussion—yeah, he wasn't really into taking on a burden like that for them. But for Zoe? It felt like a victory of sorts. He'd need to take those thoughts on a long jog after this mess settled down a bit.

"Gage Harrison?" A female voice spoke past the background noise of metal on metal and low-pitched conversations.

"Yes, ma'am."

"Dr. Kealoha was admitted for shock and exhaustion. We were having trouble getting her vitals regulated, so she accepted sedation. will reassess in the morning."

"She's sleeping now?"

"We have her in room 606 with an IV running, so we can adjust her meds as needed. She's resting comfortably."

He remembered how vulnerable she looked on the gurney. How fragile. "Can I come and sit with her?"

"We have an open visitation policy. But between the hours of 9 pm and 5 am, you'll need to show your ID and sign in for a visitor's pass."

His nerves iced. "And anyone can sign in during that time? Anyone can come see her?"

"Yes, sir."

"You know that Dr. Kealoha was attacked, and that's why she's in the hospital, right? Is there anything that can be done to increase her security?"

"I'll bring it to the security officers' attention. We can restrict her nighttime visitation to you and Colonel Guthrie, who is also on her directives list. I'm not sure what can be done during regular visiting hours, but I'll ask."

"Thank you."

After tapping a finger on the screen to end the call, Gage opened his gallery to take a good hard look at the pictures he'd snapped of the men who had come after Zoe. Of all the questions asked and answered that night, the one that poked at him was whether these guys had been American. Prescott was insinuating that there might be a foreign group interested in Zoe, or maybe not Zoe, as much as her research.

Gage scrolled through his contacts until he got to Titus Kane, a retired Marine Raider now functioning as a force commander for Iniquus. Iniquus was an entity that signed both private and public security contracts with deep-pocketed sources. They often served as intermediaries when the governmental alphabets weren't playing nice in the same toy box. Iniquus was free to cut through the red tape and push the envelope on what constituted the letter of the law to take down bad guys, especially in politically delicate areas of the world. With Titus's encouragement, Gage had recently interviewed for a job with them. Iniquus had a sterling reputation, and they treated their operatives with respect and provided them with ample resources to get their jobs done. Gage still had another month to decide whether or not to re-up with Uncle Sam. But for now, it was those resources that Gage had his focus on.

"Kane here."

"Do you ever sleep, man?" Gage leaned his head back against the wall and closed his eyes.

"Just drinking my morning joe. I'm on graveyard tonight. What's up?"

Gage quickly briefed Titus on the evening's events. After a long pause before Titus said, "Glad she's okay, man. You followed protocol and took photos and fingerprint ID?"

"Affirmative. The tangos were painted, so it's hard to see the planes of the face. The ear pics are pretty clear. I was hoping you'd give the data a whirl through your search engines. See if you couldn't pop up an ID."

"Roger that. Send them through. I'll get on it before I punch the clock."

"Thanks, man."

"Sempre Fi, brother."

Okay, that's good. That's a step in a forward direction. Gage needed to take another step, and another, and another until he figured out who had gone after Zoe and how to keep her safe. He was up and pacing. He felt caged in and wanted to be out beating the bushes for whoever pushed the buttons to make those tangos jump. He'd learned the hard way on his very first deployment; you had to chop the head off the snake to kill it.

Gage ran through the hospital conversation again. Who was this Colonel Guthrie to Zoe? Why was he on her advanced directives list? Was he someone from DARPA? Gage knew a guy named Colonel Stan Guthrie. His unit had run parallel ops on occasion with his. He liked the guy; they got along just fine. He moved to the counter, dragged Zoe's purse over, and fished out her phone. After swiping the code onto the screen to access her contacts, he looked up Guthrie.

Gage examined the icon next to the Colonel's name. Same guy. He wondered if the hospital had gotten in touch with him and if he knew what was going on. Gage considered calling, but then, he didn't know what kind of relationship the colonel and Zoe had.

Zoe and Gage had never had the "exclusivity" discussion, but he had been monogamous with her. Since he met Zoe, all other women had fallen off his radar. Of course, his decision making wasn't necessarily Zoe's decision making. Gage typed the Colonel's address into Google Maps. He wanted to look Guthrie in the eye when he told him about Zoe's attack, get some kind of read on what their relationship was all about.

What the hell else am I going to find out about you tonight, Zoe?

4

GAGE

"HOOAH, SON. IT'S A MIGHT LATE TO BE RINGING FOLKS' doorbells, don't you think?"

Colonel Guthrie was dressed in blue striped pajamas and a plush robe that he held tight against the December cold.

"I'm sorry to disturb you, sir. I'm here because of Zoe Kealoha."

"Zoe?" The Colonel scanned over Gage's shoulder at Gage's car parked by the sidewalk light. "Come on in, Marine." He stepped back from the door, and Gage moved into the dimly lit craftsman-style home.

Gage shot a look up the stairs.

"You didn't wake the wife. She's off visiting her sister. I was just about to have a finger of scotch to settle me in for the night. Can I pour you a tumbler?"

"Thank you, sir, but no."

Gage stood in the middle of an oriental rug as the colonel moved to a side table crowded with lead crystal decanters. "It's nigh on zero dark thirty. I'm sure you showing up at this hour means bad things for Zoe." Guthrie moved over, so they were standing side by side and eye to eye, both just over six feet tall. "Let's have it."

"Sir, may I ask how you know Zoe? Do you work together?"

"I recommended her for her current position. At DARPA, I'm her direct supervisor. Her dad and I were in boot camp together. He was smart and got out once he scratched twenty years onto his belt. Every time my contract comes up, I get bitten by the same damned bug and sign up for another round." He took a swig from his glass. "When Hani Kealoha and his wife were headed back to the islands to retire, he asked me to keep an eye on Zoe for them, be there if she needed me." The colonel's face grew stern. "You're here, and she's not, so what's going on? And how did you come by my name as having a connection with Zoe?"

Gage gave him a sanitized version of the night and concluded with, "Both of our names are on her hospital directives, sir. I got your address from her phone. She's being treated for emotional shock after the break-in. She's also suffering from exhaustion from lack of sleep. I thought it would be best if I came by in person on my way to the hospital."

The colonel knocked back the rest of his scotch. "Not hurt, though, you say? Just nerves and exhaustion?"

"Yes, sir."

"Good. That would be one hell of a phone call to her parents."

The front window lit up as a car pulled up on the front lawn and parked kitty-corner in the grass. "What in the hell?" The colonel moved to throw the front door wide. He stood with his lips pushed into a tight pucker. Gage could hear a car door open.

"Chuck, you son of a bitch. What the hell are you doing on my lawn, you drunken shit-for-brains?"

A man in a grey suit staggered toward the front door. The

colonel glanced back toward Gage and scowled. "Son…" His head swung around to the drunk, staggering up the stairs. "God damn it."

Gage got the message. "Would you mind if I helped myself to a glass of water in your kitchen?"

Colonel Guthrie reached out and thumped Gage's shoulder. Gage moved toward the back of the house, where he expected the kitchen would be. His ears pinged when he heard the colonel say, "Senator, you're going to get arrested for DUI, and you don't need that kind of publicity."

"She's *dead*," the senator sobbed.

"Who, Barbara? Shit, Chuck, come on. Let's sit down before you fall down."

"Not Barbara. I told you… Oh my God, I loved her. I really loved her."

"You mean—? Oh, holy hell."

"I stopped by a pub for a beer and a steak. I'm looking up at the news, and there's her picture. They said she's dead." A long pause was punctuated with a groan. "I have hearings in the morning. She was my main researcher. Somehow, I have to sit there and face the day without letting anyone know how much she meant to me. I won't be allowed to grieve. We went over all of those notes together. How can I look at my notes without remembering her beautiful black eyes? How silky her hair felt as she let it paint over my stomach?"

"All right, stop. Facts. You were having an affair with your researcher. She died tonight—"

"Her picture was on the news," the senator slurred out. "They're saying it's under investigation. They'll find out that she worked for Montrim Industries and that she was a whistleblower. They'll dig deeper, and they'll figure out we were lovers. My wife is going to know. My career in politics is over. *Over*. Just as I was primed to stop Montrim."

Gage was prowling the kitchen. The senator had said three things that made him think that this was about Zoe—the woman had black eyes, she worked for Montrim, she did research. There was also that conversation between the FBI and DCPD, where a misunderstanding was supposed to be seeded about Zoe's possible death. Had the reporters run with that idea? Had they reported it as a suspicious death? Or was Gage overreaching because everything for him revolved around Zoe right then?

"Chuck, listen to me, you have to lay low, let this storm pass —give the Montrim fight to someone else."

Gage moved on silent feet into the hall and was now plastered against the wall leading to the living room so he could hear better.

"I have to go after them!" the senator roared. "They're playing with apocalyptic weapons of war. Look at the experiments they're doing with weaponized sound waves."

"Ah, but it's better than nuclear, isn't it?" the colonel asked calmly, reasonably. "You need to let this crusade against Montrim go. Think what they're doing for us. If we had that sound technology, we could wipe out the enemy and leave their infrastructure unscathed. And there would be no lasting residual effects on the environment. Think of the soldiers' lives that would be saved." Colonel Guthrie was talking logically, which Gage thought was a waste of breath. "Sure, the area would have to be repopulated from the bugs to the animals, to the humans. But it is so much better for the world than nuclear. In this day and age? You can't *not* have a deterrent." Guthrie stopped and laughed a thin, forced laugh. "Listen to me trying to reason with a drunk. Chuck, let's talk about this when you've got your wits about you."

"We tried it already with the nukes, and where did that get us?" the senator asked dolefully.

"The sound deterrent is formidable and one of the best weapons possible to create a post-nuclear world. There would be no nuclear showdown. We'd simply deploy the sound waves before they pushed their buttons."

What in the hell are they talking about? Could Zoe be working on apocalyptic weaponry? As gentle as her soul always seemed to him, that...that was a mind-blower.

"See? Saying it that way, you've convinced yourself, and you can convince others that it's benign. Simply wipe everyone out of a certain area, and we can move in. But you're talking about *every living thing*. Women, children, infants in arms. *Genocide*. And it's so much easier to make the decision to use sound weaponry over nukes because we wouldn't have the ongoing radioactive consequences. Thereby making it more likely that it will be used."

The colonel's voice came from over in the corner where he had poured his drink earlier. Gage could hear a glass stopper being pulled from the neck of a decanter. "Okay, devil's advocate here. If we don't get there first with the research, someone else will, and we'll have no defense against this thing. Are you willing to let China get their hands on this technology first?" There was a pause in which Gage imagined the colonel belting back his drink. "Senator, why are you screwing up my lawn in the middle of the fucking night?"

"I need you. I need you to come and testify at those hearings."

"Senator, honestly, I've told you. I will not testify against Montrim. I'm not ready to retire yet. And me going up against the defense contractors? I'm not suicidal. Look, it's almost two in the morning. You're sloshed. Why are you here?"

"Please, Stan, I'm drunk. I'm sick with grief. I can't face my wife tonight. Can I stay?"

The colonel released an exasperated sigh. "The guest room is up the stairs, second right."

Gage moved back into the kitchen, yanking his earbuds out of his pocket and sticking them into his ears. By the time the senator was climbing the stairs. Colonel Guthrie had made his way to the back of the house. Gage stood at the kitchen door, looking out on the manicured garden with his head gently bobbing as if to a good tune.

"Sorry for the interruption. What were we saying?"

Gage pulled the buds from his ears. "Did your friend leave?"

"He's upstairs, sleeping it off."

Gage nodded as he stepped forward, his hand extended to shake with the colonel. "Okay, I'm on my way to the hospital. You have company, so I'll call you if anything concerning comes up."

"Thanks, Marine, I'd appreciate that." Colonel Guthrie shook Gage's hand, then he moved to a shelf and picked out a card from a small stack. "This one has my private number on the back." He handed it over, then tapped it when Gage had it in his fingers. "It will get me on the phone instead of an answering service. Use that if you need me."

Gage moved through the front door, down the steps, and over to the senator's car. As the senator had made his way to the house, he'd left the car door standing open. A wallet lay on the ground. Gage picked it up and gave it a quick once-over. He reached into the slit meant for business cards and pulled them out, turning them over and fanning through the stack until he found three where "private cell" was handwritten on the back along with a number. If he ever needed to ask the senator a question, Gage didn't want to be last in the queue on some aide's list of people to ignore that day. Gage pocketed one of them, slipped the rest in place, then put the wallet on the floorboard. He pulled the keys from the ignition, set them next to the wallet, and quietly closed the senator's door.

Gage climbed back into his SUV, feeling like he was waiting for a grenade to explode.

5

THERE WERE NO CARS ON THE HIGHWAY AS GAGE DROVE TO Inova Alexandria Hospital and parked in the garage. The closer he got to Zoe, the louder his danger signals pinged. He met with the security guard at the front desk and was relieved that the guy did a thorough job with the identification process.

"Has anyone else been in to see her?" Gage asked.

"Not so far, sir." The guard passed him back his military ID and driver's license.

Gage gathered his things and made his way to Zoe's room, nodding at the desk nurse as he passed by. Standing by Zoe's bed, the room dark except for a dim utility light, Gage's gaze followed the tubing from the IV bag down to her elbow. She had curved into a ball around her pillow, her long hair fanned across the white sheet, her face peaceful and still. He put a hand on her back to feel the reassuring rise and fall of her breathing.

Gage swallowed down the bitter taste that sat on his tongue. He didn't know what to think. He scanned the room, then moved to a chair in the far corner. Pulling out his phone, then sliding down to rest his head on the back of the seat, he splayed his long legs out in front of him. He'd learned how to relax and rest his body whenever possible to recharge for the next battle. And Gage knew in his gut that there were more battles to come.

He checked to see if anything had come through from Titus. There was nada. Next on his list was finding out who the senator was talking about when he said his lover had died. He started with local News Nine and on their website's front page was a picture of Lily Winters, Zoe's college friend who had stayed with Zoe while she left a bad marriage and found a place of her own. Lily had moved out of Zoe's apartment…what? Maybe three weeks before?

The news reported that Lily Winters had fallen onto the Metro platform without enough time for anyone to jump to her aid. Gage hit the arrow to watch the video that came with a "Sensitive Subject Matter" warning label. The sound of a reggae band loudly playing the steelpans came to an abrupt halt when a scream went up. Someone had recorded Lily lying on the tracks, looking like she was unable to move. Adrenaline? Drugs? Alcohol? Gage registered fear in her wide-open eyes and raised brow, so he put an x over the second two options. The crowd was yelling for her to get up, to hurry, as they looked down to where she lay beneath them.

As the light of the subway powered forward, their cries became a horrifying mantra, like a choir they sang in unison, "Stop! Stop!" They leaned together out into the open space, waving their arms frantically to signal the engineer to apply the emergency brakes. It must have worked because the subway seemed to slam to a halt. The video panned back to Lily, who had managed to get herself up on her feet. She stretched her hands toward the men who would pull her to safety. She took a single step forward. The video bounced up, missing the last moment as the subway hit Lily and came to a stop a mere two or three feet further down the track. Screaming could be heard from the platform, anguished cries of disbelief.

Lily was dead. Shit. Gage wiped his hand over his face. He didn't really know her, but from brushing by her in Zoe's hallway or grabbing a quick breakfast before he took off for Quantico. She seemed like a nice person. Intelligent. Sarcastic with a bawdy laugh. He seemed to remember that she worked as an accountant. Had she said she worked for Montrim? He didn't think so. Gage glanced over to where Zoe's unmoving body lay under the hospital sheet and cotton blanket. He was going to have to tell Zoe about her friend before she heard about it online. Zoe was still in recovery from her own shocking experience, and now here was another one for her to assimilate.

Gage did another search and decided that Lily's death was the only one that was being reported locally that night. Lily must be the Senator's mistress and the whistleblower. *Maybe*. Gage realized he was jumping to conclusions.

If Lily was the mistress, she must have been trying to help the senator take down her employer. If the employer was Montrim Industries, well, that was a major player in the vast military complex that Eisenhower had warned the country about over fifty years ago.

Zoe worked for Montrim. Or at least, she had an access badge. He wasn't clear who exactly Zoe worked for. He looked at the time stamp on the subway video, twenty-three twenty hours. Only an hour and a half after he'd opened Zoe's door and neutralized the tangos. Was it possible the intruders weren't after Zoe at all? Maybe they had been tasked with taking Lily captive. She had been living in that apartment up until recently. Someone could be working from old intel.

Gage wanted some answers. How did Lily land on that subway rail? Why couldn't she move to get up? Was she really the woman who was sleeping with Senator Chuck Billings? Or was Gage pushing to put two and two together when that wasn't the equation at all? He'd know whether Lily was Billing's lover if he could get a look at her phone. Gage pulled the business cards he'd been collecting tonight from his pocket, wondering which one might be his ticket to some answers. He picked out the one for Special Agent Damion Prescott, moved into the hall so as not to disturb Zoe, and tapped in the number.

"Prescott here."

"Special Agent? This is Gage Harrison. Have you got a minute?"

"Where are you?"

"Up at the hospital. Zoe's been admitted for shock and exhaustion. She's asleep right now."

"I appreciate the update."

"Sir, I'm wondering if we couldn't give each other a helping hand." Gage scrubbed his fingers over his eyes.

There was a pause. "How's that?"

"I came by some information that might be helpful. A correlation that you might not turn up on your own. But there's something I need in return."

"Withholding information on an ongoing case is a serious problem, Major." Prescott's voice was shaded a bright color of "don't fuck with me."

"There's a woman in the Alexandria, Virginia morgue who may have a connection to the case. I'll be happy to explain that connection if you can help me get a look at her phone. I want to see who she's been calling."

"When was she taken in?"

"Around midnight."

"Tonight? Is this Lily Winters and the Metro rail accident?"

"Yeah, I'm not convinced it was an accident as much as an

on purpose."

"Huh. And you think this is connected to the Zoe Kealoha attack?"

"I'd have to let you draw your own conclusions, sir. But yes, that's what I think. Is it possible to meet me down at the medical examiner's office? I need to be back to the hospital by zero five hundred hours."

"Because?"

"That's when the guard at the front desk loses his ability to keep Zoe's room free from bad guys."

"Got you. Lily Winters was hit by a subway. Her body's going to be crushed. Exactly what information do you think you're going to get from seeing her?"

"My understanding, sir, is that any personal effects that belong to the deceased are gathered up and taken with the body to the morgue. Isn't that the case?"

"Yes, if they find something."

Gage leaned into the wall as a janitor pushed a bucket on by. "My theory can be proven if I can see her phone."

"If her phone was with her, it's bound to be destroyed. What do you think's on it?"

"Corroboration of a connection that I'm trying to make for you." Gage was growing impatient with this back and forth.

"The Medical Examiner's Office doesn't open until eight. Chances are good that we won't get anywhere until then. But I get that your window is tight. We can take a run at it. Worst case, they turn us away. Or the phone isn't functional." Prescott paused. "But whatever the outcome, you're going to make the connection for me."

"Agreed."

It was a long shot. But at least he'd squeezed the trigger. Now Gage needed to wait and see if he got a bull's eye.

6

GAGE'S FOOTSTEPS ECHOED OFF THE CEMENT RAMP AS HE JOGGED toward his car. He didn't have time to play around. Zero five hundred hours was moving up fast. His tires squealed as he took the corners to the exit at speeds not intended for a hospital parking garage. Without having to dodge traffic, and by playing fast and loose with the red lights, he was parked and climbing the stairs just behind Prescott.

Prescott flashed his badge. The security guard pushed the door wide.

"We don't open 'til eight, sir."

"I'm working with Homicide Detective Kirk Browning on a case of national importance. It's time-sensitive. I just need a quick answer from the medical examiner, and then I'll be out of your hair."

The guard gestured toward the sign-in book and gave Gage the stink eye while Prescott scrawled illegibly over the line. Without asking for directions, the special agent stalked toward the elevator, obviously familiar with the building. "We'll go in together, and you're going to keep your mouth shut. I'll do all the talking. Got it?"

"Yes, sir."

The elevator pinged; there was a heavy thud, then the doors hesitated for an overlong pause before they squealed open. Prescott put his hand out, letting Gage walk in first. "The phone holds the key?" Prescott asked after the doors shut again. "How are you going to access it?"

"Lily Winters and Zoe Kealoha were friends—"

Prescott let out a low whistle. "No kidding? Huh."

"I've seen Lily unlock her phone before. If she didn't change her code, I should be able to get us access."

"There's more to that story than Zoe and Lily are besties."

"Not besties. Friends. But yes, I'll tell you more after I see the phone and can confirm what I think I know."

The doors slid open, and Prescott gestured to the right. They walked down the empty hall to a double door where Prescott punched a button that buzzed an alarm. He took out his FBI badge and held it close to his face as he looked into the camera above the doors. They were beeped through.

"Dr. Tooker, good to see you again. Looks like I woke you up. I'm sorry." Prescott grinned and held out his arms to give the woman a hug.

It was the sour-faced woman with tightly permed hair who had collected the bodies at Zoe's condo. Gage had seen her from where he'd sat on the guest room bed, out of the way. She squinted her eyes at them and grunted.

Prescott let his arms fall as Dr. Tooker made her way to the light switches and flipped them all on. "We open at eight. How'd you get past the security guard?"

"Charm." Prescott dipped his head sheepishly. "I know this is unconventional, Mandy, but I'm on a case that's time-sensitive.

Someone's life could well rely on my getting answers fast. I depend on your goodwill to help me out."

"Goodwill at three a.m. is going to be hard to come by. What exactly do you need? I put your guys in the fridge, and that's about it. Autopsies in the morning."

"I'm interested in the Lily Winters case. Is her autopsy scheduled too?"

"She'll be number three in line. Her body's not in good shape. I'm not sure what you expect to get from seeing her."

"Did she come in with personal effects?" the special agent pressed.

Dr. Tooker moved toward the refrigeration unit and pulled open a drawer with a black body bag. "I found her purse beside the tracks. She must have dropped it as she fell in. The straps were cut off by the subway, and it's filthy from getting dragged, but the bag itself is intact."

"I need to see her phone," Prescott said with a chummy smile.

Dr. Tooker rolled her eyes at him, then unzipped the body bag. Gage looked down at Lily's corpse and didn't recognize her. He barely recognized her as having human form. He wondered if she had committed suicide like the news reporter had suggested. It was a pretty gruesome way to go. He shook his head.

His mom died in a car accident when he was fourteen. That's what the police called it, an accident. She was driving too fast while intoxicated and hit a tree without wearing a seat belt. She died on impact. Gage imagined that much like Lily's body, his mom would have been equally gruesome.

Of course, what the officers didn't know was it hadn't been an accident at all. When he had come home from school, he had found two notes side by side. One was a note from his dad saying he'd found his true love and had left them. "Left her" is what it actually said. But the "them" was implied. The other note was his mom saying how she couldn't live without his dad, so she'd decided to end it. Gage never told the officers about the notes. He'd ripped them up and flushed them down the toilet. With no family to call on, Gage was shipped off to a home for boys, where he lived until he went to college.

Gage was glad that Lily—whether this was suicide, a terrible accident, or something darker—didn't have children left to wonder if their mother had known they'd loved her. Or the even bigger question—why she had decided to leave them. Gage knew why his dad left; he was an asshole. To be honest, Gage had been happy when he read his note saying he was gone. But his mom? That one haunted him.

The medical examiner turned and handed out nitrile gloves, which they pulled on, then she moved the purse to a stainless-steel tray. The phone was nestled in the inside zippered pocket. Dead.

"No battery," Dr. Tooker said and raised her brow.

"iPhone. You don't happen to have a charger, do you, Mandy?"

Dr. Tooker moved toward her desk and unplugged her phone. "Yes, if it'll get you out of here sooner, and I can get some sleep."

Gage's gaze scanned over to where an unmade cot stood in the corner. Obviously, there for the medical examiners who were on night duty.

As soon as the phone blinked to life, Gage unlocked it and moved quickly to Lily's list of recent calls. As he scrolled through the screen, Prescott and Gage each took photos with their own phones.

"Hey, who is this guy with you?" Dr. Tooker asked.

Prescott didn't look up from their task. "Some random homeless dude I found on the sidewalk. I told him if he could wait a few minutes, I'd buy him some breakfast. You know I have a heart of gold and can't stand to see my fellow man suffering."

Dr. Tooker snorted. Her phone buzzed, and she moved to answer it. Gage scrolled back through the last month of numbers before he moved to messages and did the same. Either Lily deleted her texts on a regular basis, or she just didn't like to text. She didn't have much there for him to record. Most of the names looked like family members.

"Okay, Damion, that was a call about a traffic fatality. I need to head out, so we need to zip Lily Winters and her things back up." She moved over to them and took the phone away, pulling her cord from the bottom. "It's time for you all to leave. If you need anything more, you can show up during regular hours." Dr. Tooker put the purse back with Lily's remains.

Prescott leaned in to Gage. "You get what you need?"

"Not sure."

"It'll have to do." Prescott put his hand on Dr. Tooker's back as she pushed the drawer in place. "Mandy, thank you as always. I owe you a drink. A stiff one." He added with a wink.

Dr. Tooker snorted. "Funny." Then she grabbed her keys and pushed the two men through the door.

Dr. Tooker turned right. They turned left to move back to the elevator and out the front door. As they reached the street, Prescott broke the silence. "You still have time before five. Let's grab a quick cup of joe. You must be dragging ass."

He was tired, but Gage had been trained to fight for days and nights on end, through pain and exhaustion. He had to admit, this was a different kind of tired. It wasn't physical as much as emotional. This whole experience was eye-opening. He hadn't realized how much Zoe meant to him. How invested he felt in her well-being. Even though Gage didn't seem to have even a basic grasp on who she was. Right now, he'd move mountains to keep her safe. Gage looked up the street toward an all-night diner and nodded his head in that direction. With their hands pushed deep into their pockets and their heads tucked into their collars, the two men moved through the early morning chill.

Inside, Gage ordered a tall coffee to go. Black. Prescott lifted a brow and then ordered the same. "Anxious to get back?"

"Yes, sir."

"You're worried about her safety. And you should be. Until we can get a better feel for what's going on, the FBI considers Zoe to be in imminent danger. I'm working on arrangements for a safe house for her. I need you to call me as soon as she's getting ready for discharge."

Gage accepted the thick paper cup from the waitress and reached for his wallet.

Prescott put his hand on Gage's arm to indicate that he'd get the bill. "Zoe's wearing a wedding ring, and you're one of two people on her hospital list. To some eyes, it might look like you're married." Prescott pulled a ten-dollar bill from his wallet and exchanged it with the server for his to-go cup. "Who's she really married to?"

"She's not. Guys think that an attractive woman on her own is an opportunity. Zoe hates it when strangers talk to her. She wears the ring as a deterrent. If they bug her anyway, she tells them her husband's a Marine Raider. That usually does the trick."

Prescott put his loose change in the tip jar and put the bills in his wallet. Nodding at the door, they made their way back out to the street. "Does that bother you? Zoe insinuating that you're married?"

"I don't think she's ever insinuated anything about me personally. I think my job gave her a title that sounded like muscle would be applied if anyone bothered her. And I can promise you it would be."

Prescott tipped his cup for a sip. "I can see that." He stopped under a street light. "Did you find what you thought you would?"

"Yes, sir." Gage put his coffee cup on the ground near his feet. He pulled out his phone and picked the image that had three calls to a single number unidentified by name or icon just hours before her death. He reached in his pocket and pulled out a business card with "private cell" scrawled in blue ink.

Prescott's gaze slid between the two. "Whose number is this?"

Gage flipped the card over to show the name *Senator Charles Matthew Billings* on the front. "I overheard a conversation, but I didn't have a lot of context. You need to take this as a step above pure speculation."

"All right." Prescott leaned his shoulder against the streetlamp post.

Gage picked up his coffee. "A couple of hours ago, Senator Billings told a friend that he was having an affair and that the woman died last night. She was his lead researcher for the Montrim Industries trial being held by the Senate oversight committee."

"You said Lily and Zoe were friends and that this could have something to do with Zoe?"

Gage took a sip from his cup. "I'm not sure. I don't want to run you in the wrong direction because that might endanger Zoe."

"Spit it out. We'll use an abundance of caution with all our decision making."

"Lily died not two hours after I neutralized the men in Zoe's apartment."

"Seems a hell of a coincidence. But I'm not sure—"

"Up until a few weeks ago, Lily was living with Zoe while she got her feet back under her following a divorce."

"Lily lived with Zoe. Two thugs break into that apartment. Lily dies shortly after. Crap. They might have been going after Lily, and Zoe happened to be there."

"It's a possibility. Or the two things might have nothing to do with each other."

Prescott's phone buzzed. He slid it from his belt holster and stepped away from Gage. "Prescott here...I don't care. We need this in place...well, jump over his head to someone who will authorize." Prescott threw an exasperated arm in the air and let it land on his head. Pulling the phone back to his ear, he growled, "Do it." He hung up, strode down the sidewalk, then turned and stalked back to Gage. "The safe house wasn't authorized. I'll keep working on it. It shouldn't take me long. Sometime later today, probably. Can I depend on you to keep Zoe in your sights until then? Let me know if anyone else tries to contact her or goes to see her?"

"Roger that." Gage looked down at the time, zero four thirty-five hours. "Shit. I've got to go." With a backward wave, Gage jogged toward his car. He had to get back to Zoe. Now.

7

GAGE

No sooner had Gage found his place in the corner of Zoe's hospital room than the door pushed open. Gage was immediately moving to get between whoever this new player was and Zoe.

"CIA, son. Relax." The guy moved farther into the room. "The name's Parker." He yanked out his wallet-badge and flicked it open for Gage to see. Parker nodded toward Zoe's sleeping form. "She looks like she's getting some rest. Good. Good." He pulled a chair from one end of the room all the way over to place it directly beside the chair Gage had occupied seconds before. He patted Gage's chair. "Let's chat."

Gage crossed his arms over his chest to make his biceps bulge in a prominent display of physical capacity. He leaned his shoulder into the wall to let the agent know he wasn't going to be compliant. Something about this guy set off his warning signals. Could be. Gage acknowledged to himself that he was primed to be combative from his night of adrenaline and confusion. He'd see how things progressed before he kicked the guy out on his ear. Right now, curiosity had the edge. He wanted to know why the CIA would be visiting Zoe before sunup.

"Hell of a shock, what happened tonight." Parker crossed his ankle over his knee and adjusted his trousers. "She's been working around the clock on her project. But you already know that, eh?"

Gage didn't answer.

"I understand from the DCPD, she's been diagnosed with exhaustion." There was a pause, and Gage could feel Parker gathering carefully selected words. "Sleep deprivation does terrible things to the brain. Makes people paranoid, creative about reality, overly emotional, poor girl."

Gage said nothing.

Parker cleared his throat. "Ironically, being exhausted also makes sleep come harder—nightmares and sleep talking are common. It's good that she's getting the meds she needs to get some rest." Parker crossed his arms casually. "You sleep over at her place much? Ever know her to have problems like that? Talking in her sleep?" He quirked a brow. "If so, we should let the doctor know so he can adjust her protocol."

Something in the studied ease in Parker's body made Gage shake his head. "Not that I know of. We don't really have that kind of a relationship."

"No? I thought you were the boyfriend." Parker canted his head, the look on his face saying he didn't believe Gage for a second.

"We see each other. I don't think I fall into the boyfriend category. She's pretty busy, and our schedules don't always mesh. I'm jumping between Lejeune and Quantico. She's up here in Alexandria."

"What do you know about her job? She must have told you something," Parker asked.

What did Gage know about her job? Well, he didn't know she was a damned Ph.D., that's for sure. She'd told him she worked in a lab. A "lab tech," she had called herself. But lab techs don't have doctorates, and they sure as hell don't have top-secret clearance or the CIA and FBI buzzing around.

"She does something with robotics, I think. We really don't talk about our jobs," Gage replied.

Parker stood and gazed down at Zoe. "I bet you don't do a lot of talking about anything at all, eh?" He sent Gage an I've-got-your-number grin, and Gage wanted to slam his fist into the guy's jaw.

Parker moved back to his seat to answer a text, and Gage looked down at Zoe's drugged state.

Gage had lied to the CIA operatives. He was definitely Zoe's boyfriend. His mind jumped back to one of the last conversations he'd had with Zoe. Gage had asked her a question about some-thing random. She had been staring at the wall and pulled out of her trance to ask, "Do we have to talk?"

"No. Not if you don't want to." He'd chuckled at her candor.

"Good, thanks," she'd said as she opened her computer.

"You know, my friends think I'm the luckiest guy in the world."

She'd turned and raised her brow. "I don't know your friends." She didn't say it like a bitch. There was nothing bitchy about Zoe. Her voice had been pleasant and matter of fact. She saw the world through Zoe-colored glasses. Pragmatic. Non-judgmental. Clear about parameters. Hoping everyone would respect hers in return.

"They've seen your picture."

"All they could get from that is what I look like, right? That's kind of a shallow way to decide if you're lucky or not." She tipped her head and looked at him with curiosity. "Why were you showing them my picture?"

Gage smiled over at her. "Putting a face with a name. You know, their girlfriends want to talk to them constantly. Ask them how they feel about stuff."

Zoe's eyes turned thoughtful. "Communication is important to maintaining a healthy relationship."

Gage's smile turned into a grin. "That kind of sucks since my girlfriend hates to talk."

"Girlfriend, huh?"

"Okay?"

She turned back to her computer. "I guess. Now can you leave me alone?"

That was Zoe, in a nutshell. He got that Zoe spent a good part of her time in her head. He was sort of medium on the introversion continuum and liked the time he spent rattling around in his own brain.

At the time, he had been happy about his good fortune in finding a woman who put out zero in the way of couple-vibes or demands. There was no honey-do list or expectations. It was all just…fun. He enjoyed Zoe.

He had flopped back on the couch, thinking he really was a lucky guy. He found Zoe to be an odd mix of edgy and sweet, and it intrigued him. Now that Gage knew she was involved in something damned serious—possibly life-threatening—he wished he'd asked more questions instead of just heading back to base when she'd had trouble sleeping. What had she been wrestling with? Did she know she was in trouble? He had thought that their relationship was comfortable and fun. But that had changed seven hours ago when he crushed some guy's windpipe to save her.

The doorknob turned, and Gage took advantage of the

distraction to step back into the shadows. A head peeked around the doorframe.

"Grossman, good. What've you got?" Parker waved the guy in.

"Besides acid indigestion? I've got a deadline in my rearview mirror." He strode over to the bed. "How's she doing?" he asked Parker.

Parker raised his wrist to check the time. "She has another few hours before they let her wake up."

Grossman reached over to Zoe's IV and read the prescription label on the bag. "Good." He nodded. "This'll wear off quick and won't give her a hangover. She'll be functioning again in no time. So she was hysterical? Where are the bodies?"

"The medical examiner took custody of them. The DCPD and FBI are working on identification."

"Shit."

Parker turned and gestured toward Gage. "And this is the hero of the night." The tone he used seemed to pass information from Parker to his colleague. "Gage Harrison, meet Jim Grossman, also CIA."

When Gage took a step forward and extended his hand for a shake, he made sure his face wore the impassive mask he'd used to become his unit's poker champ.

"You're the guy who took down the kidnappers? Hell of a feat, soldier. You did Uncle Sam proud tonight and did your nation a huge favor."

Gage detected the ember of a lie in the way Grossman squeezed his hand a little too hard and a little too long and stared into his eyes with a flint-edged gaze. Gage didn't trust this guy any more than he trusted Parker. "I'm a Marine, not a soldier. Just glad I got there when I did."

"Are you standing post?" Grossman asked.

"I'm going to stay with Dr. Kealoha until she's released."

Grossman pursed his lips, then focused on Parker. "I've got a fire to put out. We need to know when Dr. Kealoha wakes up so we can have a chat." He pointed at Gage. "You don't have clearance to be in here for that."

"Sir, I'll wait and ask Zoe what she wants."

Grossman and Parker exchanged another silent look.

Gage had relied on his ability to read body language to stay alive during his three deployments to the Middle East. He couldn't always pick out the words when people spoke in their particular dialects, but he always knew when to dive and cover. And Gage knew that Parker and Grossman had their fingers on their triggers. They were dangerous as hell.

A nurse popped the door open. "Gentlemen, I need to hang a new IV bag and check vitals."

"That's okay, ma'am, we're headed out. Loverboy over there," Parker rolled his head toward Gage, "can't be persuaded to leave the good doctor's side. I'm afraid you're going to have to put up with him."

Grossman and Parker each reached into their wallets and produced business cards. "We'd appreciate a call when she wakes up. You can buzz either one of us."

Gage accepted the cards. He needed them to help him keep track of all the players. One after the other, the scrimmage line was filling up in front of him. He watched as the agents walked out of the room. The CIA handled America's foreign intelligence. Why were they operating on US soil? And why the hell would foreigners want to kidnap Zoe?

8

As the nurse checked Zoe's vitals, Gage paced. From their timekeeping and their concern about the aftereffects of Zoe's medicine, it seemed to Gage that the CIA was working something urgently sensitive. Gage peered through the blinds at the dark parking lot but saw nothing that drew his attention. He thought about Grossman saying, "our girl." Could Zoe be a CIA asset? Hell, could she be an operative for the CIA? Maybe she was playing on the spooks' field. Gage's cellphone vibrated in his pocket. He swiped his screen to read the incoming message.

Titus: **What's the sitrep?**

Gage texted: **FUBAR, sir. 2 CIA were here.**

The reply came immediately: **CIA?**

Gage: **Asked a lot of questions. Advise.**

Titus: **I'd keep a tight watch.**

Gage: **Any progress on the IDs?**

Titus: **Nothing domestic. Parameters have been
expanded to international. It's going to take time for
the computers to search. More as I have it. Out.**

Gage glanced at the nurse, who sent him a shy smile. "I'm
not Doctor Kealoha's nurse on duty. That's Stacy." She pointed
to the board with the name written on it. "She got hung up with
another patient, so I'm filling in. If you have any questions, I'll
tell Stacy, and she'll come in and talk to you."

"How do you think she's doing?" Gage asked, tucking his
hands in his pockets.

"From these readouts, Dr. Kealoha's fine. She'll be right as
rain after her rest. Her vitals are looking good. This new IV bag
is for hydration, not sedation. She should stay asleep for a while,
though. We'll let her wake naturally." The nurse turned and
cleansed her hands with hand sanitizer before she pushed her
computer station into the hall, holding the door so it would close
silently behind her.

Gage pulled his chair back over to Zoe's bed and sat down
with his elbows on the safety bar and his chin on his fists. He
desperately wanted to smooth the hair out of her face, to run a
hand down her back, to pull her into his arms. But she needed to
be whole and healthy to deal with this situation, and he didn't
want to rouse her from her sleep.

The CIA asked if she'd been having nightmares and talking
in her sleep. A sign of exhaustion. *Why aren't you sleeping, Zoe?
Huh? What's on your mind? You're always so laid back...*

He tried to think back to when this had started. The last time
he'd tried to spend the night was the worst, but she had been

flopping around for the previous month. Before that, she had slept like a rock.

Spending the night with a woman wasn't something Gage did as a rule. He'd found that women read too much into their relationship if he woke up beside them. The act of spending the night led to too many future plans. It was easier to go home and keep the boundaries stable. Less confusion. Less upset when he had to leave on assignment and had no details to share about his comings and goings. There were no promises he could offer that he'd come home safe and sound. He didn't have the kind of job that lent itself to reassurances.

It wasn't like that with Zoe. She was uncomplicated. He stopped to laugh at how wrong that statement was. She *presented* as uncomplicated, he amended. Their relationship had been uncomplicated, at least.

Zoe seemed self-satisfied. She seemed to have complete faith in his ability to do his job and get home. There were no tears or angst. It was easy, really easy to be with Zoe. Their relationship was such a relief to him, and he'd never really reflected on his spending the night. Getting up in the morning and heading back to Quantico didn't have emotional weight. He never felt like he was leading her on because she didn't seem to have an agenda for him. His mind flitted back to thoughts of the CIA and FBI. Wouldn't that be the attitude an operative would have? Seemed to him that might fit.

He scrubbed his hands over his face. He needed another cup of coffee bad, but hell, if he was going to leave her alone to roam the halls and find a machine. He looked out the window as the tops of the trees started to show an outline against the blue-black sky. He slowed his breathing and let his mind wander. Sometimes when he was on the battlefield, taking a moment and listening to his thoughts instead of raging forward against the enemy gave him the perspective he needed to make good choices. Oddly, what he was thinking about were those trees.

When he was at UVA, taking the obligatory literature class to meet his requirements, he had been struck by a poet that... Gage leaned his weight onto one hip and pulled his phone from his back pocket. He pulled up a search engine, then stared at the ceiling. He couldn't remember the poet's name. The only thing that came to him was "marriage" and "oak tree." He typed it in with little confidence. But the second link on the list was "On Marriage" by Kahlil Gibran. Gage read the short poem.

SING AND DANCE TOGETHER *and be joyous, but let each one of you be alone,*
   Even as the strings of a lute are alone though they quiver with the same music.

"LET each one of you be alone," Gage murmured. He liked that phrase. Back in Charlottesville, it had been an epiphany. It had led to him breaking up with the girl he'd been dating for almost two years. She was beautiful, smart, witty, and athletic, but the more she scripted their future, the more heavily she leaned on him. Almost every decision she made, she filtered through him—from her choice of majors to what to wear when they went to grab some pizza. It seemed to him that the longer they were together, the more she was devoid of her own opinions; she deferred to him too much. It was her background and upraising, he knew. Her mother submitted to her father in all things, and that had worked for their marriage.

Gage didn't want anything to do with that kind of a relationship. It felt burdensome. It was a responsibility he'd never looked for and didn't feel comfortable shouldering. He wanted to be with someone who brought new perspectives, ideas, and interests to the relationship, expanding his paradigms rather than absorbing his thoughts and tastes until they weren't two people but one.

His girlfriend had thought that was the goal—to make two into one. But this poem defined for Gage what he wanted in a relationship—someone who was strong. Independent. Someone who knew her own mind. Had her own friends and interests. And they could share, or they could just be amicably and happily together without needing to share it all. His world shouldn't construct anyone else's world. Being in Special Forces, he couldn't guarantee the person who walked out the front door would be anything like the person who came home. If he came home at all.

Gage had searched a long time to find someone strong enough to stand on her own and not fold under the weight of a relationship with him. He thought he had found it a time or two. But as the relationship became more serious, the women Gage had dated seemed to morph and change, as if to make themselves his ideal—not realizing his ideal was that they simply be themselves. Sometimes he found himself falling into that trap, too, shifting for a time to become something he wasn't in order to preserve the peace or maintain the status quo. But inevitably, that strategy would backfire. Who had the tenacity to maintain a charade like that?

AND STAND TOGETHER YET NOT TOO NEAR *together:*
   For the pillars of the temple stand apart,

And the oak tree and the cypress grow not in each other's shadow.

THAT'S the line he remembered—trees not standing in each other's shadow. Standing strong by themselves. Zoe had that inner strength. She was happy within her own skin and didn't seem to need outside validation. It was a very appealing trait.

He stared down at the words of the poem without really seeing them. Zoe seemed to be perfectly content on her own. She also seemed to be perfectly content when he was around, even if they were just two bodies in the same place. He closed his phone as Zoe gave a little moan and straightened her legs. He watched to see if she was coming to, but her lips parted in a sigh, and she continued to sleep.

Gage thought back to the last night they'd spent together, the one that ended with him stomping out of her condo at zero dark hundred to drive back to Quantico to hit the racks when she was tossing around and keeping him awake. He should have stayed and tried to find out what was going on with her. A missed opportunity, in retrospect. And he shouldn't have missed it

She had been quiet that day. That wasn't unusual. When they were at her place, he'd usually read or whatever, and Zoe would wander around in her own little world. He'd stay quiet and out of her way when she got that look in her eye when she pulled her brows together and stared into the distance. He had a sister who was an introvert, and he knew that expression meant Zoe needed to spend time alone in her head. He got it. At least, he thought he did. Now? Shit, nothing was clear. What had she been thinking about all those times, staring at the wall, mumbling under her breath? Warfare?

He watched the slow rise and fall of Zoe's chest and shook

his head. He couldn't believe that this woman, who never had a bad word for anyone, who wore a sweet Mona Lisa smile as her natural facial expression, could ever contemplate creating the level of destruction that Colonel Guthrie was encouraging. Could she?

9

A KNOCK SOUNDED AT THE DOOR. GAGE WAS OUT OF HIS CHAIR in an instant. *Speak of the devil.* Colonel Guthrie stuck his head around the frame. Before he could speak and maybe wake Zoe, Gage was at the door, moving the colonel back into the hallway.

"Just checking in. How's our girl?"

That was the second time that morning that Zoe had been referred to that way, and it was like nails on a chalkboard to him. Zoe was no one's "girl."

"She's doing fine. Sleeping."

Colonel Guthrie held out a cup of coffee and a bag with a bakery monogram on the front. "The coffee's black. I didn't know how you took it. There are cream and sugar in the bag with a breakfast sandwich. I thought you'd probably need a pick-me-up by now."

"Thank you, sir."

The colonel rocked back on his heels and shoved his hands into the pockets of his coat. "I haven't called over to Hawaii yet. It's about midnight over there right now. I didn't want to pull her parents from their bed and have them worried all night—not until I talked to Zoe myself or had something a little more definitive."

"I'm told she's fine."

The colonel nodded. A close-lipped smile stretched across his face. Worry clouded his eyes. "I've known Zoe since she was in diapers. And even though she's nearly thirty, I can't seem to make her age past her fourth birthday in my mind." He looked past Gage into Zoe's room. "Almost thirty. Huh. Doesn't *that* feel like a kick in the nuts?" He scratched the line of his jaw. "You'll keep me in the loop with what all's going on? If she needs anything at all, you'll reach out?"

"Yes, sir. I have your card."

"All right then. I'm heading to the office. Thank you, son. I appreciate all you've done. All you're doing." He slapped Gage on the shoulder and headed down the hall.

Gage moved back into the room and pulled the business cards he'd accumulated over the last eight hours out of his pocket. A police detective, a colonel, a senator, a special agent with the FBI, and not one, but *two* CIA operatives. He fanned them out. With all these experts worried about Zoe's wellbeing, you'd think he held a winning hand. It felt more like a shitstorm to him.

Zoe moaned, and Gage moved to her side.

"No one will know." She whispered it so softly that Gage wasn't sure he'd heard her right.

He crouched by the bed, so his ear was near her lips. "Know about what?"

"Sphecius…" She lifted her hand and rubbed the tip of her nose. Her eyes were still closed.

"Sfeeseeus? Is that what you said?"

When she didn't reply, Gage tried to sound it out and come up with a spelling that seemed reasonable. Google was good at filling in the proper word if he could get his guess anywhere close to being right. He couldn't remember seeing a word that began with "sf," so he tried "sph" like sphere. Did she mean sphere? Maybe she meant "spacious." "Sphecious," he typed. Google sent him to a Wikipedia page for a wasp, genus Sphecius. He looked over the description—large, solitary, ground-dwelling, predatory. This couldn't be right. She worked with robots. *Possibly* worked with robots.

Very quietly, so as not to fully wake her, Gage whispered, "Hey, Zoe? Do you know what Sphecius is?"

"Wasp…wasps." She sighed and seemed to fall deeper into sleep.

His phone buzzed, and Gage moved to the far corner of the room. "Titus, man, I was about to call you."

"Yeah, well, I've got some good news and some bad news."

"Shit."

"That about sums it up. Is she still conked out?"

"The nurse stopped sedation a while back. She said Zoe's just sleeping now."

"Didn't you tell me that the special agent on the case was setting her up in a safe house? This might be the time to give him a call and rock Zoe on over there."

Gage was on immediate alert. "What did you dig up?"

"The two guys that you killed last night? They're MIA, assumed dead."

"Come again?"

"They're listed as Israeli Special Forces, killed in a bomb attack. We'd need DNA to make it one hundred percent, but with the combination of the ear scan, face scan, and fingerprints you sent, we're still hitting probabilities in the low-nineties on both of them."

"What could they possibly want with Zoe?"

"Good question. Why don't you get her moved, then call me back? I already talked to command and was given permission to lend Iniquus assistance, pro bono. They don't like the idea of foreign mercenaries playing with our DARPA scientists."

"Prescott told me this morning the safe house plans for Zoe have been nixed. I'm on my own to protect her for the moment. Surely if they knew who these guys were, it would change their minds?"

"I don't think it's wise to wait on FBI red tape to get sliced. I think you need to shake her awake, get her dressed, and move on out the door. The hospital leaves her too vulnerable, with too many ways to make bad things go down. I'm headed your way. I'll take you to an Iniquus location. That should buy us some time to figure out what's going on."

"Thanks, man, I owe you. She's in room 606 at Inova Alexandria. Hey, on the off chance, have you ever heard the word Sphecius?"

"Sphecius? No. You can tell me where you heard it when I pick you up. I'm heading for the garage now."

As he hung up the phone, the door pushed open slowly. Gage shook his head. This hospital room was like a circus tent. Ring one—CIA. Ring two—DARPA and the colonel. In two strides, he was jerking the door open to see who was in ring number three. A small man, with the pointed face of a weasel and wiry frame, stood outside the door. "I was told this was Dr. Kealoha's room."

"That's correct. She's asleep. May I help you?" Gage held the door, so the man couldn't see in and stared him down. The guy was dressed impeccably and had the polished feel of a man who enjoyed being pampered.

"Oh, ah, no. I came to check on how Dr. Kealoha is doing." He reached into his coat pocket and pulled out a card.

"Topher Bilik. I'm the director of one of Dr. Kealoha's ongoing projects at Montrim." He held out his card and adjusted his body into a posture of power. At least that's what Gage thought the guy was doing. Gage took the card and slid it into his pocket without a glance. He didn't offer up his own name in return.

"Zoe works at Montrim," Bilik added, then tilted his head, trying again to peek around Gage's muscular build into the hospital room.

Gage stared at the guy, wondering why the heck he'd showed up to see Zoe at this hour of the morning.

"How is she?"

"Fine." Gage arched his brow. "How'd you know she was here?"

The man took a step back as if thrown off balance. He quickly recovered himself and offered up a plastic smile. "Oh, Colonel Guthrie called me last night."

"Last night?" Gage tilted his head. "What time last night?"

Bilik scratched his upper lip. "Early this morning, I guess."

"He woke you up with this? There's nothing wrong with her."

Bilik seemed to realize how odd that would be. He tried to change the subject. "Is there anything Dr. Kealoha needs? She's a shining star at our organization. We want to make sure she has everything she could possibly need."

"Why would Colonel Guthrie wake you up in the middle of the night?" Gage wouldn't let it go. "Why couldn't it wait for morning? Why did he call you in the first place?"

The man gave him a bloodless smile. "If you'll be so kind as to pass my card to Dr. Kealoha and let her know I stopped by? I'll call her on her cellphone later." He turned, and with his arm up in a goodbye, he skulked toward the elevator.

Gage shut the door and moved back toward Zoe, wishing she'd come to. He held his phone between his palms and stared out the window. Too many players were worried about Zoe's wellbeing, and Gage had lead in his belly. It was the feeling he got on a mission when there were bad things on the horizon. He furrowed his brow as he dialed his superior. "Sir? Major Gage Harrison here. I'm respectfully requesting leave to take care of a situation of exceptional circumstance." His gaze fell on Zoe as she stretched out her legs and blinked her eyes open.

10

ZOE

The better the fruit the more wasps to eat it

— GERMAN PROVERBS

ZOE SQUINTED AS SHE TOOK IN THE INDUSTRIAL EFFICIENCY OF the hospital room. Lying there, she worked to understand her surroundings. She remembered being brought in on a stretcher, but everything seemed fuzzy—her memory of why, and the things around her.

"Here you go, Zoe." Gage stood at the side of her bed, placing something in her hands.

She sighed with relief as she realized they were her glasses. "Thank you." She sounded a little tipsy to her own ears. Whatever they gave her last night had done the job. Zoe remembered talking to the nurse in a darkened room, and now she was awake again with the sun streaming through her window. Time had moved forward without her. She glanced over at Gage, who wore a bemused look on his face. His eyes, which could magically change from blue to green to black as coal, were locked on her.

Right now, she could easily read affection and concern in their depths, and also a little bit of that look he got just before they… Zoe felt her cheeks turn pink.

Gage chuckled. "I'd pay good money to know what you're thinking."

"Have you been here for a long time?" She glanced at the wall clock, then over to Gage. He wore the same clothes as last night, along with the rough shadow of an unshaven face.

"In and out since last night. Mostly in. I wanted to keep an eye on you."

Zoe pushed the button on her bed, so she could sit upright. She crossed her legs under the cotton blanket. "All right, Captain America, what happens now?"

Gage sent her a curious look. "Why did you call me that?"

"What?"

"Captain America."

"Oh." She tilted her head and examined him. "Must be the body language."

"Body language?"

"Do you have to repeat what I say? It's irritating."

Gage raised a brow.

Zoe scrubbed a hand over her face. "Okay, body language, in one of my robotics classes, the professor was really into discussing body posture and facial displays so that we could help humans connect with the robots."

"Why would he care about humans connecting with a machine?"

"We were working on a prototype for domestic help. A robot to interface with families. I got into the habit of watching bodies and faces for my research."

Gage shook his head, and Zoe read that as "you still haven't answered my question."

"Your body language, especially right now, reads as trustworthy, intelligent, courageous, and having deep affection for me. You know, a total Captain America." That last word caught in her throat.

Gage chuckled. "You don't think those are good things?" When she didn't answer, he added, "This is an odd conversation. Zoe, you don't flatter people as a rule."

The corners of her mouth tugged down and pressure built behind her eyes.

He cleared his throat and wrapped his hands around her guard rail. "You're obviously not trying to stroke my ego." The statement sounded like a question like he'd found some puzzle that needed solving. "You're usually not sarcastic either. I don't know why the look on your face is throwing me so hard. I hate that you're frowning at me. You've never done that before."

Zoe blinked back tears. "I've never felt this way before." She reached behind her and pulled her pillow around so she could hug it. "I am so deeply, profoundly grateful." She sniffed hard. "Beyond words. It's actually kind of like a tsunami rolling through me right now." She attempted a quivering smile and something that sounded like she wanted it to be a laugh. "Yeah, I feel like I could be swept away and probably drown in all of these emotions."

Gage waited silently as she fought for some semblance of control. When her breathing came a little steadier, he leaned forward and kissed her forehead. Something happened with that kiss. Some kind of promise was made. He pulled her head to his chest, where she could hear his heart beating. He was so steady.

After a long moment, she got hold of herself. She sat up and pushed her hair back over her shoulders as she asked, "Has anything happened since last night? Did they find out what those guys wanted?"

Gage's face shifted to stoic. He cleared his throat. "Zoe, I have something I need to tell you."

She raised a brow. Then a quick knock on her door and the entrance of a nurse stalled any further exchange.

"Good, you're awake. I'm doing the last round before I go off duty, and you get a new nurse. The doctor is right behind me." She pushed her rolling computer system beside Zoe's bed. "Unless there's an issue, it looks like you'll be discharged this morning." The nurse glanced over at Gage and smiled. "Good morning."

Zoe considered the way the nurse's tired countenance brightened like her happy pill suddenly kicked in and realized that Gage had caught this woman's attention. While the nurse documented numbers on her computer, Zoe considered Gage. He was cute. She could see why the nurse would perk up at the sugar rush of some unexpected eye candy. Cute was probably the wrong word. Cute really didn't belong to a man with Gage's hardened warrior's body. His face was ruggedly handsome, more so now that he was sporting stubble on his normally clean-shaven face. She guessed the cute description came from his smile and how his eyes crinkled at the corners when he was amused. Gage's eyes were his best feature, she thought. Well, no. He had some other features that sat at the top of her list too. As that thought came to mind, Zoe caught Gage's gaze, and he winked. Her pink flush turned to bright red, and he started laughing. The nurse glanced up with a question in her expression, and Zoe looked away quickly, fiddling with her fake wedding ring.

"Can I ask you to wait outside for a moment, please?" the nurse asked Gage.

Gage crossed his arms over his chest. He took on the feel of a boulder that couldn't be moved. Entrenched. This must be one of his war faces. Gage had used a different war face last night, and it was intimidating as all get out. Zoe had grown up in the defense world. She knew that Gage belonged in the sphere of the elite soldiers, but it had been a concept rather than a reality for her until last night. To meet Gage, well, he was an easygoing guy. Her old roommate, Lily, had called him affable. Zoe could get on board with that adjective. But now, she also saw him as deadly. He had killed to save her. Tears prickled the corners of her eyes. Her breath caught in her throat. How did you thank someone for something like that?

"I think Dr. Kealoha would like some privacy while I remove her catheter."

"Oh, yeah, right." Gage rose to his feet, towering over the petite woman.

The nurse smoothed her hands down the front of her blue scrubs and tilted her head back, so she could smile up at him. "Thank you, this won't take long."

THE NURSE WAS EFFICIENT, perhaps a little brisk. Zoe could understand that. They were on duty for twelve hours at a time. If Zoe had just finished a twelve-hour shift, she'd want to get off her feet too. Zoe definitely understood the toll that long hours at work could take. She had been pushing hard to get her project in place. She wanted to be done, done, done with her contract, and move on. She needed a project outside the world of military research that was more life-affirming, like what she'd done in biomedical engineering. She would do anything to go back to when she signed those darned DARPA contracts. She'd rip them to shreds and march right out of the office. Now she was hospitalized for exhaustion and, call a spade a spade, hysteria. "Shock" was prettying things up a bit. What she was was a big, fat mess. But not for long. Soon she'd have her prototype in the field. Then she could hand things back to DARPA. She planned to take a long vacation to somewhere where she could be alone with nature, and alone in her head where she was happiest. Then she could make some decisions about what her future looked like.

As the nurse exited, Gage came back through the door with a doctor Zoe hadn't met.

"Dr. Dithers," he said. "I'm the hospitalist on duty." The doctor stood at the end of the bed and talked to the clipboard he was scribbling on. "Are you ready to head home? You're feeling okay?"

"I am, thank you."

"All righty then. If you'll sign this, you're good to go." He held out a plastic clipboard and pen for Zoe. "You'll want to follow up with your physician about your sleep issues, and consider seeing a mental health professional if you notice any adverse effects following the break-in. It's best if a counselor works with you earlier rather than later. It leads to a better outcome."

Zoe offered him a tightlipped smile and signed her name without reading the document. She watched the doctor move out of her room, then threw the covers off. Last night, she had been wearing Gage's black sweats with no shoes or coat. Maybe Gage could pull the car up to the exit, and she could run out. She hated hospitals, and the sooner she was out of there, the better. But she also didn't know where she would go. Home didn't feel safe.

Gage lifted her overnight bag from beside the chair and placed it on the bed. "I brought you some things. I hope that's all right."

Zoe opened the bag, chewing on her bottom lip as she flipped through the neat piles Gage had placed inside. Wow, he brought a lot of outfits. It looked like he'd packed for the week and not just a twenty-minute trip across town. "There are a lot of clothes here."

"Special Agent Prescott said you might be moved from the hospital to an FBI safe house. I wanted to make sure you had what you needed."

Zoe's mind galloped at a rate that made it hard for her to pin down any thoughts. Finally, she landed on, "You make it sound like there was a change of plans."

"Not a big change, but Iniquus will be putting you up in one of their places instead of the FBI."

"Iniquus is the security group you were interviewing for, right?"

"Right. A friend of mine, Titus Kane, is a unit commander there." Gage pointed toward her door. "He's in the hall, waiting for us."

Zoe lifted her favorite plum-colored hoodie and hugged it to her chest like a teddy bear. "I'm confused."

Gage put his hands on his hips and sent her an appraising look. "We're all confused. But we'll figure it out. The first step is to get you somewhere safe so we can all share information and come up with a plan. I need you to get dressed, okay?"

She reached behind her to yank the ties and release her hospital gown. It slid to the floor at her feet. She stood there naked, with goose flesh rising across her skin. There was a tingling in her scalp, and her mouth had gone dry. The full burden of why she was sedated last night was coming back to her. Two massive goons had broken into her apartment, and Gage had killed them to protect her. Tears prickled the corners of her eyes. *He needs me to get dressed so he can get me somewhere safe.*

She searched the bag until she found the stack of bras and

underwear. She saw that he'd brought her what she considered her "date night" panties and not the comfy cotton hipsters she wore for every day. She pulled out a pair and sent an "Oh, really?" look over to Gage. It was her way of trying to normalize a situation that was everything but normal. "You don't want to give me a few minutes of privacy so I can get dressed?"

Gage let his eyes slide slowly over her naked body. He frowned and shook his head, though his eyes were bright with merriment. "No can do, ma'am. I've been tasked with guarding your body."

He was teasing, but a new vulnerability raked over her.

"I put your toiletries bag in the outside pocket—it's got your toothbrush and stuff."

Quick as she could, Zoe dressed. A hasty brush of her teeth and hair, a zip of the case, and she was almost ready. "You picked all of my favorite outfits." Zoe crouched to pull on her boots.

"Well, I picked the things I see you in most. I wanted you to be comfortable."

She stood and flipped her hair back out of her face. "You pay attention to my clothes?"

"It's my job to be observant." He raised his brows in silent question.

Zoe nodded. "I'm comfortable, thank you." That was only partly true. Her clothes felt comfortable, but she herself was not. She had no idea what to think about a move to a safe house.

Gage picked up her case and reached for her hand. Zoe grabbed it like it was a lifeline.

He puts his hand into a wasp's nest.

— Hungarian Proverb

ZOE FELT CONSPICUOUS WALKING OUT THE DOOR, FLANKED BY two powerhouse men. She wasn't exactly diminutive. She stood five-foot-ten, but the heels of her boots put her over six feet, nearly eye to eye with the guys, but while they embodied latent force and solidity, she was stumbling along, twitching at every movement and sound.

Titus was a little overwhelming. He had a shaved head and a square jaw. A scar wrapped around one side of his neck and stood out as a pink and white slash against his coffee-colored skin. Zoe wondered how someone got close enough to slice him. His single facial expression seemed to be a glower. But maybe it was the circumstances. Maybe he'd soften around the edges when she was tucked into his safe house. He made Zoe nervous.

Sandwiched between the men, they all moved as a single unit, taking up space on the sidewalk, then in the garage.

Titus had brought a gunmetal grey SUV that looked like it was going to war. At the sight of it, Zoe started to shake. As she climbed into the back seat of the vehicle, she wondered about the choice of cars. They wouldn't exactly blend. It would be hard to lose someone in this thing if they were being chased. Zoe couldn't imagine that it could go very fast. Of course, if the worry wasn't about blending and outracing and was more about providing cover and protecting them against being rammed off the street, this might be good. Or maybe this was simply what Titus drove every day, and there was no thought process at all.

Zoe settled in. The heavily tinted windows gave the passengers in the back some concealment. No one would know she was there unless they were already being followed. Gage tipped her overnight bag into the cargo section, then shifted in beside her. Titus would do the driving. Before they took off, Titus handed a pistol to Gage and a couple of extended magazines. "There's an MP5 under my seat if you need it. Mags are in the seat pocket."

So this is what people mean when they say quaking in your boots. Zoe yanked her seatbelt hard across her hips to help hold her in place.

Titus spun the wheel, and they moved onto the street. As if synchronized, Gage looked right while Titus scanned left. Then Gage scanned left, and Titus looked right. Zoe focused on her white-knuckled grip on the seat belt.

When they finally reached the highway, the men seemed to ease a bit, even if the shift was microscopic. Titus adjusted his rearview mirror and used it to stare at her. "You can settle in. I'm going to take you on a little tour to make sure we didn't pick up a tail."

"A tail?" She threw her body around to look out the back window.

"Normal operating procedure. Hotel Iniquus is in Maryland,

outside of town, and we don't want to lead anyone to your safe house."

"Of course, thank you," she whispered.

Gage had reached into his pocket and pulled out a bunch of business cards. He laid them out on the seat between them. "Here are some players with a big interest in you. Do you know them?"

Zoe read them over. A detective. The colonel. Prescott, well, she had sent him an SOS. Parker and Grossman, the CIA shitheads. Topher Birch. He had spoken with Gage? And why was Senator Billings's card here? A frown pulled between her brows.

"Do you trust these people?"

"I'm not sure." Zoe's voice trailed off as she sunk deeper into her head, trying to figure out the connections. How did Gage get all of these cards?

"Do you think it's possible that the intruders were sent by someone you know?"

Zoe shot Gage a look of dismay. She had no idea. Her eye caught Titus's in the rearview mirror.

"Are you still fuzzy from the meds?" he called back over his shoulder.

"I can't feel my lips." Zoe wasn't sure if that was the meds still at work in her system or her anxiety.

"Coffee?" He moved to the far right-hand lane.

"Bless you." Zoe turned to look out the window and rested her forehead on the cool pane.

"Zoe?" Gage called to her quietly. He unraveled her hands from the seatbelt and laced his fingers through hers. She closed her eyes. "Zoe. I have something I need to tell you." His voice was as gentle and smooth as lake water on a summer night. She could float on it in perfect peace, staring up at the wide expanse of stars. That's where she imagined herself to be. Willed her mind to go. She didn't want to hear what he had to say. She knew whatever it was was bad. Fog coated her thoughts like it had last night when she couldn't even remember how to dial 9-1-1.

She didn't respond. Gage didn't push. Yet.

They went through the Starbucks drive-thru. Titus ordered her some food as well as coffees all around. She took the food bag gratefully and ate. After a while, when she felt she'd worn the cowardice mantle a little too long, Zoe looked over at Gage. She forced the corners of her mouth into the semblance of a smile. "Okay, I'm ready. What do you need to tell me?"

Once again, Gage reached for her hand and placed it between both of his and rubbed. "Zoe, you're as cold as ice."

"I'm all right. Can you just spit it out? My imagination is creating some pretty demonic monsters in my head."

"It's about Lily."

Zoe blinked. "Lily Winters?"

He nodded. "I'm so sorry, Zoe, but Lily died last night."

Zoe opened her mouth, but nothing came out. None of the questions that pushed themselves forward demanding to be answered found a voice. *Are you kidding? How could this happen? Are you sure? Did she suffer? How did you find out? Where was she?* All Zoe could do is jerk her head back and forth in some kind of denial. As if to say Gage was lying to her. But Gage never lied to her. Ever.

"She fell onto the tracks in the Metro and was hit by a subway before she could be helped."

"That's really…" Zoe's words trailed off as she searched for a word. The right word. "That's really an improbable way for her to die."

"The news said that she was leaving the theater. The Metro

station was crowded for that time of night as people were going home from the performance. She was at the front."

Zoe shook her head.

"Is there any question in your mind—is there any chance at all that she might have committed suicide?"

"No." The word burst out of her mouth without any thought. She should reflect on it before spouting off. She should be clear and precise. She pulled her hand free of his. She needed to process what had been going on in Lily's life. Lily had divorced. But Lily was happy now that she was no longer tied to her domineering husband. She liked her job; she'd had a new project that kept her busier than usual. But she seemed excited by what she was doing. She had a new man in her life, Charlie. "No to suicide. I'm pretty sure I can say no. Just yesterday morning, she sent me a video by mistake when she was trying—did you pack my phone? I can show you."

"I put your phone in your purse, but it's on airplane mode. Let's leave it there for now."

Zoe blinked. Did he think someone was tracking her through her phone? That was the only reason that she could come up with for his saying not to use it. Her heart rate was off at a gallop.

"Can you tell me about what you want me to see?" Gage asked.

Zoe turned and searched the traffic out the back window as if she knew how to spot a tail.

"No one's following us," Titus said as he flipped on his blinker and moved toward an exit ramp. "We're almost to our destination."

Zoe swallowed hard. "Yesterday morning was um... Thursday morning. Lily was supposed to go out of town tonight with Charlie, the guy she's been seeing. He was taking her to a little bed and breakfast on the Maryland coast."

Gage leaned forward. "Charlie?"

"Yes. Lily was so happy about it. She sent me a video she made for him by accident. What she really meant to send me were pictures of her trying on outfits. She wanted to make sure she was packing her cutest clothes, so she was trying them on and snapping pictures and sending them to me." Zoe thought back to the pictures. Lily's face had shined with expectation and joy. It was the happiest that Zoe had ever seen her. "She didn't commit suicide. And it sounds like an improbable accident, even if the Metro was crowded." Zoe rubbed a hand over her mouth and nose. They had gone numb again. "You remember that Lily lived with me. Is it possible…"

"I've considered that the people who broke in were coming after Lily and not you. It is possible. But we're only at the beginning of trying to understand what happened. So it's best not to jump to conclusions."

"No. Data needs to be thoroughly examined before a conclusion could possibly be drawn." Dread was the only word that Zoe could come up with to describe this feeling. Horror, maybe. She felt like she needed more oxygen than what she could get through her nose. She opened her mouth to take in big gulps of air.

"Zoe, look me in the eye. Right now. Look at me." Gage's voice pulled her from a very distant place.

She worked to comply. But she felt like she was drowning. Like she couldn't get her head above water. She was flailing and floundering, desperation flooding her system. "I think I'm going to be sick."

Titus was on the side of the road in a split second. Gage reached past her to shove the door open, then held her hips while she leaned out and gagged up her just consumed breakfast. When the horrible retching calmed, Titus handed her a bottle of water.

She swished and spit, dragging her wrist across her mouth. Zoe reached for the door handle to pull it shut, but she didn't have any power in her arms. She was powerless.

Gage reached out and shut it for her. He trapped her chin in his fingers and swiveled around so he could scrutinize her. His eyes were deep blue right then, and they shined with concern. Zoe felt like she should be handling things better. In her world of science, she liked to see cause and effect. Zoe preferred when things were linear and defined. What was happening in her head and in her body was chaos, and she hated it.

Titus swung the SUV back into traffic. "This is an over-whelming situation, I know. I have lots of experience at this, so does Gage." He nodded Gage's way. "This isn't a movie where a good guy shoots a bad guy and then moves on with their day, completely fine. This is what happens in reality. Your reactions are absolutely normal. Okay?"

Zoe could see Titus in the rearview mirror. He wore the same expression he'd worn since she met him in the hospital, impenetrable and stern.

His voice, though, conveyed humanity if not warmth. "Gage says you're a scientist. Mental health research tells us that it's important in the long run that you don't stifle your emotions and play brave. That reacting like this is actually a good sign. It's psychologically healthy. I'm proud of you."

Weird that he should be proud that I'm quaking and puking, Zoe thought as she nodded her acknowledgment to Titus.

He caught her eye in the mirror. "We're here with you. You're safe. But you need to go ahead and let your body do what it needs to do. Don't force those feelings away. Be brave. Be strong. Deal with them as they come. Can I depend on you to do that?"

Zoe nodded again like she had any control over her body's reactions at this point.

Titus reached for his coffee mug and took a long swig. "Lots of nutritious food. Lots of sleep. Some exercise. You don't want a big old case of PTSD, now do you?"

Zoe shook her head, not trusting herself to speak.

"Good. And thank you for not puking in my car." He rolled his lips, and if Zoe squinted, she could actually see the shadow of a smile there. Gage was holding her hand as they powered down the road a short distance and came to a halt.

Titus popped his seat belt and turned toward them. "This is it."

12

Repeated visits to the mud pit enable the wasp to build its house.

— **AFRICAN PROVERB**

TO CALL THIS A "HOUSE" WOULD BE AN INCREDIBLY ELASTIC stretch of the word. Zoe stood in front of what looked like an abandoned manufacturing plant. White paint curled and hung from the metal exterior. Rust accented the door with bright orange streaks along its hinges. "Safe" seemed right, though. No one would suspect that anyone inhabited the interior other than maybe a rat colony. Zoe felt her nostrils flare and her nose wrinkle at the thought.

Gage pulled her bag from the back of the SUV and came to stand beside her. Zoe sent him a wide-eyed gaze. She wondered if this was going to be a dump and run. Were the guys going to open the door, wish her well, and go home to their own beds? *Gage didn't sleep last night. He's been up protecting me. I should hope that he'll go and get some rest.* Though it felt abundant in its selfishness, what Zoe really hoped was that he wouldn't leave her there on her own.

Titus moved to the back of the vehicle, where he removed a computer case. As he strode forward, keys in hand, he aimed for a doorway partially hidden by what had been a fire escape. The door screamed its resistance when he pushed it open. In single file, they moved into the open space. There, in the center of the enormous factory floor, was what looked like a large cube. Titus entered a code on the door handle and pushed it wide as he snapped on the lights and gestured Zoe in.

Night and day. That's the only way to describe the transformation that took place as she stepped from the filthy factory into the apartment. It was an open space with a modern, clean design. The high ceilings gave it an open, airy feel, despite it being windowless. The wall color was the cool tone of tropical water, set off by crisp white woodwork, that felt soothing and fresh. The furniture looked comfortable. There was a wall of floor-to-ceiling bookshelves with a library ladder attached to a rod so it could slide along them. As Zoe moved farther into the space, she saw that the kitchen was up-to-date with stainless steel appliances and granite countertops. There was a bar. Zoe considered and then discarded the idea of a shot of vodka.

"There are three bedrooms, each with their own bathroom." Titus indicated the three doors on the far side of the room. "When the safety door to the inner complex is properly shut, there are no telltale signs that anyone is in here. No lights. No movement. The walls are built to be noise resistant instead of noise canceling. That's so you can have some sense of what's happening outside the cube. It means no yelling. No blaring music or television. You need to keep it down. But you don't have to tiptoe around."

Zoe opened and then shut each of the bedrooms. The last

one, larger than the others, squeezed her heart. It held a queen-size bed, a bunk bed, and a crib inside. A family had been in hiding with little kids. She sniffed the air. It had the slightly stale scent of a hotel room with a whiff of lemon. She moved to the kitchen and found a powder room and a broom closet. Zoe swallowed hard. "Wow," she said as she turned back to Titus, wondering how long she'd have to hide out here.

"Here's the plan." Titus put his case on the table and pulled out a computer. "Gage has to get down to Quantico and sign papers so he can take leave and pick up his duffle."

Zoe's eyebrows were up to her hairline. *Gage is leaving me here*, was her knee-jerk reaction. It was quickly replaced with gratitude that he was going to use his leave to help her. She wondered if she actually *needed* help. Could the bad guys have really been going after Lily? Had someone actually killed her? Surely that was an accident. A horrible, horrible accident, Zoe reasoned, to keep a new wave of bile from crawling up her throat.

"I'm going to take your phone back to Iniquus and get it checked by our forensics department. Then I'll pick up some food and bring it back. What I need you to do right now, Zoe... Zoe, look at me."

Zoe dragged her gaze over to Titus and worked to focus on him.

In a voice even more quiet than his usual low tone, he said, "I need you to make a list of what you'd like to have on hand. Let's say enough food for a week to be safe. A grocery list. Include any toiletries, medications, anything that you need to be comfortable." The timbre of his words forced Zoe to focus on his lips to hear and understand him. Her mind was stuck on the fact that they both planned to leave. She'd be there alone. She pulled out a chair at the dining table where a pad and pen lay ready for use.

Zoe had no appetite and no desire to menu plan. Her list started: *fruit, vegetables, kefir, pasta, coffee…*

"While I'm gone, you can use this computer to do research. *But*, Zoe, this is extremely important. Do *not* contact anyone. Not in any way, shape, or form. You are not to go on *any* social media platform. No Twitter. No Facebook. No Google+. I'm trusting you. Normally, we don't allow Internet in our safe houses. But I think it's important that you have this for your research. You can access news sites, for example."

"Zoe, do you know Charlie's last name?" Gage's question seemed to come out of the blue.

Zoe shook her head and added: *sandwich rolls, deli meats, and cheeses, eggs…*

"Do you know how Lily and Charlie met?"

As she scribbled *chocolate. Lots of chocolate. Wine if it's not already here*, she said, "All I know is that he was considerably older than she was, and that felt a little weird to her at first. Why?" Zoe sent Gage a hard stare.

"I have a theory about who she was seeing. I have some circumstantial evidence, but—"

"Evidence? Do you think this guy might be responsible for Lily's death? He wasn't with her at the theater, I can almost guarantee. Lily said Charlie was getting ready for some big political showdown. He wasn't coming up for air until the weekend."

"She never posted his picture? How long had they been seeing each other?" Titus asked.

"No to the pictures. I can't remember the time frame. It would be on Lily's calendar, though."

"We don't have access to that," Gage replied.

"Sure, we do. Lily has it on Google calendars." Zoe gestured toward the computer. She turned to Titus. "Can I go on Google calendars?"

"You have her password?" Gage asked.

"She has so many passwords to remember at work that she just has a single password she uses in her personal life—outside of her banking, of course."

"Does anyone else have that password besides you?" Titus asked.

Zoe shrugged. "I wouldn't know."

"Okay, first things first. I need you to get into Lily's accounts, her email, her calendar, everything you can access," Gage said. "I need you to take screenshots of everything. We need to get that locked down before anyone has a chance to wipe it."

"You think someone would?"

"We don't know what's going on. The important thing here is that we preserve everything ASAP in case it turns out there's something significant in play."

Zoe pushed the list toward Titus and waved her hand, gesturing for him to hand her the computer. "I'm not that particular. Get whatever's easiest at the store. I can make do."

Titus pushed the computer toward her. "Glad to see you have your priorities straight."

Titus ripped the list off the pad. The men moved toward the door. Zoe refused to watch them leave. She pulled up Lily's accounts, not taking enough time to read them as she did a screengrab, dumped each image into a folder, and moved on to the next. Zoe imagined that she was racing some nefarious character in some underground dungeon, trying to beat her to the information, and her fingers flew over the keyboard. Lily was dead. That was a fact. Gage had said he went to the morgue and saw her body himself. Why would he do that? How could he do that?

Surely this is just an exercise in... She shook her head. What word did she want? Over-cautiousness? Conspiracy? Paranoia? Who would want to kill sweet Lily? She was a CPA, for goodness sake. She liked cats and hot cocoa and reading romances. She grumbled the entire time she exercised because she hated it so much, but she never missed a day because it was on her list of things to do. And nothing made Lily more anxious than not marking off every last item on her to-do list. Reliable Lily. Generous Lily. Funny as all get out Lily with her dry sense of humor. How could she be dead? Zoe pulled the pad of paper over and wrote: *Check Lily's "to-do" list.*

As Zoe pressed save and moved on to the next screen, she wondered about Lily's ex, Graham. What a misogynistic creep. Zoe had never figured out how those two had fit together as a couple. Obviously, they hadn't. Their marriage hadn't lasted long. Zoe picked up the pen and wrote: *Is there any way to get a hold of the security tapes from the Metro?* Then she moved on with her task. Zoe wasn't sure how far back they needed the calendar. She arbitrarily cut it off at two years. She closed the screen then went to Lily's Hotmail account.

Lily was very organized about her accounts. Everything was in nice neat little folders, and her mailbox was basically empty otherwise. Since Lily had last logged in to her account, there was just some spammy crap about lady Viagra, timeshares, and some guy who was willing to share his five-million-dollar windfall from Zaire. Lily hadn't been dead long enough for more items to accumulate. Time was doing odd things in Zoe's head. It seemed she had been living this ordeal forever. But no, she reminded herself, this had all just happened last night. *Two men broke into my apartment, Gage killed them, and you died, Lily.*

That the events happened in such quick succession made them seem like they absolutely must be connected. But she wouldn't jump to conclusions. Her mind had been data-driven for so long, it would be odd to suddenly give in to this emotionality. The sooner that Zoe could connect with her rational mind, the sooner she'd feel more comfortable. She looked around the safe house and felt the solidity of the emptiness. How alone she was. Normally, that was what she craved—time without interruption so she could be in her head moving things around. Now? It was seriously creeping her out.

Zoe forced her attention onto the emails. There were too many to open and capture them all. That would take days. Did Titus mean for her to get *all* of them? The folder for the vet, she could probably overlook because Lily's ex got the cat in the divorce. It was a hateful cat who destroyed the furniture and loved to jump onto counters and bat your drink to the floor. *Enjoy the cat, Graham.*

Zoe skipped over the folder from Lily's sorority and the one from her synagogue and moved to the one marked XX. She had saved the first three items when everything in the folder disappeared. Zoe pressed undo and saw the icon swirling, and for a moment, the folder filled again. Once again, the items disappeared. One by one, Zoe watched all of the folders being discarded. The "deleted items" folder now numbered in the thousands.

"No. No. No!" Zoe yelled at the screen as she tried to figure out a way to save them from being destroyed, but once the last file had been emptied, even the one from the vet, the discard folder went to zero. Zoe stared at the screen. Who would do that? And why? She clicked around to see if there wasn't a ripcord she could pull, some parachute that would open and save the email.

But she couldn't find anything. They had been purged from the system.

As a last-ditch attempt, Zoe pressed refresh. The screen brought up the sign-in page. *That's odd.* She typed in Lily's email address and passcode, and the red font in the box said that the password was incorrect. She tried again. Still incorrect. Someone had changed the password. It wasn't enough that the files were emptied, but now she knew there was no way to retrieve the information.

Who would do this? Why would they care?

She tried Lily's other accounts, her to-do list at Evernote, her cloud files. Even her Picassa folders. All gone.

To Zoe, it felt like Lily had slipped right between her fingers and disappeared into nothingness. *Lily is dead.* Zoe couldn't make herself believe it. "Dead," she said out loud, hammering the word into place, trying to pin it to a hard surface so it wouldn't keep floating away like a dandelion in the wind. Zoe pulled her knees to her chest and let the tears flow freely. *What happened to you, Lily?*

13

Laws catch flies, but let hornets go

— **RUSSIAN PROVERB**

ZOE UNCURLED FROM THE BALL SHE HAD MADE ON THE COUCH. She'd needed to pull the plug and let some of the grief in her chest drain away. She had allowed herself to moan and sob, trying to keep the decibel level within the confines of the safe house walls. She was glad no one was around. She wasn't a woman who felt free exhibiting her emotions. She was publicly pragmatic and only very privately expressive. She had known Lily since they were in undergrad together. Lily was one of a handful of people that were in Zoe's comfort zone. That she allowed to see her cry. Or laugh with abandon. Or be a bitchy, hormonal, ice-cream-eating mess.

Was. Were. Lily would always be thought of in the past tense now.

Zoe moved to the bathroom and splashed cold water onto her face. As she slid her glasses back in place, Zoe saw her eyes were swollen and her face splotchy. She wondered if Lily was being autopsied now. If the medical examiner could say from the evidence how this had happened. She had to force her thoughts away from the visual of someone doing that to Lily's body.

Zoe's thoughts turned to Lily's mom. She'd have been given the news already. *I bet she had other plans for this weekend. Something different than organizing her daughter's funeral.* Zoe shook her head. She wished she could be there for Lily's mom. Lily's mother, being Jewish, believed that autopsies weren't to be performed. But as a questionable death, the authorities would have no choice. It seemed like salt in a wound. Zoe wondered if she'd be able to go to the funeral. She hoped so. Zoe moved

Zoe sniffed loudly, squared her shoulders, and sat back at the computer into the kitchen to get a glass of water. These kinds of thoughts weren't helpful. Helpful would be figuring out why someone would want to wipe all of those emails. She put Lily Winters's name into Google to see if there was more information about the event available. "Event" was a nice, safe, scientific word. "Event" allowed Zoe to stay analytical. That was a better place for her to be. Especially holed up all alone in a safe house.

Zoe clicked on the top article on the Google suggestions list, the "Breaking News" article from CNN. Odd that Lily would be mentioned on CNN. There was a video of Senator Billings standing behind a podium. His wife, dressed in black, stood next to him. She looked like crap. Like she was still in shock from some horrible event, and Zoe wondered why she was torturing herself by appearing in public when she was obviously going through a private hell.

The senator cleared his throat. "I stand before you today with a heavy heart. Last night, a wonderful person, an amazing person, lost her life in a terrible accident on the Metro line."

Zoe watched the senator's wife. When the senator said "wonderful" and "amazing," Barbara Billings curved her stomach in as if she was being punched. Mrs. Billings struggled to hold her shoulders back, to keep her lips from quivering. It was horrible to watch, and Zoe wanted to turn her head and give this woman some privacy but simply couldn't.

"Lily Ann Winters was working with me on a project of immense import to the United States—indeed, to the world's security. Her research was invaluable to the American public." He gripped the podium and rocked back on his heels, then forward. His head dropped. He no longer stared defiantly into the camera lens. "Over the time that I worked with Miss Winters, I was moved by her patriotism, her strength of character, and her sunny personality. I grew to love Lily very much. Lily and I developed an intimate relationship. It was improper of me to stray outside of my marriage of twenty-two years. It was improper for me to fall in love with a colleague. I have nothing more to say on the subject, other than that it was Lily who shined brightly at a time when I was surrounded by the darker forces of humanity. I deeply cared for her. She made me happy. Her death is a great loss to me and to the American public."

The camera panned to Senator Billings's wife, whose face had turned ashen. She was swaying like a metronome, back and forth. A woman in a red trench coat stepped up behind Mrs. Billings, placed a folding chair behind her knees, guided her to sit, and kept a steadying hand on her shoulder. Mrs. Billings kept staring forward, never looking to see who had saved her from a faint. *What kind of jerk would put his wife through a press conference like this?* It was inhuman. Zoe felt like a voyeur peeking through a window into someone's very private pain and felt ashamed to have in any way participated in it.

"How could you have been involved with a married man, Lily?" Zoe muttered at the screen, her mind racing, searching for scraps of conversation that they had shared. "That was so antithetical to your values. Barbara Billings is obviously devastated. You'd never do that to anyone. Ever." *What the heck is going on?*

"As much as I would like to have some time to mourn Lily's death and to work through this with my wife," Senator Billings continued as he turned, and for the first time, realized that Mrs. Billings was physically and emotionally collapsing on national TV. He stared at her for a moment, then looked at the person holding his wife upright, then moved back to the mic. "Our nation is in peril. I will be conducting the first day of Senate hearings into the kinds of weaponry that Montrim Industries is developing and the—"

There was a light knock on the safe house door. Zoe pitched herself out of the chair and away from the computer, her gaze swinging around the room for a place to hide.

"Zoe? Titus Kane. Open the door."

Titus. Zoe felt a little foolish. Her nerves had been spiking since the night before. And maybe there was a tinge of guilt mixed in for having watched the CNN report. Zoe moved to open the door.

THE CUPBOARDS WERE FILLED with the copious amounts of food Titus brought in with him. He handed her a bag that must have contained a good five pounds of chocolate. *Thank God*, Zoe thought.

"Let's talk about your phone."

"Did you bring it back?"

"No. You had an app on there to follow you via GPS. Another one that allowed people to see what numbers you called and who called you. And a keystroke app."

"Someone was tracking my texts?"

He nodded. "Who would want to keep tabs on you?"

Zoe shook her head.

"Montrim?"

"I don't work for Montrim. I merely have lab space at Montrim. They shouldn't care what I'm doing."

"The military?"

Zoe shook her head again.

"What about those operatives from the CIA?"

Zoe rolled her lips. *Yeah, it could be them. It very well could.*

Titus's phone buzzed. He pulled it from his belt and checked the screen. "Gage is heading back and asking if you need anything. It can't be anything from your condo. If it's being watched, we don't want to lead anyone to your location."

Zoe scratched at her head to stop the prickling sensation. She looked over at the bottle of wine Titus had put on the counter. She needed something to take the edge off. "I'm good."

"Pour yourself a glass if you think it will help. When Gage gets here, we need to assemble what we've gathered and put it all on the table so we have a better idea of what's going on. I'm going to go get him."

"Get him? Why get him?"

"His car hasn't been swept yet, so we don't know if someone planted a tracker."

Oh. Zoe moved toward the kitchen and put her hand on the bottle. *Maybe two glasses.* On second thought, Zoe actually had no intention of drinking any alcohol. She needed her thoughts to be sharp. Focused. Pragmatic. She didn't have Titus and Gage's Special Forces skillsets, but she did have a very good brain. Would that be enough to keep her safe?

Fire drives the wasp out of its nest.

— **ITALIAN PROVERB**

"ZOE." GAGE'S EYES WERE NOW GREEN WITH SWIRLS OF BLUE. They seemed turbulent, like a storm kicking up waves of concern. "I need you to trust me. This isn't going to work unless you do."

Titus leaned in. "Do you trust Gage?"

Zoe twisted her fingers together in her lap. "With my life —obviously."

"Now, I need you to trust me." Titus was using his soft voice again. The one that forced her to lean forward and pay complete attention.

She wrinkled her nose. She didn't like this particular tactic. Zoe wanted to be able to hear and let her mind churn at the same time.

"I'm going to be truthful with you. Gage trusts me—of all the people he knows, I'm the one he called to help protect you."

Zoe frowned.

"He turned to me because I'm the Commander of Panther Force—an elite group of former Special Forces who work for Iniquus."

Zoe nodded. She knew who Iniquus was. Not only had Gage interviewed with them recently, but they had been in the paper and on TV. She had never heard anything but glowing terms when it came to Iniquus. Sometimes the admiration seemed to tip into adoration as if the men and women of Iniquus were superheroes. By all accounts, they were the good guys. The ones who fast-roped off helicopters and swam two miles in the dark of night to save families kidnapped by pirates off of Sudan. The ones who searched for a missing teammate through tropical storms in the Gulf, even though everyone knew there was no hope of survival. And they were as red, white, and blue as the American flag. Titus was with Iniquus, and Gage had called him —Zoe had never for a moment doubted that she was safe in his hands.

"Now, here's the part that might have you changing your mind about who to trust. Iniquus is headquartered here in DC, and we work as a liaison between different government entities. Gage, can I see those business cards you've collected?"

Gage reached into his pocket and handed them over.

"The FBI, the CIA, the military." As he spoke, he laid down a corresponding card from each. "The legislature, the police. We contract with all of them. They're our bread and butter. We also do security for people who need us in the corporate world. Montrim is one of our customers." He laid down the last card in his hand with the name Christopher S. Bilik beside the red foil Montrim logo. "We often go overseas with Montrim executives to provide security in hot spots, though I've never met Mr. Bilik. I have worked for all of these organizations. Knowing this, are you still okay with Iniquus protecting you?"

Zoe pulled her gaze from Titus and let her eyes rest on Gage, looking for any sign that he was conflicted. She found only resolve on his face. "Yes, thank you," she replied. "I appreciate your help."

Titus's calloused palm gestured over the cards. "I know how they work. I know how they play. And right now, I know you're a hot commodity for someone. All of them have the capacity to have gone after you last night. Or it could have been none of them. It could very well be some outside entity that hasn't landed on our radar yet. That's what we need to start working on now. I need a better handle on what you do and who you think might have targeted you."

Zoe looked between the two men. They both sat at the edge of their seats, their elbows balanced on their knees as they leaned in, closing the circle like a football huddle. Zoe didn't know where to start.

"You both think it was me that was the target and not Lily?" Zoe shut her eyes as she realized how much she had willed the opposite to be true. In her mind, she had decided that some bad men had come after Lily, and, for whatever reason, Lily was the victim of a tragedy. But if Lily had been the target, it would mean that Zoe was not. That she could go home and feel sad but safe.

"Not after I found the spyware on your phone. You're a person of enormous interest to someone. And we need to know why." Titus hammered his words as if he were nailing a sign in place.

She had allowed herself to lapse into wishful thinking. She had lined up what little information she had and written a story that fit her purposes. It was an unscientific approach, inconsistent with how her brain usually worked. But her brain was usually building and testing ideas in a laboratory, not facing off against bad men with criminal intent.

Facts. Science. Logic. Even if Titus had asked her to be brave enough to experience her emotions and deal with them in the here and now, she thought that it was probably a bad strategy. First, she didn't like to swim around in her emotions. And second, the emotions clouded her thought processes, entangled them in superfluous data, drove her down roads that were dead ends, like the one that went, "surely they were coming after Lily, and I'm safe." Nope. Zoe needed to plant both feet in reality.

She took a deep breath and imagined herself in front of her whiteboard, working out a problem. But the faces of the dead men in her bedroom, and Gage's war face when he'd dragged her out from under the bed, formed a barrier between her and logic. Okay, shoving her emotions aside might not be possible. She'd work on tucking her reactions away the best that she could. She cleared her throat and looked at Gage. "Ready?"

His eyebrows came down low and flat, and he nodded.

"I'm a scientist." She pushed her glasses up her nose into place. "I do research and development in micro-robotics. I went to undergrad with a dual major in biomedical engineering and software engineering. Lily lived in the dorm room next door to me freshman year. We liked each other because we both kept our heads in our books. She was working on a degree in accounting. But I'll get to that in a moment." Already her thoughts were jumbled. She needed to untangle the knots to make this as simple and thorough as possible.

Gage stalked over to the table and snapped up the pen and pad. He read over the two items Zoe had written there, then flipped that page over to a fresh sheet as he sat down beside her.

Zoe rubbed sweaty palms over her thighs. "My senior year, I

was working on my honor's research project, investigating the usefulness of biomarkers that I'd discovered in human blood."

Titus raised a questioning brow. She held up a hand and said. "First things first. What are your clearance levels?"

Titus put his hand on his chest. "I'm top secret and above."

Gage nodded. "I'm top secret."

Zoe nodded. Top secret. They were safe to read into some of the program. Certainly not all of it. Gage and Titus would need enough to know the who, what, and why of the people who had their business cards on the table. They didn't need to understand the scientific minutiae. Zoe stared at the floor between her feet and was grateful that both of the men gave her time. She decided she needed to walk them through her timeline.

"I was doing some research one night for an ethics paper, and I came across something called the Innocence Project. This project's goal was to free those imprisoned for crimes they didn't commit. About seventy-five percent of those who were later exonerated had been convicted based on eyewitness testimony. Eyewitness testimony depends on human memory, and we know, without a scientific doubt, that human memory is malleable. Memories can be seeded and otherwise changed by the passage of time, the lighting, the person's mood, their profession, or more insidiously, the choice of words in a police officer's question. That's what I ultimately wrote my paper about, the ethics of using information that we can scientifically prove is flawed to take away someone's freedom." Zoe pushed her hair behind her ears, then got up to pace. She wanted to move away from the intensity of the men's scrutiny. It felt too heavy, and she needed to move her muscles and look at furniture rather than their faces.

"DNA testing is newer than some of the Innocence Project cases that I read about. DNA is costly. The labs are backed up sometimes by a year or more. A lot of people simply don't have access to getting their DNA tested to substantiate their innocence." Zoe looked up, and the men nodded. "I had been doing experiments on blood biomarkers. For example, I developed a method to tell if blood came from a female or a male."

"These are hormones?" Gage asked.

"No, hormones fluctuate and can be changed. For example, if a person is undergoing gender reassignment and is using hormone therapy, then that changes the blood levels outside of the norm for birth gender. The markers I identified are stable within the subject over time. They cannot be altered by manipulation."

"Would you be able to give me examples of some markers?" Gage asked.

"Well, two that you might know about are blood types like A, B, or O and their corresponding Rh factors. That's positive or negative. I'm A positive. Gage, you're O positive."

Gage sent her a speculative look.

"It's on your dog tags. Those biomarkers are the ones that most people know about. I have more. Lots more."

"All right. Biomarkers. Go on," Titus replied.

"In grad school, my thesis was built around developing a presumptive field test for law enforcement, so they could rule out an individual who had come under scrutiny for a crime."

"Do biometric blood analysis in the field," Gage said as he scribbled onto the pad.

"My aim was to develop a field rule-in rule-out test. It's meant to merely be a presumptive test."

Zoe had paced to the far side of the room, and Gage swiveled to look at her. "What does that mean exactly?"

"In forensic science, they have the ability to do some testing at the scene of a crime. If, for example, they see something streaked on the floor that looks like blood, they can use a reagent to test it. The results are not definitive—they will simply tell the forensic tech that either the substance *isn't* blood or that the substance possibly *is* blood. If they get a positive presumptive test result—mind you, it could be a false positive—then the tech knows that they should process the area as if it were blood and take the information back to the lab for further analysis."

Gage scribbled some more words onto his pad. "And this applies to your blood biomarkers, how?"

"Let's say that a tech picked up some blood on the scene, and the police have someone in hand they think is associated with that blood. The officer could ask for a blood sample. It would be a quick finger stick and a couple of drops of blood. The tech could then compare the suspect's sample to the blood on scene and decide right there and then that no, there is no possibility that this is that person's blood. Or yes, there is a possibility that this is the person's blood, which would signal a need to order a DNA test. This presumptive test would help a lot of innocent people walk away without having the time and expense of proving their innocence. It would also save time, money, and effort for law enforcement, the American court system, and even the U.S. prison system. Even though this only accounts for a small subsection of crimes where blood was left on scene by the perpetrator."

"There has to be blood on the scene?" Titus asked.

"For my test? Yes. It can't be a DNA sample from skin or hair follicles or secretions like semen. My test only works on biomarkers found in human blood."

"I can see that having an amazing effect on law enforcement and their ability to manage their resources better," Titus said. "I notice that you keep saying America and the US in reference to law enforcement uses for your test. Why is that?"

Zoe looked at the ceiling. She was still grappling with what to tell them. Zoe could hear the wall clock tic-tic-ticking; other-wise, there was absolute silence. The more she explained, the more her nerves tingled. Hadn't she signed contracts that stipu-lated that to share any of this information outside of the very tight circle of people who signed the contract along with her would be an act of treason? Would she go to jail because she was trying to save her own life?

15

Today butterflies, tomorrow wasps

— NAMIBIAN PROVERB

AFTER A LONG MINUTE SITTING IN SILENCE, TITUS PUSHED THE conversation forward. "Were you able to make it functional?" He had leaned back in his chair, swiveling this way and that to follow Zoe as she paced. It made her feel like she was a duck in a carnival shooting game. She wished he didn't scowl so much.

Zoe pursed her lips. "I'll get to that. But there's another big step that comes next." Yup, she was going to take the leap. She had no way of seeing over the edge anyway, no idea where this was going to land her. "Christmas of my senior year, before I got my bachelor's degree and entered grad school, my parents came to visit me from Hawaii. We went to Washington D.C. for a few days to see the sights. One night, we had tickets to a concert at the Kennedy Center. Colonel Guthrie and his wife, Maeve, joined us for the show and then a late dinner." Zoe stopped to clear her throat. She realized she'd been using a lot of filler.

Telling a broad story as a means of stalling. She knew Gage had probably picked up on the change from her normally succinct exchanges. Zoe sought out his gaze. She read curiosity and worry in his expression, but also affection. She sent him a little smile of gratitude.

"Over dinner, my dad was asking how my research was coming. I was explaining the biomarkers and how I was investigating the efficacy of using them in the forensics field, and what I planned to do in grad school to further that research. At the end of the night, Colonel Guthrie asked me to come and talk to him before I headed back to school, and I did. He thought that having a compendium of information about the unique markers could have a big impact on the war on terrorism. He envisioned having a parallel system to CODIS. CODIS being the FBI's database of DNA. I told you about the Innocence Project and that gathering DNA has prohibitive issues, mainly the backlog and expense of testing it. But testing my markers could let the government know if this was a likely person of interest or not. Colonel Guthrie envisioned a military application for building a library of blood biomarker data to try to identify terrorists. The problem for the military at that time was that it is very hard to identify the bad guys in the field. It's still a problem with groups like ISIS. Their traditional dress and facial hair make it very hard to photograph them and use facial recognition software or ear identification marks."

Both Gage and Titus nodded their heads.

"One of the things that I found was that ninety-one percent of the unchanging biomarkers I identified are familial. The remaining nine percent are unique to the family member."

"What aspects are you measuring?" Titus asked.

Zoe blinked. How did he expect her to describe what she had developed to someone who didn't know squat about the subject?

"That's classified. I'm sharing the absolute minimum for you to understand. And I'm probably breaching my contract by explaining this much."

"Right now, law enforcement uses familial DNA to identify a suspect," Titus said.

"Right, exactly. But there are groups that don't want everyone's DNA to be gathered and stored, even if someone is convicted of a crime by a court of law. They think it's unconstitutional, and the question needs to be decided by the Supreme Court. DNA, at this point, is our best identifier. We do need to be very careful about how we use DNA. My tests aren't the same. They can't be used—they were never intended to be used—to identify someone as the culprit. If anyone tried to do that, to use my test to prove guilt, I'd go to court myself to fight it."

"How did Colonel Guthrie think your tests could help in a war zone?"

"He's a director of DARPA. They subcontract with other entities who do defense research and development. They, for example, subcontract with me. One of the companies they work with is Montrim Industries. Colonel Guthrie wanted Montrim and their contractors to develop a system like the FBI's CODIS. Only this would be for blood biomarkers. Running DNA on everyone is too time-consuming and expensive."

"Who is *everyone*?" Titus asked.

"Everyone in conflict zones."

"What?" Gage's eyes went wide.

"Montrim sends in teams of health care workers contracted by the US government to help with the whole "win the hearts and minds" campaign. They go village to village, set up a tent, give everyone in the village a basic medical once over, offer them health care intervention, antibiotics, immunizations, vitamins, stitches—whatever is needed. As part of the field exam, they do a blood glucose test. Blood glucose is measured by poking a finger and putting a drop of blood onto a sample strip, which is then analyzed by the machine and the number displayed. The newer strips take the tiniest bit of blood to sample. Older strips, however, absorb a blood sample large enough to analyze for the biomarkers."

"Right there in the field?"

"No. The analysis would happen back in the Montrim laboratory. Each of the strips was carefully stored, documented, and brought back to Montrim for testing. The results were stored in a computer database."

"That sounds like what they were trying to do with Osama Bin Laden." Gage leaned forward and posted his forearms on his knees. "Collect DNA samples from the compound where they thought he was hiding. They sent the people in disguised as health workers."

"Montrim started collecting the samples in late spring of that year. The CIA had access to the data, and when they killed or captured enemy soldiers, they took samples to add to the database. In April, the CIA decided to gather information from the Bin Laden complex. I only know this because I was in grad school then and a field test machine. It was a rough prototype, not a sleek finished project. They had to hook it up to a computer screen to read the answers, but it was workable. I only had the one. I allowed the operatives to use it for a 'special project' so they could get their results immediately. They came to me, and I trained them on using the machine. They took it away and then brought it back unused. I put this all together as the news reported Bin Laden was killed by SEAL Team 6. Later, Colonel Guthrie, who had facilitated the CIA's access to my machine, confirmed my suspicions." Zoe shrugged. "Colonel Guthrie said agents went to the complex under the same ruse that Montrim had been using in Iraq, Syria, and Afghanistan. But they were shooed away before they could get a single blood sample."

Gage shook his head. "Yeah, but the US didn't have a sample of Bin Laden's DNA or blood to compare."

"We had familial samples. If they got blood from the children, they'd do the presumptive test. If that was positive, they'd send the samples back to the US for DNA analysis. Of course, just because Bin Laden's wives and children were in a complex didn't mean Bin Laden was there. But it would have been a big clue. And the presumptive tests would tell them whether or not they should go through the effort to test for DNA."

"That's nuts, Zoe." Gage was grinning.

Zoe frowned back at him. "What is?"

"I thought you cleaned beakers in a lab. But instead, you were one of the masterminds trying to take down Bin Laden."

"Yeah, right. That's like telling the Sig Sauer manufacturer that he's responsible for the Bin Laden takedown because he built the gun strapped to one of the SEAL's ankles. I'm just the geek girl in the lab, trying to help the Innocence Project."

"I'd like to go back to discussing Montrim and their database, if you don't mind, Zoe," Titus said. "Montrim set this all up. And you said you were developing a field test. I'd like to hear more about that and where you are with your research currently."

"Hey, Zoe, are you okay?" Gage had fixed his gaze on her face. "Maybe you should stop and eat something."

Zoe didn't want to be "that girl"—the one who was delicate and needy. So even though Gage was right, and she was feeling shaky and sweaty, she wanted to power through this explanation. "I will in a second. Titus, to answer your question, biomarkers were proving helpful in the war against terror. But there was still an unfortunate gap between the time that blood was collected and archived in the States and getting the info back to the boots on the ground. DARPA pushed me to move forward with my long-term goal, helping law enforcement. In order to be of consequence to law enforcement here, and to the armed forces in the Middle East, they needed instant analysis, giving law enforcement the ability to hold a suspect rather than having to let them go while tests were being run."

"You're very careful about using the term law enforcement, so I'm assuming that this wasn't for the police," Titus asked. Zoe could see his mind churning.

"Right," she replied.

Gage picked up one of the business cards on the coffee table. "So for the FBI, like Special Agent Damion Prescott?"

Zoe debated whether she should respond.

"Did you work with Parker and Grossman?" Gage pointed at the cards.

"No, I don't work with the CIA. But you were right about Prescott. He's in charge of the FBI's side of the field trial. It's been going on for a while."

"This would save so many resources. It's an amazing invention. I'd like to get my hands on this for Iniquus," Titus said.

Gage pushed the business cards back into a nice, neat row. "How did Prescott know you were in trouble? How did he get on scene so fast?"

"When I was under my bed, I sent him an SOS text."

"And he wanted to safeguard you because of this tech. I wonder why he couldn't come up with a safe house."

"I have no idea. Sorry." Zoe clapped her hands on either side of her head. "I really need to stop talking and get something to eat." She glanced toward the kitchen. As she said that out loud, she became acutely aware of the nausea that she felt when her mind got so busy that she forgot to take care of her body. She needed fuel. Now.

"I need to call Prescott," Gage told her as Zoe made her way into the kitchen. "Ask him if he has anything new."

"Yeah, I'd really like to know too." She yanked the fridge door open.

"But after you eat, I need you to tell me how Lily is involved with this. You started this whole story with Lily living next to you in the dorm and said that you'd get to her in a moment."

Zoe gathered what she needed for a sandwich. She snagged a nectarine and bumped the door closed with her hip. "When I started my doctoral program, Lily had just graduated with her MBA, she'd taken the CPA exam and had that certification, but she was up against a really difficult job market. Competing against people who had ten years of experience under their belts, while she was still wet behind the ears." Zoe slapped a quick sandwich together, and she took a big bite. She gave herself a moment to chew and swallow before she said, "Usually, UVA's Darden program is a launching pad to the best jobs in the US, but with the recession in full swing and industries putting a moratorium on hiring, there weren't any job openings to compete for. She told me that she had gotten a bite from Montrim Industries and was in town for an interview. We had dinner, and she asked what I was working on."

"Which was?"

Zoe took another bite to buy herself some time. Should she? Shouldn't she? She swallowed and then took a few breaths with closed eyes. The full force of both of the warriors sitting in the living room was overwhelming. She looked from one face to the other. She really didn't have a choice. Zoe sucked a deep breath through her nostrils, and on the exhale, she said, "WASPs."

16

Titus lifted his chin in Gage's direction to catch his attention. After years in battle, where micro-gestures protected their locations from enemy eyes, it didn't take much to convey a message. Gage shifted silently toward his buddy while Zoe was busy eating.

"You said you got data off Lily Winter's phone. When was that?" Titus asked under his breath.

"This morning in the morgue."

"You had help?"

Gage moved Special Agent Prescott's card over to him.

"They should have information from the autopsy by now. If Lily's death was an accident, it changes the dynamics of this situation. How about you give this guy a call and see if he won't share his intel."

Gage palmed the card and moved past Zoe, who sat in her own little bubble, munching her sandwich. He made his way to the bathroom and opened his phone. The call didn't go through. He tried Titus's number and got the same.

Gage moved to a bedroom and tried again. His alarm bells

were ringing hard. He stood in the door, his eyes on Titus until Titus turned toward him, then got up and strolled his way. Gage looked over at Zoe—she was off in Zoe-land, thinking her thoughts, letting the gears grind and turn.

Titus moved through the door and shut it soundlessly behind him.

"My phones not functioning. No bars, where there had been four bars when I was here earlier. No connection. Unless you've got something going on here security-wise, I think someone's messing with airwaves in the area."

Titus did a quick check on his phone. When he looked up, he caught Gage's eye and held it in a split second of silent communication. They had a plan and moved on it.

Gage surveyed the front room as he scooped up the business cards and shoved them in his front pocket. He swung his jacket on and snagged Zoe's from the hook by the door.

Titus was busy packing the laptop and pad of paper, Gage and Zoe had taken notes on. He grabbed Zoe's overnight bag and tilted his head toward the bedroom on the right. Gage put his hand under Zoe's elbow, his index finger making a hush sign. He swept the last of her food from the counter, dumping it into the garbage. Everything was cleared as if they had never been there except for the groceries in the fridge—nothing he could do about that.

Zoe's eyes widened, asking him what was going on. He didn't have an answer other than the prickle that made the hair on the back of his neck stand up. It was the feeling he got when someone had a bead on him and was about to squeeze the trigger. He moved Zoe to the room that Titus had disappeared into, back to the open door of the bathroom. He could make out Titus's silhouette behind the rippled glass shower doors. He steered Zoe into the bathroom and shut the door.

Inside the tub, on the back wall, Titus had opened an escape hatch. Gage pressed Zoe forward, over the lip of the tub, and into Titus's waiting hands. Titus whispered in her ear and pushed her toward the opening. She lifted one foot into the hole, then she was climbing down a ladder. Titus nodded toward Gage, who followed her down. Titus handed him the computer, followed by Zoe's bag then her coat. Gage, in turn, handed them down to Zoe's outstretched hands. Titus entered the tunnel, then pulled the hidden door shut and locked it from their side, preventing anyone from following them along this escape route. Gage and Titus made quick work of the ladder, coming to rest in a dark underground tunnel. With a snap and a shake, Titus's face lit up in the pink glow of a chem-light. He handed it to Zoe.

"What's happening?" In the dim light, it was hard to read Zoe's face, but to Gage's ear, her voice sounded firm and strong.

"Looks like someone's jamming the cellphones. Someone might have located this safe house," he whispered.

"Are you sure there's not an issue because of the materials used to construct the place?"

It was cold in the tunnel. As Zoe spoke, Gage handed her her jacket, and she quickly pulled it on.

"Or maybe it's our distance from cell towers? Or a carrier malfunction? There are reasons for not being able to make a phone call other than there being wolves at the door, right?" she asked.

"Could be, but it's always good practice to go over an escape route. Let's chuck this up to doing a drill." Titus pulled a bullet-proof vest from a hook on the wall. "Here you go, Zoe, it's going to be a little big, but you can make do."

Gage rocked back on his heels, watching Zoe getting strapped in. His mind, though, was securely on how the heck someone had followed them. Gage had watched every move that Titus made. Titus was on point with his counter-surveillance maneuvers. Gage's mind went back to Titus's explanation to Zoe of all the ways he could be entangled by his past associations with everyone who had a hand in this game. He considered the possibility that Titus had compromised them. But if he had, wouldn't he have made up some garbage about having cellphone issues in the safe house? Iniquus, as a company, and Titus, as a commander, were above reproach. Gage sincerely believed that, or he wouldn't have interviewed to be on the teams, and he wouldn't have called Titus to help Zoe. *But you also thought Zoe was just a lab tech.* Yeah. He was definitely questioning his own sense of what was true and what was not. "How do you think they found us, Titus?"

"I don't know, man, we'll work on that later. Right now, the plan is to follow this tunnel. It'll take us to an exfil house about a klick to the north. Once we're topside, there's a landline I can use to send an encrypted message, call in the cavalry. You got a weapon on you?"

"The pistol from earlier."

Titus reached into the front pocket of his tactical jacket. "Here's an extra magazine, sixteen rounds. Zoe? We're going to move forward now. I've got point. Gage's going to bring up the rear. Gage and I have our weapons in hand, and you have the chem-light. If we run into anyone down here, I need you to underhand throw the chem-light toward them, try to get it to roll toward their feet so we can see where to aim, and they can't get a good bead on us. As soon as that light leaves your hand, duck behind us, get flat on the ground up against the wall out of the way of our feet. Do you understand the plan? You don't deviate, no matter what genius idea pops into your head. We're working as a team, and that's your only role. Got it?"

Zoe nodded her head. Her teeth were chattering so loudly that Gage could hear it echoing off the walls of the tunnel.

"Tell me the plan," Titus commanded.

"If someone's there, I throw the light, fall to the ground, and get flat up next to the wall."

Gage had given those same instructions about a dozen times as he moved assets out of harm's way. It sure felt like a different ride when he was in a tunnel under Maryland soil, protecting the woman he loved. Gage let that last thought filter through his head, and he tucked it away to examine later when his nerves weren't so raw.

"Good." Titus pulled the go-bag over his shoulders, reached for Zoe's hand, and planted it on his back. "Don't let go unless you're throwing the light and diving for cover. I need to know I haven't lost you, and I don't want to keep turning around to scan. Got it?"

"Yes," Zoe whispered.

They moved forward at a slow jog. The floor was muddy and slick. In places, they needed to duck their heads a little to move under the joists that kept the roof from collapsing. The farther into the tunnel they moved, the stronger the smell of rot and decay.

Their footfalls echoed through the space. Zoe's breath came in ragged huffs. Gage was counting paces. He jogged at sixty-six paces per hundred meters. Titus said they should be there in a klick. When they reached around the six-hundred pace mark, Titus had slowed his speed perceptibly. He probably felt Zoe getting tired. She was running with twenty pounds of metal around her chest. At pace six hundred and ten, the quality of the air changed. Another fifty paces, and they came to another ladder.

"Hang tight," Titus whispered as he clambered up the rungs.

Zoe held the chem-light above her head as Titus moved cautiously to the top. He pushed the trap door open about an inch, enough to get eyes on the floorboards and see if there were any enemy boots in sight. They stood as still as statutes, ears straining. Finally, Titus pushed the door all the way open, letting natural daylight stream through the hole. Zoe moved to follow, but Gage's hand on her shoulder held her back.

Overhead, they could hear the soft pad of stealthy feet as Titus checked the house. Gage felt like a mouse caught in a trap. Gage had used his elbows to skim the narrow sides of the tunnel the whole way, looking for a possible turnoff. There seemed to be only two ways to get in and out. Gage didn't like this level of vulnerability. He liked options. Sweat dripped from his neck down the back of his cotton shirt. He was antsy to get topside and was about to take action when Titus's head poked down the hole.

"Clear," he called down.

GAGE LEFT ZOE'S OVERNIGHT BAG IN THE TUNNEL, TO BE retrieved when things were safer. He zipped the computer into his jacket, shoved his pistol into his waistband, and scrambled up the ladder and out of the hole, relieved to fill his lungs with fresh air.

He scanned the room. They were standing in the corner of a minimally furnished bedroom containing a painted iron bed, a faded quilt, and a cross on the wall. He followed Zoe into the living room, where she plopped onto a threadbare recliner, her eyes searching his face for answers.

Titus pointed his finger to the olive-green rotary phone hanging on the kitchen wall. "I sent a distress signal to my team. They're en route. We'll have backup within the half-hour. Do you have cell service now?" Titus asked as he pulled his phone from his pocket and pressed a number, said, "Systems check," and moved his phone back to the holster on his belt.

Gage rang Titus's phone. When it rang, he swiped the red button and put his phone back in his pocket. "The cell jammers aren't working out here."

"That was a drill," Zoe whispered. "We ran down the tunnel so we could try it out and make sure that the plan worked, right? No one went to the factory to find me, right?"

Gage took up watch at the side window where he had a clear visual of the road that ran along the front of the house. Trees dotted the broad expanse of the front yard. His head was on a swivel.

Titus was the one to answer her. "Zoe, we don't know who wants you or what their resources are. We need to err on the side of caution. You have some powerful people in play. Powerful resources."

"But how?" Her voice warbled. "No one followed us."

Titus moved from window to window, lifting the curtains a fraction of an inch, checking the perimeter, and letting the fabric fall back into place. "No one followed us on the ground."

Gage pulled a heavy, chest-high bookcase away from the wall.

Zoe sat in the corner of the room, looking lost. "What does that mean, Gage?"

"Someone could have had us on satellite and been following us remotely. It's a huge stretch. I didn't tell anyone that I called Titus. We left my car back at the hospital, and when Titus picked me up from Quantico, I left my SUV in a garage near the Metro line. In order to follow us, they would have needed to identify Titus and his SUV as part of our team. Zoe, come here. I need you to come sit in this corner."

"That all seems very improbable." She moved to the corner and wrestled herself down. It wasn't easy with the bulk and rigidity of the bulletproof vest.

Gage had to grab her hands and lower her into position.

"The probability of all that happening is very low," she said again.

"Very low. Move up against the corner, Zoe. I'm going to push this bookcase across the space."

"But why?" she squeaked as he moved the case into position.

He knew she hated small spaces. Hated the feeling of being confined or trapped. Even clutter around her apartment made her uncomfortable; that's why her place was always minimalist and clean. "I'm sorry, sweetheart. I know this sucks. But hopefully, it won't suck for long."

"Have you got her situated, Gage?"

"Yeah. What have we got for weapons?"

"I'll give the house a shake. You look in the jump bag and see what you can come up with."

Gage pulled the hook and loop closure open on the front of the bag to find a loaded revolver. He leaned over the top of the bookcase. "Zoe?"

She stared up at him with wide eyes.

"Have you ever shot a gun before?" Gage couldn't imagine Zoe with a weapon in her hand, even if she'd grown up in a military household. She was a bookworm, not an adventurer. But over the last few hours, Zoe had been busting his preconceived notions left and right.

She twitched her head to indicate no.

"Okay, this is a revolver. It's very easy to shoot because it never jams. But the downside is you only have five bullets, and it has a kick." He reached down and positioned her hands properly around the grip. "If someone is pointing a weapon at you, look at his stomach. Not his face or his eyes, Zoe. Force yourself to look at his stomach, then reach out like you're pointing your finger at him, and pull the trigger."

Her knuckles were white as she squeezed the gun between her hands.

"Deep breaths. We don't know what's going on right now.

We're just trying to be prepared for anything, right? Panther Force is only a short distance out. We should hear them roaring up the road any minute now. Noise out front can mean good guys. Breathe, Zoe. Are you breathing?"

"Trying to."

"Good. You're doing great. I'll be back to check on you in a bit."

Titus was coming out of a side room with a shotgun and a box of shells. He hunkered into the corner that had a view of the front door and was shoving the shells into his pockets.

"Do you hear engines approaching?" Titus asked.

Gage stilled. Yeah, he could hear them. He leaned over the top of the case. "I'm here, Zoe. I'll protect you. I won't let anything bad happen to you."

Zoe said nothing in return, just looked up at him with her glittering black eyes.

Titus swung his head, telling Gage to cover the back. Gage moved into position.

The house fell silent. Those engines should have driven by the house by now. Gage's senses expanded, sucking in information around him. The bird calls, the leaves blowing across the lawn, every small intonation was analyzed. Gage knew this feeling well. His body was primed for battle. He settled down into the steady count of combat breathing, keeping his mind oxygenated, keeping his body relaxed. Time moved forward, and nothing changed. He wondered if what he and Titus had heard was a roadway nearby that he couldn't account for from the small visual field he had in his position. From what he could tell, anyone coming up the back had little cover. The tree line looked a good fifty yards away. A side street was to his right.

Gage glanced at his watch. "If your team didn't hit traffic, they're only a couple minutes out," he whispered in Titus's direction. Gage turned his head toward Zoe's hiding spot. "Soon, Zoe, okay?"

Zoe didn't answer, but he could imagine her nodding her understanding.

The light on the side table went out. Gage took a step back to get Titus in his view. Titus moved to the phone, lifted the receiver, and after holding it to his ear for a moment, he shook his head and put it back in place. They both checked their cell phones again. Nada.

"Jammers. This isn't your guys, is it?"

"No way," Titus responded. His gaze shot back to the bedroom with the escape tunnel, and he tipped his head. Did Gage think that would be a good option?

"I'd rather not, man," Gage said. "Going down that hole feels like being a fish in a barrel."

"I'm not going back down in the tunnel again," Zoe's voice rose from behind the shelves.

"Titus, man, if they were able to cut the power and the phone lines, they must be close." Gage licked his lips. He slid his phone from his belt and pulled up the number for Special Agent Prescott. He followed Zoe's lead from last night and texted **Zoe SOS**, pressed send, and stuck the phone back in his pocket. Since texts were delivered asynchronously, there was the slight chance that it could slip through, and if not, at least he knew the text would keep trying until it was able to be delivered. These bastards couldn't keep jamming the airwaves forever. Eventually, Prescott would get the heads up.

"Titus, I've got a black SUV coming up the side road. Could it be one of yours?"

"Black, not grey?"

"Black, Durango."

"Not mine. I have the same coming up the front. Counting two heads. Yup. Here we go. Automatic rifles."

"Zoe?" Gage called, his voice gruff. "I need you to lay on your side with your back to the bookcase. I want you to pull your knees to your chest and tuck your head down tight. If there are any bullets, they'll need to get through the books and wood, then they'll hit your vest. Stay tucked tight. Tell me when you're in position." Gage worked to make his voice strong and easy, as if this was no big deal. It was a pretty damned big deal. The SUV had pulled behind a copse of hardwood trees, and Gage counted three heads coming up the back. His pistol and limited ammo would be shit stacked up against MP5 submachine guns that his three had in hand. All three men hid their faces behind black ski masks. They moved in practiced formation, leapfrogging each other to get closer to the house.

"How would they know we're here, Titus?"

"I don't know, man. We'll have to drill down on that question after we put these tangos to sleep."

"Where's this cavalry you promised us? Times up. They're supposed to be here by now."

"Focus," Titus growled.

Gage watched as the first guy in full tactical uniform jumped the garden fence and ran for the door. Gage massaged the trigger, waiting for the perfect headshot that would take out this guy's nervous system. He needed to make sure there was no last-minute burst of ammo spraying the clapboard walls that offered almost zero in the way of real protection. Those bullets would strafe the house, taking out everyone inside. Just as Gage was about to squeeze the trigger, pink mist engulfed the man's head. The tango's body slumped to the ground.

One of his teammates turned and fired in the direction of the bullet's origin. Gage knew the first man was downed by a sniper rifle. Some guy in a ghillie suit was probably prone in the field, just waiting for someone to run in his direction.

"Heads up, Gage. We've got company. The cavalry you were doubting is here. They're dressed in grey camo, Iniquus uniforms. You touch one hair on one of my guys' chinny-chin-chins with your fucking Lauchheimer Trophy shooting skills, and you'll be facing a wrath worse than hell, my brother."

"Copy that." Gage shook his head at Titus's mention of his elite shooting award. He hoped to hell those skills would serve him now. The two remaining tangos were moving in fast. Gage flung himself behind the window frame, hoping for some modicum of protection. The two men split up. One fired toward the woods, forcing anyone back there to duck and cover. The other was racing toward the kitchen door. The tango's MP5 swept high. These men were too well-trained to be shooting so poorly. Gage thought the guy was probably trying to force their heads down, their bodies behind cover. Keep them from shooting. It didn't seem like he intended to kill everyone in the house. Gage thought back to the bag brought in by the two Israelis the other night. It was packed to capture. They were coming to take Zoe alive. As for Titus and him, these guys probably didn't care about their health as much.

The tango was on the patio now. He stopped for a nanosecond glancing down at his dead teammate. As he hopped the body and put his foot on the porch stair, a grey-clad hulk swung around the corner and tackled the man to the ground. Gage had a bead on the guy near the field. He pulled the trigger and saw him fall and roll. When he got up, he gripped his shoulder and took off toward the Durango.

Bullets strafed the house from the front. Gage could hear the plinking of metal and exploding glass. From the front room, the sound of Zoe mewling temporarily dragged his attention away from the fight. When he spun back, he saw the tango slip through the Panther's grasp and leap through the door. Gage brought his fist up and clocked the man with a hard right hook across the jaw. His knuckles slid across the knitted surface of his mask. Gage readied an uppercut, but before he could deliver it, the tango dropped. The Panther shot through the doorway, flinging himself on top of the unconscious man. He cuffed him and gave him a pat-down before he unceremoniously hauled the guy the rest of the way into the house and shut the door.

Gage ducked and ran for the front room.

"Clear," Titus yelled as he popped the front door open for his team members to come in.

Gage dragged the bookcase out of the corner. Zoe was flailing. With practiced hands, he checked her for bullet wounds. There on her back, he could see where three rounds had flattened into shiny silver circles against the plates of her protective vest. He yanked the closure until he had her free of her armor. She put her fists to her chest and sucked in air. He pulled her into his arms and buried his nose in the warm silkiness of her hair. "I've got you, Zoe. You're safe now. I've got you," he whispered.

Slowly, Zoe was able to catch her breath. She clung to Gage, and every time he said, "I've got you," she seemed to climb a little further out of the place this attack had driven her.

Titus moved to stand next to the two. "Gage, man, we've got to get her moved."

ZOE

They are flies that are born of a wasp

— INDONESIAN PROVERB

BEFORE TITUS COULD HUSTLE THEM TOWARD THE CAR, SPECIAL Agent Prescott arrived on the scene, lights flashing. He stood beside the century-old magnolia tree, where Gage introduced him to Titus Kane. Titus gave a two-sentence overview of the attack.

"You got here fast," Gage said.

"The SOS text system isn't the best, but it's working." It seemed as though the moment the black SUV took off from the side street with its one occupant, Gage's text went through. Prescott had traced the number and raced to their location, which fortunately wasn't that far from where he was working. "Are you okay, Zoe?" Prescott asked.

Zoe felt like she was on some kind of hallucinatory drug. She nodded in reply. She was glad for Gage's hand resting between her shoulder blades. It was her anchor.

Prescott sent a glance toward the bullet-ridden front of the little white cottage. "How many are in custody? How many killed?"

"Panther Force didn't sustain any casualties. Zoe took three bullets in her vest. She'll have bruising tomorrow. Of the tangos, one neutralized, one in custody. Three got away, going opposite directions in two vehicles. We didn't chase them down. We weren't going to split our forces if they had a B team heading in. But we got photographs of their license plates."

"Send those over to my phone, will you?"

"Done," Titus responded.

"Shit." Prescott shook his head. "I wish I knew what was going on. DCPD wasn't able to come up with IDs on the men that broke into Zoe's apartment. They aren't in any of our systems. It doesn't mean we'll stop working on it, though, Zoe."

"Iniquus has that, sir," Titus said. "I'll send their identifications to you as well. Right now, what you need to know is that they were documented as Israeli Armed Services. The two men were listed as being MIA, assumed dead in an explosion."

"How did Iniquus swing an identification, where the DCPD and FBI couldn't?"

"Gage took photos of faces and ears and rolled fingerprints after he neutralized the danger. With those three data points, we're confident in the IDs churned out by our computer system," he said obliquely.

Zoe turned her head to catch Gage's eye. When did he have time to do that? She didn't remember him doing that. *Thank goodness* he did that.

Gage looked down at her and dropped a kiss on her forehead.

"Israeli?" Prescott shot a glance at the house. "All right." He took a couple steps away from the men and posted his hands on his hips while he looked up at the sky, making some decision or other. "This is getting complicated as hell, with a lot of foreign intrigue, and a lot of American interests at play. Let's start here for now. How did Iniquus get involved?"

"We heard from Gage that a DARPA scientist was in danger, and Iniquus stepped in with pro-bono security when the FBI fell short." There was no censure in his voice; Titus was merely stating facts.

Prescott chewed on the inside of his cheek. "Is Iniquus willing to continue playing a security role?"

"For the time being," Titus said. "Of course, if this is going to be long term, you're going to need to shift this case to the US Marshal Services."

"But we have some time to try to figure this out?"

"What are you thinking?" Titus asked.

"I'll call in an FBI cleanup crew to come take care of this. If anyone heard gunshots and called the police, we can wave them off." Prescott sent a glance up and down the street. "Doesn't look like that's going to be a problem, though." He focused back on Titus. "We take the suspect to Iniquus headquarters, put him in one of your interrogation rooms, and see if we can't convince him to talk. We take Zoe to your headquarters, as well —she'll be safe and comfortable there for the moment until we can get her rehoused. And we get started piecing the story together. As Zoe names names, I'll have one of my FBI team run by and pick them up for a friendly chat to see if they can add anything to our understanding. All very nice, polite, and civilized. Folks will probably be better about spilling their guts in one of the Iniquus conference rooms than they would if we were asking questions at FBI headquarters, where they'd probably lawyer up. Iniquus has the same ability to record and remote view as we do."

"How do you think they found us?" Gage asked.

"Had to be trackers," Prescott said. "Did anyone sweep you?"

"Titus looked at Zoe's phone, and it was compromised. It's still at Iniquus," Gage said. He looked for Titus's nod that that was the case.

"But not you and your clothes?"

"No. Why would we?" Gage asked.

Titus rubbed a hand over his chin. "You were rubbing shoulders last night and this morning with a bunch of people who seem to have a lot riding on Zoe Kealoha. You brought in a pocketful of high-powered business cards. And most of those people have access to tracking technology." He looked over at Prescott. "I've got equipment in my SUV. We'll give them both a check before we move them."

"Let's go ahead and take care of that sweep," Gage said, "and get this show on the road. I don't want the three that got away to come back with a bigger team and bigger weapons. We don't need a showdown out here."

Titus moved to his SUV, driven over by a Panther, to gather his equipment. Prescott was on his cell, barking orders. Gage stood in place, muttering in her ear, "This kind of thing was all so normal when I was in the Middle East. It feels pretty foreign here at home."

Zoe leaned back into him, and he wrapped his arms around her armor-plated vest. She wondered how in the world they were going to keep her safe without putting themselves in even more danger.

Anger is as a stone cast into a wasp's nest.

— MALABAR PROVERB

A HANDFUL OF COVERT TRACKING DEVICES LAY ON THE KITCHEN table. Titus, Zoe, Gage, and Prescott stared down at the collection.

"Unbelievable." Titus laced his fingers behind his head and leaned back in his chair. "This SNAFU is going to be the subject of a command leader meeting. Obviously, a body sweep needs to be part of our intake protocol."

"Seems like a one in a million shot that something like this could happen," Prescott said.

Titus focused on him. "It only takes one."

"Now we know why we had time for Panther Force to get in place. They tracked the safe house but couldn't follow us when we were in the tunnel, no radio signal that deep down."

One of the Panthers, a guy they called Thorn, tall and lanky like a basketball player, knocked on the doorframe leading from the dining room to the kitchen, and caught Titus's eye. "Sir, I'm back from the safe house."

"Find anything?"

"Yes, sir, everything was intact at the original site. But they were about to make their play."

"Signs?" Prescott asked.

"Det cord and C-4 on the factory door. Not the side entrance we use for in and out, the main door that was soldered shut. Boot prints in strategically triangulated observation points. Tire tracks to two SUVs parked on the far side from where you drove your SUV, Commander. From the rutting, it looks like they took off in a hurry."

"You were on foot when you escaped. How did you beat them here?" Prescott asked.

"We were only a klick by tunnel, which was dug as the crow flies, but it's a seven-mile detour by car. They had to gather the team, find our location, develop a new plan, and execute. The SOS Gage sent to you slipped through almost immediately, so it looks like the fates were shining a little luck in our direction."

"What are you thinking, Gage?" Prescott asked.

Zoe turned to Gage to see his fierce as hell combat face.

"I don't like how close we came to not having the present outcome. I'm used to close shaves. But in the rubble of Kabul, that was the expectation. On American soil, I didn't anticipate a foreign enemy to be gunning for us. And I didn't expect to be protecting precious cargo."

"Precious cargo," Zoe repeated, trying out the words.

"Zoe, you're classified as precious cargo," Titus said. "It means we're tasked with keeping you safe. Okay?"

Zoe gave a quick nod, not sure how to respond. Was she okay with that? Well, she'd rather be someone's precious cargo than a hunting trophy someone bagged. But who? Who wanted her enough to chance gunfire in the middle of the day? And C-4, for heaven's sake. She looked down at the trackers on the table. "And each of these devices was placed by different people?" Zoe asked.

"No, these two are the same. One planted in your jacket and one in Gage's. So it's probably the same person who planted these," Prescott answered.

"Well, one of these is obvious." Gage picked up Christopher Bilik's business card. "Can anyone explain how this is a tracker?"

The four of them stared at the card. Gage turned it over and held it up to the light. He examined the thickness. It looked and felt like every other card in the pile.

Prescott turned to Zoe. "Ideas?"

Zoe took the card from Gage and ran her thumb over the print and graphic. She was alone in her mind, where she was comfortably free of others' intrusions, though she knew that the men sat still and silent, waiting for her to come back into the room with them and offer up an explanation.

She waved the card in the air. "An EMF detector would be needed to confirm." She let her gaze circle the table, taking in the men who sat with her. "Have any of you heard about smart dust?"

Three heads shook in reply.

"Hmmm. Well, it's the only thing I can think of right now."

The men waited patiently.

"I thought smart dust was still conceptual in its communication's application." Zoe laid the card back on the table. "There was a grad student working on a silicon chip, which she exploded by accident, destroying it. But through that accident, she realized that the individual pieces could work as sensors. Those sensors have real-world applications now in many scientific ways, such as detecting tumors." She fell silent.

The men watched her as she ran the pads of her fingertips over the card like she was reading braille. She pursed her lips in concentration.

"Zoe," Gage reached for her hand. "You're going to have to make a connection for us between the discovery and this card."

She looked up. "It would just be speculation." Zoe didn't like theory and speculation; they could throw thoughts in incorrect directions. She liked facts and clear data. Sitting at this kitchen table, without scientific equipment, she had a hypothesis, and that was about it.

"That's okay," Gage said.

Zoe put the card back on the table. "A collection of micro-electromechanical systems can form a simple computer."

Prescott reached for the card and ran his thumb over the print like Zoe had. "Small enough that it could be embedded in this card or even the ink on this card?"

"They are light enough that they can remain suspended in air," Zoe replied. "The concept is used to gather information in environments that are hostile to life."

"How small would this be?" Titus reached for the card so he could feel the print as well.

"I'm just *speculating*." Zoe needed them to hear the word again. They needed to understand that she didn't have the answers. Shifting her weight from one thigh to another, she said, "That's not good science."

Prescott leaned forward. "We're throwing ideas on the table. No one's going to call these actual facts. Why do you want this card to go through the EMF detector? What do you think we might find?"

"It could be that the foil on the "M" is an antenna to augment the capacity of a tracking system built on smart dust research."

Prescott reached to take the card from Titus and stared at the logo. "It would need a power source."

"If it were me? I'd go for kinetic energy or possible light power. No, not light. The card will be in a place that gets little to no light in someone's pocket or wallet. Kinetic energy. That's what I'd develop."

Prescott lay the Montrim card on the table. Gage pulled out the other business cards that he had in his pocket. "Let's see if we can figure out where the other trackers came from." He laid the cards in a straight line down the middle of the table. "Zoe sent me a text. I went to visit her. There were two attackers. Neither would have been able to plant a tracker on me. The next people I encountered were the DCPD." Gage moved the detective's card to the front of the line. "Detective Adamson and I had a close encounter in the kitchen. I have no idea why he would plant a tracker on me."

"He wouldn't," Prescott said. "Let's take him off the table."

Gage scooped the card up and put it in his pocket. "And you were there too, Prescott. Later on, I met you for our field trip."

Zoe wondered what kind of field trip Gage had taken in the middle of the night with the FBI special agent.

"None of these are mine." Prescott flicked his finger at the tracking devices. "I had zero reasons to track you. I know Zoe from her work with the blood biomarker field analysis. I went to her condo, following her SOS text. I met you later because you had a weird correlation between—" Prescott cut himself short when Gage glared in his direction. "I'm involved now because you sent a second SOS text. And frankly, I'm looking forward to getting caught up on what this is all about. Why is there Israeli interest in Zoe?"

144 | FIONA QUINN

"I think we're all are looking forward to understanding this better." Gage picked up Prescott's card. "That takes you off the table too." Gage moved that card to his pocket. "Leaving Zoe's place, my first stop was Colonel Guthrie's house."

"Why did you go there?" Titus asked.

Zoe turned interested eyes on Gage. "How did you know I know the Colonel?"

"I called the hospital to see if they would give me an update on you. They were able to tell me what was going on because I was listed on your advanced medical directive."

"That's right, I filled that out as a requirement when I set up a lab at Montrim. I also listed Colonel Guthrie," Zoe said as the light went on in her head.

"I found his address on your phone and went to tell him what had happened in person." Gage moved the colonel's card forward. "While I was there, Senator Billings showed up drunk on the colonel's lawn. I removed myself to the kitchen while the colonel sent his friend upstairs. I found the senator's wallet on the grass as I left and took a card. It wasn't offered to me. I was never in the same room as the senator." Gage pulled Charles Billings's card off the table and put it in his pocket.

"Next, I went to the hospital. First Parker, then Grossman came to visit. They both came right into the room. Grossman mostly stood by the sink except when he shook my hand. I don't see how he could have planted a tracker on me. But I'm going to leave him in play." Gage pulled that card to the side. "Parker, on the other hand, made himself at home. The next person to visit the hospital was the colonel." Gage tapped the card. "Then Bilik from Montrim. We know he handed me his tracker, embedded somehow in this card."

"The CIA were the only ones who walked into the hospital room?" Prescott asked, pulling Parker's card to the center.

"That's right, I spoke with everyone else at her door."

"Then the CIA would have had the opportunity to plant the pair of trackers in the coats, one for Zoe and one for Gage." Prescott put the matching trackers on that card.

"Which leaves two more trackers and one card," Titus said.

Prescott moved the tracker that was found in Zoe's watch to the side. "This was done in the past. Not last night." He put the last tracker they'd found on Gage onto Colonel Guthrie's business card. "Now isn't that interesting. Why did he go by the hospital in the early hours of the morning? Didn't you already tell him she was fine?"

"He brought me some coffee and a sandwich. He came to check up on her."

Titus leaned forward. "So he expected you to be there. He knew what had happened. He knew you were going to be protecting her. Did he know you contacted me?"

"I didn't mention you, no."

"He wanted to know where you were taking her," Titus said. "Still, why would he plant a tracker? I'm not so sure about this one."

"I'm more confident in the ones planted by the CIA. They definitely wanted to know where she went." Prescott sent a speculative look Zoe's way.

"But there's also the tracker that was in my phone, that Titus found, and now the one in my watch." She pointed to where her watch lay on the table with its back removed. "People could have been tracking me for a very long time."

"Lots of interest in your whereabouts, Zoe. We need to know why."

This tracker information was a lot to take in. Why did people feel a need to follow her? She felt gray as if all the color had been wrung from her body. Gage reached out to run a calming hand down her arm and lace his fingers with hers. She squeezed his hand between both of hers as she looked at the Panther Force men posted at the doors and windows. "This is an inappropriate location for that discussion."

"Understood," Titus said. "We'll have you in a secured location soon. Now that we have a good idea how they found you at the safe house, we can do a better job of keeping you protected."

"Sir, an FBI panel van just pulled up," a Panther called from the front room.

"That's our cleanup crew," Prescott said.

Titus picked up a box that would thwart the tracking signals, placed the devices inside, and shut the lid. "Now everyone will know we've found the trackers. Whoever sent the teams in knows they blew their best chance at their grab, not once but twice." He glanced around the table. "They know if they're going to get to Zoe, the time between our leaving this house and getting her squirreled away is probably their only window of opportunity. I imagine they're scrambling to find a way to snatch her from us. Time to head out."

Where the wasp has passed, the fly sticks fast.

— FRENCH PROVERB

THE FBI PANEL VAN SAT TO THE SIDE OF THE CIRCULAR driveway. Prescott went out to talk to them, and two of the Panthers had gone to bring their vehicles around. Gage and Zoe waited off to the side.

Prescott jogged back to the front door. "Okay, we're set," he called loudly enough for the entire team to hear. "The clean-up crew will take care of the body."

"*Body?* What body?" Zoe spun around, searching for an answer.

"Let's get saddled up and head out," Prescott finished without answering Zoe.

"Roger that." Titus moved through the door as two charcoal grey SUVs pulled in. "Prescott, you got restraining systems? We don't have paperwork to carry the prisoner with us."

"Yeah, let's get him strapped into my vehicle."

Titus turned back to the house. "Okay, bring him out."

Gage maneuvered Zoe out the door and toward the car that would take the middle spot in the convoy. It sat center stage on the sparsely graveled drive.

Zoe turned to watch as one of the Panthers led a man out the front and down the cracked cement walkway. Prescott reached out and plucked the ski mask from his head, exposing the beginnings of one hell of a bruise, a split lip, and a swollen jaw that hung at an improbable angle.

"Zoe, do you recognize this guy?"

With Gage pinned to her side, Zoe moved closer to scrutinize the man's face.

"No. I don't know him," Zoe said as the man licked his lips suggestively. When his leer became a wink, Zoe had the urge to slap the smirk off the man's face. Gage beat her to it with a straight punch that crushed the man's nose. Zoe jumped back out of the way of the spurt of blood that shot from his nostrils and dripped down the front of his shirt. The man would have gone down except for the Panther's tight grip.

"Goddamnit, Gage. You broke his goddamned nose." Prescott threw his hands in the air. "Now, he's going to bleed all over my goddamned car."

"Sorry about that," Gage growled. He was eye to eye with the man who tried to shoot his way into the house to get to her. Gage was palpably seething with violence, and Zoe thought he was having a hard time stoppering it.

Titus patted him on the shoulder. "Stand down, Marine. Get Zoe into the car."

Gage turned. "Fucker," he said and spat on the ground. He reached for Zoe's hand. Gage stalked down the sidewalk, and she two-stepped to keep up.

A Panther opened the SUV's door and pulled the center bench seat down. "You'll be in this one, ma'am." He extended his hand to shake with her. "My name's Thaddeus Crushed. I go by Nutsbe."

"Nutsbe?" Zoe said wonderingly, then she put two and two together. "Oh!" She grimaced.

He crawled into the far back with a chuckle and pulled the seat into place.

"Go ahead, Zoe." Gage held out his hand, gesturing her in.

She moved to the far side of the center bench. Gage folded himself in beside her.

A second Panther came over. "Hey, man." He reached out and fist-bumped Gage. "I heard you might be joining our team, dude. Did you think you'd get better cred if we saw you in action?"

"How am I doing?" Gage asked.

"So far, alive and kicking, and that's about all anyone can ask. Ma'am, I'm Brian Ackerman." He reached past Gage to shake her hand. "They call me Brainiack." Brian, like the other Panthers, looked like he spent a good deal of time keeping his body finely tuned. His tactical jacket was unzipped, revealing how his uniform compression shirt showed off his pecs and washboard abs. His eyes were sharp, and he wore an air of competence like a second skin. Gage would fit right in with these warriors. But she couldn't imagine Gage ever leaving the Marines. She wondered why he even went for the interview. Maybe it was curiosity.

"Zoe," she said in a near whisper.

Brainiack nodded, slammed Gage's door shut, and jumped in the front seat as Titus jogged over and flung himself behind the wheel.

Titus cranked the engine and pulled out behind Prescott.

"Forty minutes, so settle in," he said as gravel crunched under their tires.

Prescott held the lead as they pulled away from the little house. The special agent had another Panther sitting shotgun. Zoe hadn't seen the team all in one place. She turned and scanned the car behind them. There were two more heads. So six Panthers, one FBI agent, and one marine. She should feel safe. *Should.*

"Gage, are you sure the prisoner is secure? Could he get over the seat and out the back door?"

Nutsbe answered from the back. "The tango is shackled to the floorboard, his hands are cuffed to the rod above his head, and he's safety-belted for good measure in the far back seat."

"Okay. Thank you, Nuts—um, Thaddeus."

"Tad will do, ma'am, if you don't like my call name," he said with a grin.

All of the men seemed vigilant. Competent. Ready. She was the only one who was shaking. Gage sent her a searching look, obviously trying to see how she was handling things. Zoe didn't have it in her to lie, to let him think she was a brave little soldier. She was nothing of the kind. She didn't inherit any of her father's military blood. She turned her face to look out the window and wished for the sanctuary of her laboratory.

As they drove, Zoe's limbic system was lit up. Sweat dampened her underarms and thighs and the small of her back. She licked her lips; her mouth had gone oddly dry. She felt like a woman crawling through the desert, desperately hoping to get to water. As they merged onto the highway, Zoe realized that she was having a lot of desert thoughts. The stories her subconscious had pushed forward last night had helped her immensely in her condo when her body went stiff, and all she had by way of defense were memories. With them, she had evaded capture or injury.

She would have survived on her own had she not sent that "come and get me" text to Gage earlier that evening. After all, she'd heard them say that she wasn't there. Her ruse had worked.

But, had Gage not shown up, the would-be kidnappers might well have headed on to plan B.

Before they got the chance, Gage killed them. Gage *killed* them. She closed her eyes. They were Israeli soldiers. They had been assumed dead. Now they really were dead. And who knew why?

Zoe hated the tortured loops her brain was making. She wanted to be back in her life from twenty-four hours ago. Twenty-four hours, could that be right? She lifted her wrist to check the time and remembered that Titus had taken her watch and its tracker away from her. She pushed back her hair, now damp and stringy, getting it out of her face. She'd really like a shower. And some water. That thought brought her right back to deserts.

Traveling in a convoy reminded Zoe of the photos her dad sent to her and her mom from Iraq and stories she had heard on painful anniversaries when her dad drank too much. Her dad had been on a detail that ran VIPs down the hellish twelve-kilometer road that stretched between the heavy fortifications of the Green Zone and Baghdad International Airport. It was extremely dangerous. Getting from the airport to the Green Zone safely was not a given. Insurgents targeted the area because of the military convoys and high-profile visitors. Suicide bombers, roadside bombs, even random shooters were the norm, not the exception. Her dad drove a hillbilly, armored car. That was when a normal military vehicle was retrofitted with anything the soldiers could find in the scrap pile to give themselves a chance at survival.

She turned toward Gage. He was leaning forward, scanning to the right. Zoe looked back at Tad. His eyes were busy looking everywhere around them. "Tad, is this a normal SUV, or is it tricked out with bulletproof panels?"

He maintained his focus on his surroundings but said, "Not armored. No, ma'am, But it's got bullet-resistant glass and run-flat tires."

"Thank you." Zoe turned to look out her window again. They were side by side with an eighteen-wheeler, so she didn't have much of a view. A country music soundtrack played in her mind. Zoe wasn't a big country music fan, but this playlist was the tear-jerker that her dad played on endless loop every painful February 26th. It was the only night of the year when he became an angry drunk. Mean. The only night when her mom would slip out to call some of Dad's buddies to come talk him down while she came into Zoe's room, locked the door, and climbed in bed with her.

"This isn't your father," she'd whisper into Zoe's ear. "This is the anger."

When Zoe was three years old, Dad's twin was stationed in Dhahran, Saudi Arabia, when a missile destroyed the barracks, killing twenty-seven and wounding another ninety-eight Americans. Zoe hated this memory. It reminded her of vulnerability and craziness. Well, she guessed that was fitting since she did feel vulnerable and crazy. As they drove forward, Zoe's mind insisted on thoughts of Iraq. Why?

Zoe scanned her memory. She knew that Operation Desert Storm was over two days after the barracks attack. Her teachers on base had made sure that date was drilled into her head. After the Iraqis announced they were withdrawing from Kuwait, they fled down Highway 80.

It was a huge Iraqi convoy of tanks and armored vehicles,

fleeing troops, and trucks. Allied forces bombed them from the air. It became known as the "Highway of Death." The PR was a nightmare because the airmen bombed the front of the convoy, blocking forward movement, and then bombed the rear, stopping the Iraqis from turning around. For two days, they bombed everything in between. Most of the Iraqis fled into the desert on foot. But there were miles of destruction. It looked like the Americans were having a turkey shoot. That wasn't the truth of it. But that wasn't really the point here.

Zoe cleared her throat and once again wished for some water. "Could someone please explain to me how this works? How does the convoy stay safe if someone were to try to attack us?"

Tad was the one who answered. "Prescott's the only vehicle with lights and sirens. The plan is to only use them in a tight space. We're doing our best to keep a low profile, which is why we left the SUV back at the house. Our goal is to never come to a complete stop. Our route keeps us to the highways as much as possible, but highways can't get us entirely from point A to point B. There are two times when we'll have to deal with stop signs and traffic lights. No matter what, we'll stay bumper to bumper in those spots to avoid the risk of the team getting divided."

"Thank you," Zoe replied. He didn't add, "And possibly conquered," but Zoe heard it in her head.

It really was a complicated time of day to not get cut off from one another, Zoe mused. People were pouring into the city, looking forward to a Friday night of restaurants and entertainment, while others were trying to leave work early for their weekend away from the congestion of the city. Brainiack had told her that Iniquus was positioned on a green space along the Virginia side of the Potomac. That seemed like where the congestion would be concentrated.

Gage reached back behind him, and she slid her hand into

his. She knew that his right hand held the pistol just beneath the window line, out of sight but at the ready. They were moving off the highway to the first of the small towns they needed to traverse. They flew through the stop signs and traffic signals with the help of Prescott's blue lights. They traveled in tight formation. In and out. Zoe had held her breath the whole way. As soon as their tires hit the highway and their speed was up to seventy, she breathed again.

They drove on for another twenty minutes before the blinker click-clacked, signaling their move up the ramp.

"Your heel jackhammering the floorboard is shaking the whole SUV, Gage. What you got going through your head?" Titus asked.

"This is too easy, man. We haven't seen hide nor hair of these guys. This is their last shot at Zoe and their last shot at getting their guy back before we interrogate him and make him spill. They should have been all over us by now. What have we got? Crickets. The hair on the back of my neck is standing up." He scanned the roadway. "Let's not get comfortable. If I were a betting man, I'd say it's going to be when we go through this last town."

"Well, let's hope you're wrong about that. Why don't you lay Zoe down?" Titus said. "Nutsbe told you we've got bullet-resistant glass, but its effectiveness depends on what kind of bullets they're shooting. You feel me?"

"I feel you." Gage pulled her hand toward him. "Zoe, put your head in my lap, sweetheart."

21

ZOE

Anger is a stone cast into a wasp's nest.

— MALABAR PROVERB

ZOE'S BROW FURROWED. SOMEHOW, SHE WAS JUST NOW realizing that there were eight men putting themselves in danger for her.

That was ridiculous.

She resisted his tug. She wasn't worth anyone's life. Not these Panthers, not Damion Prescott, and certainly not Gage.

Gage pulled her hand harder until she fell into his lap.

This is what people meant when they wrote, "her heart was in her throat." It always seemed like such a metaphorical phrase, but this felt literal. Zoe's head rested on Gage's muscular thigh, the seat belt bit into her hip, and she had no good place to put her long legs. Gage ran his fingers through her hair, leaving his hand on her back. She tucked her head down and covered her face with her hands, hating the fact that he knew she was crying.

The convoy slowed. "Not too close, Titus," Brian's low voice wafted back from the front. "Let's leave a little get out of Dodge room if it comes to that."

"Yeah, I hate to say it, but back in the sandbox, the hair on the back of Gage's neck was a damned good barometer on what was coming our way. I'd get my barrel up a little higher."

The exchange was so low; she knew they didn't want her to hear. But adrenaline, she'd found, had wild amplification qualities.

"Yellow light. Keep the gas pedal down, man," Brainiack muttered.

They powered through, with horns honking on either side.

"One down. One to go. Then we should be home free," Titus called back, then mumbled under his breath, "Come on, baby, stay green for me."

Zoe turned her head in time to see Titus pull the cord running from inside his jacket up the side of his neck. His comms popped out of his ear. He tapped a button on his dash. "Panther actual, Beta team. Control, what are you seeing?"

A woman's voice came over the radio. "Titus, you've got a cement mixer perpendicular, running south two blocks forward and an RV heading north directly behind car three. If they're working together, they can box you in at the next light."

"Alpha, copy," Prescott's voice came over the radio.

"Charlie, copy."

That must be the car behind ours, Zoe thought.

The woman's voice came back. "That scenario is a go. The cement truck is picking up speed for an intercept."

"Beta, going left."

Zoe popped up out of Gage's reach when he let go of her to

double-fist his gun. Titus peeled the car around, with a solid bump to the back fender of someone's BMW. The sudden squeal of tires and squawk of a car alarm had Zoe's blood pumping. She sat rigidly in her seat.

"Charlie, right behind you."

Zoe turned to see the third car rounding the curve with better precision.

"Alpha, backing to follow. Lights and sirens."

Moments later, though Zoe couldn't see the car, she could hear the sirens behind them as they rocketed down the curving side streets of the town. What town? She had no clue where she was.

"Control. Beta, be advised, the cement truck is in pursuit. The RV is in advance of your position. Your road curves eastward, and they have the ability to cut off your present direction of travel. The cement truck is pushing Alpha from the rear. You are in danger of being boxed in."

Boxed in. The Highway of Death.

"Alternate route?" Titus asked.

The men in the car were like the edge of a knife. Sharp. Capable of great harm. They all had a latent deadliness as they seemed to fearlessly face this danger. Focused, yes. Primed, yes. But not afraid. She, on the other hand, had the sudden overwhelming urge to pee. She crossed one knee over the other and squeezed her thighs tightly together.

"Control. Beta, be advised, two-hundred meters ahead, there's a break in the tree line. Overland, there's an open space bringing you to a dirt road. It looks tight enough for you to get through, but a tough run for the cement mixer."

"Roger that. I don't see the break. Can you count me in?"

"Control. Beta, you are coming up on the turn in four, three, two, one, hard right."

Titus spun his wheel, and the car bounced over the ditch in great leaps and bounds that threw Zoe up against the restraint of her seatbelt. Her hands reached out to grab the seat in front of her, and she was able to snatch them back in time. She didn't want to jostle Titus as he navigated the deep furrows of winter wheat.

He was aiming for a narrow break in the trees. Too narrow? It looked too narrow. Zoe scanned left and right. There didn't seem to be any other options. Their wheels were severely hampered on this terrain. Even though this was an SUV with high, wide tires, it seemed to her that the cement truck would have an easier time. She could hear the roar of its engine, and she could see how close it was pulling to Prescott at the back of their convoy.

Titus bounced and bumped into the trees. The saplings in front of them were felled and crushed. The paint scraped from the sides of the vehicle with shrill resentment as Titus gunned the engine and squeezed through. Charlie and Alpha held tight behind them, bumper to bumper.

The woman reported. "The cement truck was unable to navigate the trees. It has returned to the road and is backtracking. It's a long shot, but if he follows along that road, he could possibly take you where the dirt road meets the public roadway. Keep your speed up as much as possible."

"Where's the RV gone?" Titus asked. His voice perfectly steady.

Glancing into the rearview mirror, Zoe could see his expression was the exact same look of underlying power that it always held. Should that reassure her? She didn't feel reassured.

"Control. The RV is heading north."

"Any other cars raising a red flag?"

"I'll keep looking. I have an option for you, Beta," she said.

"Listening."

"If you go left instead of right on the farm road and cross over a field, you will come to a barn. It looks like there's a church bus parked alongside. You could exchange vehicles."

"How far out?"

"Five minutes, at your current rate of travel."

"Prescott?"

"Alpha. Ditching these vehicles sounds like a plan to me."

"Beta. Copy that. Control, can you try to make contact with that house? See if they won't lend us their bus for the afternoon?"

"Roger. Wilco." Then communications went silent. The men were silent. The only noise was the thunk of the Tahoe's over-taxed suspension system.

THE FARMER STOOD in front of the gaping maw of the old barn, signaling them forward. They pulled into the darkness and tumbled out of their car doors.

Prescott and his Panther were busy unhooking the prisoner.

The old farmer had a rotund body and a rosy face. He looked tickled pink to be on this adventure.

"Sir, Titus Kane from Iniquus. That's Special Agent Prescott, FBI. We very much appreciate your help. But, sir, there are dangerous people involved. Iniquus Control says that you insist on driving. How can I convince you to simply rent your bus to us? If there's any damage, we're well-covered by insurance."

Zoe didn't hear the rest of the conversation as Gage hustled her onto the bus and sat her in an orange vinyl seat.

Titus must have lost the argument because the gentleman, with keys in hand, was hot-footing it toward the bus. The

Panthers had piled in and sat strategically, with their weapons ready.

The gentleman cranked the engine. He tipped his head up to see everyone in his mirror as he pulled the handle to shut the bus doors. "You'll see. It's for the best I drive. This old girl can be a might ornery. And besides, if anyone looks in the window, they'll see it's me and not one of y'all driving. If you keep your heads down, we'll trick 'em for sure. Hee-hee."

Zoe bent down in compliance, confused by this man's obvious glee. An unexpected adventure on a Friday afternoon. Gage had her in the seat next to the window, and his gun was pointed out the glass over her back. Zoe whispered up to him, "Gage, is there any way they could have tracked us making the switch?"

"Probably. But there's nothing we can do about it. We have to play the hand we've been dealt."

Out they rumbled. The only voice on the bus was the soft-spoken directions that Titus gave to their driver. For a good twenty minutes, Zoe stayed bent over, keeping her head down, praying under her breath for safety.

22

GAGE

"LET'S MOVE," TITUS ORDERED. HE PATTED THE DRIVER'S BACK and thanked him again as their group disembarked. The bus had let them off at the front guard post at Iniquus headquarters. There was a change in manpower. Three vehicles sat just inside of the gate. Six men exited and moved toward the bus. "That's Tidal Force. They're going back with the bus to bring in our vehicles," Brainiack said.

Zoe nodded. She didn't look good. She hadn't said a word since she asked about the convoy strategy. They moved as a group to the new set of SUVs, drove a short distance to a building that looked like a country club with colonnaded porticos. If you didn't know its true function, you'd swear it was a place for fine dining, wedding ceremonies, and charity golf weekends. That image changed the moment they powered into the underground garage.

They took an elevator up to an atrium that was coldly modern in its décor. It reminded Gage of streamlined efficiency. Everything was gunmetal gray, chrome, and black. The men were in Iniquus battle dress uniforms. The women wore civilian clothes in black and grey. Gage felt right at home here. He looked at Zoe, with her shoulders nearly to her ears, and her stiff-legged gait, and thought she didn't get the same sense of relief from this environment.

Titus moved Gage and Zoe along the right-hand corridor. The rest of the Panthers and Prescott moved down the center corridor.

Titus slowed his step and turned until he caught sight of Zoe. "How are you doing, ma'am?"

"I could use something to eat and a nap, to be perfectly honest." Her voice was just above a whisper.

"We can take care of both. Here we go." He opened his palm as a woman rounded the corner, her face brightened with a wide smile. "You'll have time for a meal. We also have a nap pod available. It's the adrenaline spiking in your system and dropping out that makes you feel so tired. Some sleep should help. My associate can accommodate you while the team comes up with the next step."

Zoe stopped walking. "Have you any idea what that might be?"

"We need to hear what you have to say about this situation. And we need to see if there's any kind of correlation between your experiences and Lily Winters's death. You were about to tell us about a connection between you, Lily, and Montrim that went beyond school. You said it had something to do with wasps."

Zoe nodded.

Titus's colleague arrived at their side. "Commander." She beamed at Titus.

"Margot, this is Dr. Kealoha. If you could see that she has an opportunity to eat and recuperate from this morning, I'd appreciate it. Tidal Force will be back within the hour with her luggage."

"Certainly, sir. Doctor, if you'll follow me?" Margot lifted her arm to point down the hall.

Zoe searched Gage's face, clearly asking if she should go. He didn't like to be separated from her, but Zoe needed to eat and sleep. He was worried about her after her hospital stint. She hadn't fully recovered before her discharge; she was simply stable enough to be sent home. Then they lumped on more anxiety, physical action, and lack of food, and she was bound to relapse. He could do more good for her in the meetings, sharing what he learned while Zoe was in the hospital than by holding her hand. They needed to go in different directions for now.

He dropped a kiss onto her head. "I'll see you in a little while."

She took a hesitant step forward, then followed Margot onto the elevator, and she was gone.

Titus started them back toward where the rest of the team had headed. "I had a colleague pull security footage from the scene of Lily's death. And we'd like to hear what Prescott has to say about the autopsy. We need a copy of the death investigator's report. We need to know whether there is a correlation between the two incidents or not. That's key."

"Prescott agreed to this?" Gage asked, stretching his legs, so he and Titus maintained the same gait.

"He's reporting into his office and getting the files sent over now. The autopsy and cause of death are big questions, and the other one is what the heck the wasps Zoe mentioned are. Any clue?"

"None. Zoe doesn't talk about her work with me."

"You and the Zoe seem tight. How long have you known her?" Titus asked.

"We've been seeing each other for about six months."

They stopped in front of an elevator bank, and Titus pressed the up button. "Last I knew, you were stationed at Camp Lejeune."

"Yes, sir, my unit's still down in Carolina." Now that Gage was back in a military setting, his protocols snapped back into place. "I'm in and out of Quantico right now, helping to develop some new training procedures. Still feeling my way, trying to figure out whether I want to re-up or not."

"And?"

"I haven't made up my mind. I appreciate Iniquus's under-standing."

"We only invite the best of the best, Marine. We aren't taking in strays off the street. Command knows how to be patient." Titus nodded at a passing colleague who'd lifted his hand in greeting. "I guess your continued work at Quantico has some-thing to do with Zoe being in Virginia?"

"It does."

"How'd you meet Zoe? I can't imagine that you'd land in the same social circles."

"Well, it's kind of embarrassing to say, sir."

The elevator door slid open, and the men climbed in. Titus pushed the button. As they moved upward, Titus said, "Go on."

Gage looked down as a little smiled played across his lips. "Me and some of the guys were at the grocery store, and my buddy, Scab, couldn't get his engine to turn over. I was under the hood with another Marine, but we couldn't find the prob-lem. So here comes this beautiful Hawaiian girl in her little sundress. As she slid between our truck and her car, she kind of mumbled, "You shouldn't do that," as my buddy was poking around. She opened her door to climb into her electric car, and I asked her in all seriousness why he shouldn't. She had an air of competency. She wasn't flirting. She probably didn't even mean to say that out loud. She spouted out some technical reason." They stepped off the elevator and walked off, side by side.

"The guys said she didn't know what the hell she was talking about. She sighs, takes the wrench from my hand, and crawls under the hood. A couple minutes later, she comes back out, flicks a finger at Scab, and says, "Now try it." It started up like it was new off the showroom floor. I waved the guys on and stayed back to convince her to let me buy her ice cream in thanks. We've been together ever since." Gage stopped walking. He wanted Titus to absorb this piece of information. "You should know that Zoe's very happy living in her own head. There's lots going on in there, and when she lets any of it spill out, it's always interesting and thoughtful. But if you push her, she gets uncomfortable."

Titus leaned a shoulder into the wall and crossed his arms over his chest. "So, you don't push."

"Not if I can help it. I want her in my life. I'm telling you this about her because it's going to come into play. We get a room full of people picking at her, and she's going to slide into her shell. The more we can protect her from feeling over-whelmed, the better. She's an introvert from head to toe."

"You're right. That is going to make a difference." Titus went silent for a moment. "As introverted as you say she is, her circle must be very tight."

Gage didn't know where Titus was heading with this. "Yes, I'd say that's correct."

"Of the people she knows, they're probably all intellectual relationships."

"No. I don't think that's right. She has some good friends, girls she's known since she was a kid—Sydney, Jurnee, and

Holland. They Skype, and she's a different person with them, open, goofy, chatty."

Titus's scowl seemed more pronounced. "That's not your relationship with her."

"Not at all. It's just something I've observed a few times. I'm explaining this because I'm afraid I've drawn her like a nerdy caricature, and that would be a gross misrepresentation."

"But, you're invested."

Gage tipped his head. What was Titus asking him?

"What I need from you here is to tell me your level of investment with her."

"It's a hundred percent."

"Got it. Good. She's going to need someone to run interference for her. Someone that shy—"

"Oh no, she's not at all shy. She's an introvert. She likes to be alone in her head to process things—but she's definitely not timid or shy. She's a strong, intelligent, highly capable person."

"Within the sphere of her understanding. Which means she's going to need to lean on other people's expertise in this."

Gage breathed out. "That might be a stretch."

Titus lifted off the wall and started down the hall again. "Lynx," Titus called out as a young woman with long blonde hair and a bright pink dress rounded the corner. She looked surprisingly out of place.

She scooted over with a wide smile to shake Titus's hand. "I'm told I've been put on loan."

"Thank you, I know your window is a tight one, but we could use some focus. Lynx, this is Gage Harrison."

Lynx held out her hand for a shake as they continued down the hall. "I've heard your name around our halls recently, haven't I?"

"Gage interviewed for a position on Panther Force. He's still deciding whether or not to re-up." Titus pushed a door open with his shoulder. "This is the Panther Force war room," Titus said, holding the door for Lynx, then nodding for Gage to follow her in. "Lynx was snapped up by Strike Force before anyone else got a fair shot at her. Luckily, she's a good sport about being shared around. We're fortunate to have her with us, even if it has to be short-term. She has an amazing ability to solve some confounding puzzles."

"Well, thank you for that, but you're right. I'm pressed for time. Sorry." She walked toward the front of the room. "Now, before we get going, Titus, I should tell you, the good news is that Iniquus signed a contract with the FBI on this case." She focused on Titus. "It's one thing to give safe haven to one of our military scientists. It's quite another for our team to take bullets." She turned her head to include Gage in the conversation. "I'm so glad everyone came out of that okay. As far as our capabilities go, that contract means we're a go with all of our resources." She smiled warmly at Gage. "Now, we can put all of our wheels in gear." She switched her focus between Titus and Gage. "I'll stay in play as long as I can. Got anything we can start with?"

Titus held up the container with the trackers. "Are you ready for a wild story?"

23

THEY TURNED ON A JAMMER SO THEY COULD SAFELY OPEN THE box. Gage and Titus discussed what they had come up with at the kitchen table of the exfil house. Lynx bit her lip, picked up the Montrim card, and moved over to a machine on the back table. She brought it back and lay it in the box. "The tech guys are going to have an early Christmas present when you hand that to them. Wouldn't we just love to have that technology if Zoe's right? Okay, so far, I'm with you. If I were taking a stab at it, I'd line this up the same way: two CIA, one DARPA, one Montrim, and two question marks from before that day in the form of the phone apps on Zoe's cell and the tracker in her watch." A mischievous look crossed her face. "Two things," she said.

Titus crossed his arms over his chest and leaned back against the wall. "I always love what comes out of your mouth when you get that twinkle in your eye."

"Okay, first, Strike Force pulled our guy out of the yellow house. We can send in a clean-up team, and then you can use it for Gage and Zoe since it's our closest long-term secure residence."

"That'll work. I'll call Support and get them on that. Let's hear number two."

"I'm leaving here for Miami shortly." She smiled. "Wouldn't it be amusing if I had the cobblers put together a Zoe Kealoha packet—passport, driver's license, a couple of credit cards—and I bought a ticket for some random cruise that's getting ready to leave the dock? No, wait, some of those trackers were planted on Zoe and some on Gage. Make that a pair of tickets. I could get a set for Striker in Gage's name. We could take the trackers out of the kit just before I get on the plane at Reagan, so no one has a chance to come find them. I fly down, Striker and I can board the ship, place the trackers in the cabin, and slip out before it disembarks. I can let the poor cruise ship off the hook by calling and saying there was a sudden personal emergency— after they're out in International waters, of course—so there are no false alarms that two passengers were lost at sea. But whoever is trying to keep track of Zoe will have eyes on a southern prize, and it might give Zoe a little wiggle room to figure things out."

"Do you have the time to do that?"

"My schedule today is dictated by my flight. Once I'm down in Miami, though, I have a little more flexibility. Should we give that a go?"

"Thanks, Lynx, we'd appreciate it," Titus said.

There was a knock at the door. Prescott and the Panthers filed in as Lynx and Titus made quick calls to follow through with their plan.

"Special Agent Damion Prescott, may I present my colleague, Lynx," Titus said as he got off the phone.

Prescott gave her a curious look.

"Special Agent, if you would," she said and gestured to a seat at one of the worktables. "My understanding is that Dr.

Kealoha is the developer of a forensic field test that you have on trial."

"That's right." He sat down and tipped his head. Gage hadn't seen Prescott act like this before. Wary, unsure. It seemed odd. Lynx appeared innocuous to him.

"Is that the only capacity you have known or interacted with Zoe?"

He lowered his brows. "Yes."

"I seem to make you uncomfortable," she said sweetly.

"Maybe you're just not what I expected when Titus told me he was pulling in an expert."

"Yeah." She laughed as she moved to the front of the room. "I get that a lot. Okay, I've already heard about the trackers. That's all very interesting." She bent down and whispered something in Nutsbe's ear. He was sitting at a computer bank and tapped something out on his keyboard. "Titus said there might be a correlation between the death of Lily Winters and the attacks on Zoe Kealoha. To this end, he sent me some data, which included copies of Lily's Google calendar and a few emails. The emails were encrypted, so they're with the communications team for now. Our techs were able to capture images from her death on the security cameras, which I watched, along with the videos that were taken by the witnesses on site and posted online."

Gage sat to the side of the room. He'd crossed his arms over his chest and hunkered down in his chair. He was laser-focused on what Lynx was saying.

Nutsbe pressed a button. Each of the screens filled with a different image. Lynx lined up remotes in front of each. Gage recognized that the screen on the far left had the image that he had watched from Channel Nine News.

Lynx pressed the arrow. The sound of a reggae band loudly playing the steelpans came to an abrupt halt when a scream went up. "Let's start here. It's quite a crowd for a Thursday night. I checked the normal patterns on this particular track, and they might expect one or two people to get on at this time, but on this particular night, the platform is full. We know it was full that night because a local museum put on a play. I checked with the museum. This is the first time they've tried a weeknight event, and it concluded at twenty-three hundred hours. That made me wonder if the museum doesn't normally have weeknight events, and if this track typically has only one or two riders at this time, why would this reggae band be here?" She put down that remote and picked up the one beside it. "I took a look at the last thirty days of security tapes from this area. There were no other instances of this group or any other street performers in or around this Metro location in the last month. This is a security tape from earlier on Thursday evening." She pressed the button to show the band setting up. "That's twenty-two thirty hours on the dot, a half-hour before the play let out. Less than an hour before Lily's death. Let's put that on the back burner for a minute."

Lynx went back to the video that showed Lily lying on the tracks, eyes open, looking like she was unable to move.

"I've seen this video," Gage said. "To me, it doesn't look like she's hurt. It looks like something else is going on."

A light knock sounded at the door, and Brainiack opened it, accepted some papers, and brought them over to Prescott. Prescott peeked at them and then flipped them over on the table.

Lynx walked over and pointed at the current screen. "The videographer is focused on the band, and then a scream sounds, and they turn to show Lily on the track. The person filming is perfectly positioned to show Lily lying there. Notice that the videographer doesn't respond. There's no gasp of surprise. No bobble of the image. No scream or move to help. In today's society, we often see a bystander record instead of intervening, but typically you see or hear the human reaction. Not so here. Later, as we go through these tapes, you'll see that in this crowd, there are no other phones in hands at this point. Everyone else in the crowd is focused on the horror that's unfolding in front of them." She paused. "Did you receive some information you'd like to share, Special Agent?"

"This can wait. Thank you."

"Moving on, then. Gage, you mentioned her lying there. Initial thoughts might be that she lost her balance because of drugs or alcohol, but I bet when Special Agent Prescott shares his new data, it will indicate that she was substance-free or perhaps had enough alcohol in her system to account for a glass of wine. Another explanation might be an adrenaline reaction called freeze. Everyone in this room has been trained to overcome freeze, and every one of us hopes that training works. In the field, freezing can mean death. Now, if you look at Lily in this still, you see her muscles aren't rigid. They're lax. Not adrenaline freeze. Something else is impeding her ability to stand and get to those oh-so-helpful arms reaching out to her."

"That was said with a heavy dose of sarcasm," Nutsbe said, turning to look up at the screen.

"Yup, I'll get to that in a second." She started the News Nine video. "This is what the videographer wanted you to see next— the light of the approaching subway train. Everyone was trying their best to bring attention to the crisis. Again, no other phones are out. Flailing arms. You can make out the shock on the engineer's face. *Boom.* He's doing everything he can to stop the forward movement of the train. But look, Lily got to her feet. She sees hands that can drag her out of the way, and she reaches for them. The video bounces up and then back down, taking in the horrified crowd. We all know she's been hit. Lily was killed.

That's the story we're supposed to understand. A tragic accident."

"You don't think it is, though. You think someone killed her."

"I do. Let's look back at the Metro security footage. Remember, I started trying to figure out when the band had arrived because it was odd. Look who's arriving at the same time. A group of men, nicely dressed. They're all wearing similar clothes. They aren't talking, but they all arrive within fifteen minutes of each other. All in bulky clothes, gloves, hats, scarves. It's cold. It's December. No worries. But see how they're standing out of the view of the security camera? They don't get on the first subway." She scrolled forward. "They don't get on the next. But then two move to the area where Lily will eventually die, and three go back near the stairs. Here comes the crowd from the theater. They seem to be gravitating left, away from the men who are already there waiting. See these three men near the stairs? They move in such a way that Lily is herded to the right side of the platform, away from the others."

She played the rest of the security footage. They could see Lily fall. They could see hands reaching for her. It was hard to see anything else.

"Tech was able to work some of their magic for me," she said as she moved to the third screen. "This is a close up of that group of men surrounding Lily." They watched as Lily fell. The men worked to block others from getting near her. Then, when she was reaching for their arms, they pulled just out of her reach, and she was hit. "You can't see that in the normal view of the accident. Now here's something I want you to hear. I had tech remove the sounds of the reggae band and the milling crowd. Play that track, please, Nutsbe."

ZzzzzzzZzzz ZzzzzzZzzzz...

"What the heck is that?" Brainiack asked.

"Have a guess? Play it again, please."

ZzzzzzZzzz ZzzzzzZzzzz...

"A stun gun?" Nutsbe offered.

"That's what I think. It lasts for three seconds. Three seconds and a push would land her on the tracks, still conscious. But it can take up to fifteen minutes, depending on various circumstances, to pull oneself back together after being stunned. The reggae band, by the way, left before any emergency personnel arrived on scene. So let's try a hypothetical. Someone pays a band to play at this time. They're there to make enough noise that no one standing around would hear a stun gun. They also had someone in place to film their desired narrative and make sure these five men are never focused on."

"Why is that important?" Gage asked.

"The metro's security footage is kind of meh. And they have clear bystander video that tells the story. Lily's body will be crushed, so hopefully, if all goes to plan, everyone will get lazy and assume it was a freak accident. The guys position her where they want her. They stun her, push her onto the track, block anyone else from helping, then they leave. From the police report, I can put a name and face to everyone else there, but not these five, and not the band." Lynx turned a sweet smile on Prescott. "I'll bet your report says they found two tiny burns below her waist about two inches apart. Is that right?"

Prescott turned the photo over and slid it across the table. It showed two burn marks on Lily's skin. "I'm impressed."

Lynx smiled. "Looks can be deceiving, Special Agent." She seemed to find great amusement in that phrase. Gage thought there was probably a pretty good story behind it.

Lynx walked to the last screen and picked up the remote. "Now, it seems clear that Lily Winters was killed intentionally.

But the reason you wanted to know the cause of her death was that you think there may be a link between Lily's death and Zoe's attack. Commander Kane asked me to find that link."

Every man in the room pulled themselves up straight and leaned forward.

"The last thing I wanted to show you is this." There was a close up of a man's left wrist. Right where a man's watch would go, and about the size of a watch face, was a geometric tattoo.

Titus walked over to the screen. "Is this the best that tech could do with clarity?"

"I'm sorry. It is. But we can see it well enough to make a comparison."

Titus turned abruptly. "To what?"

Lynx clicked forward. There were four images dividing the screen. The top two were pictures that Gage took in Zoe's condo. One of the other images was a black silhouette. Those three each had a red X marking them as deceased. The remaining image was the man they had in custody.

Titus's phone buzzed, and he glanced at the screen.

"Two from Zoe's place, one killed at the exfil house, one in custody. All four have the exact same tattoo in the exact same place." She clicked one more time, and there was a close up of the tattoo. "At least one man involved in Lily's murder has this symbol in common with the four men who have made attempts on Zoe. It's also possible that one of these four men is also the man in the picture from the Metro station. And that, gentlemen, makes me believe that yes, these crimes are connected."

Titus pushed his phone into its holster. He stood, planting his fists on the tabletop. "Lynx, amazing as always. If Strike Force ever forgets how special you are, you've got a place on my team."

"Ha! Well, thank you. Glad I could help."

"Yes, thank you so much," Gage said.

"That call was telling me that the cobblers have the new papers ready, and they've purchased cruise tickets for Zoe and Gage through the Panama Canal."

"Oh, that sounds lovely. Maybe I won't ditch the trackers and run. I could use a bit of a vacation."

"Nope, we need you in action," Titus said. "Speaking of action, we sent a car to ask Senator Billings to come in and answer a few questions for us. He agreed and is in the interview room waiting on us."

"How'd you get him to do that?" Lynx asked.

"We insinuated that we had information about Lily's death. I'm glad we actually do. Do you have time to at least get us started with some questions?"

Instead of answering Titus, Lynx turned to Gage. "Gage, it looks like you have a thought."

"Last night, I had the chance to look in Billings's wallet. I saw a card with that symbol on it. I'd love to know whose business card that is."

"Me too," Lynx replied. "And, Commander, if the guy's already in house, I can get things rolling."

Titus led Prescott and Gage to the elevator. When they exited onto the executive floor, the vibe was completely different from the one they just left. Downstairs contained the fine-tuned, well-oiled mechanics of the Iniquus security machine. This, Gage thought, must be the floor where they collected the money to make the place hum. More in keeping with the country club façade, there were conversation areas with deep leather chairs that called for comfortable chats about where the kids went to

178 | FIONA QUINN

college and upcoming vacation plans. Gage could imagine the movers and shakers enjoying a brandy, and an imported cigar before real points of interest were hashed through, deals made, and contracts signed.

Gage looked down at his clothes, currently covered in mud and blood. He'd be more at home after a shower and a change. He hoped he didn't run into any of the executives. They had offered him a contract, an extremely generous contract, and he was tempted for a number of reasons to take it. They had understood about his being on the fence concerning his next step. They left the contract on the table until his re-up yea or nay with the Marines. Gage wanted to keep that contract open, and his present state seemed disrespectful. Titus was equally dirty, though minus the blood, and he didn't seem to care about muddy boots on the thick pile carpet, so Gage let his concerns go as they turned into a room.

The lights went on automatically as they sidled down the long, narrow gallery. Captain's chairs with writing desks stood in a nice neat row in front of a wall of darkened windows. Behind the chairs was a buffet of sandwiches, water bottles, and fruit. All three men loaded up their plates, then sat down and ate. Just like with sleep, Gage had learned many years ago that in his line of work, grub didn't come on a schedule. If you had access, avail yourself. It could be a long damned time before you saw food again.

24

As Gage finished his second sandwich, the lights in the room in front of the observation windows flicked on. Lynx came through the door with Senator Charles Billings. She waved her hand to indicate a chair to the right. This put Billings face to face with the men. Lynx sat kitty-corner at the head of the table.

Lynx struck Gage as very young, much younger than his twenty-eight years. And very innocent, especially when she smiled. She was a trap. A good one. After seeing her in action figuring out Lily's murder, he thought the whole cheerleader, girl-next-door routine was a power tool in her arsenal. Lynx wore her hair down, while other women wore upswept military styles. She had on a full-skirted, bright-pink dress, while others wore black and grey. It all seemed carefully engineered to confuse, distract, and disarm people. He hoped Zoe would get a chance to meet Lynx. He bet they'd get along very well.

"Senator, I can't tell you how much I appreciate your coming in this evening. How are you holding up?" Lynx was leaning forward. Her voice conveyed genuine sympathy and concern.

"This has been a challenging day."

"I can't even imagine. I saw your news conference this morning. I know you've been in senate hearings all day. Did you have time to eat? Can I call for some food? Something to drink?"

"No, no, thank you. I had my driver go through a drive-thru on the way over here." The senator glanced at the door, then his watch. "Will they be here soon?"

"I'm sorry. Will who be here soon?"

"I was told that Iniquus had information about Lily, and they thought it was important that I hear it privately. That's why I'm here. Where are Mr. Spencer and the others?"

"I'm afraid they are otherwise occupied. I'll be helping you today."

"*You?*" It was almost insulting how dismissive this guy acted toward Lynx, and Gage was offended on her behalf. Titus, on the other hand, seemed to be enjoying this immensely. Titus looked the way he always did, stoic and hard-assed, but having fought enough fights next to him, Gage knew the man was highly amused.

"I wanted to begin by telling you how sorry I am for your loss."

Billings turned his head away, tilting his face down.

"I heard you're staying with your friend Colonel Guthrie. I'm pretty sure I've met him before—kind of a pronounced nose, a scar on the chin, a bit of an ass?"

Lynx's pretty mouth saying "ass" had Billings turning toward her with the hint of a smile. "Yeah, that's him."

"You're going after Montrim Industries. That's a big get. A sixty billion dollar a year get. Thank you for your courage. Did the secret service give you someone to help protect you during the hearings?"

"No, why would they?"

"Sixty billion a year in military contracts…that's big. If Montrim Industries was to collapse because of the hearings…"

"No one can touch me. I'm too high profile."

Lynx tilted her head, considering him. "I can see that. But others involved with this don't enjoy such an advantage. Lily Winters, for example."

His lips quivered. "Lily's suicide is a great tragedy. I don't think I can ever forgive myself for the role I played in her death. I had no idea that she was depressed. That she was suicidal."

"Suicide? No, no, no. I heard the speculation on the news too. The pundits all think she took her life because you refused to leave your wife for her. But we both know how they blow hot air to fill the news cycle. No, Lily was killed."

Lynx let that last sentence settle in. They had been going along conversationally then, boom, she dropped the bomb. She slipped it right in, and Gage knew why. She wanted to gauge his reaction, just like he had wanted to see Colonel Guthrie's when he said Zoe was in the hospital. What Lynx got from Billings was complete bafflement. It was like watching the senator take a blow to the sternum. He actually recoiled. "What?" he choked out.

"You didn't know? Surely when you opened her video message on Thursday morning, you would have seen how happy she was. If anyone saw that, they'd know for sure that Lily wasn't suicidal."

Senator Billings seemed to realize that Lynx was much more than he'd thought she was. He seemed to be scrambling, trying to figure out the situation. His brows drew together, and he shook his head as if he were warding away her words.

Lynx pushed on with her sweet smile and conversational tone. "You didn't get her video message? She sent it first by acci-

182 | FIONA QUINN

dent to a friend of hers. Whoops! So embarrassing. But surely she sent it on to you after?"

"I didn't get a video from Lily on Thursday," he insisted.

"Oh." Lynx picked up a remote and pushed the button. "Well, let me show it to you so you can tell me what you think."

There was a still shot of Lily the way Gage remembered her, with big, black smiling eyes. As the video began, though, Gage became instantly uncomfortable. This was definitely *not* a side of Lily that he'd ever seen.

"Charlie," she crooned as she batted her lashes. "I miss you." She gathered her long brown curls and moved them off her shoulders. Lily reached down and pulled off her sweater. She slid her hands under her breasts, covered by the turquoise stretch lace of her bra, and lifted them up, pushing them together to create even more cleavage. "The girls miss you too." She pouted, then slid one bra strap from her shoulder, then the other. She reached around to unhook her bra. Holding it in place with one hand, she smiled again. "They can't wait to see you tomorrow. They want to be somewhere where they can be free and available to your hungry mouth all weekend." She flung the bra to the side and was soon pinching and pulling at her nipples. "And that's not the only part of me that wants your full attention." She rubbed the flat of her hand down her stomach to her crotch and left it there. She tilted her chin coyly. "Which parts of you would like *my* full attention? Will you send me a picture?" She blew a kiss to the screen, and it went black.

Gage had twisted to the side and was watching out of half-shut eyes. He both needed to see and definitely did not want to see that. He felt his face relax again when it turned off.

"So, no dick pic in return?" Lynx asked with not a bit of shame that she would serve up such a question to the senior senator from Wisconsin.

The senator cleared his throat. "No. Who else has this video? Is this going to be on the news? That's not how Lily should be remembered."

"We'll do everything we can to keep it in-house," Lynx said.

Prescott chuckled under his breath. "God, she's good."

Gage had picked up on it too. The ever so slight undercurrent of threat. *You answer my questions, or this might get into the public's hands.*

"You said this didn't arrive on your phone." Lynx put his card down in front of him. "This phone." She put her finger on the number printed on the front. "But what about your secondary phone?"

"I don't have a secondary phone. All of my calls go through—"

"No?" Lynx cut him off. "Not even this one?" She turned the card over and pointed to where the senator had written his private cellphone number.

The senator turned pink with embarrassment, then red with anger. He went to grab the card, but Lynx was lightning fast. Her hand covered the card and slid it back in front of her.

"Senator, would you do me a great big favor in exchange for my returning this card to you?"

The senator's face twitched, and he looked like he desperately wanted to let a slew of curse words fly behind firmly cemented lips.

Lynx offered him her innocent smile as if the only thoughts in her head were about hot chocolate and puppies. "Can I look in your wallet for a sec?"

Thoroughly perplexed, Billings reached into his back pocket and pulled out his wallet. He slid it over to her. Lynx opened it, reached right in, and pulled out the card with the symbol from the tattoos. She replaced that card with the senator's own card and handed it back to him.

As Billings put his wallet back in his pocket, Lynx positioned the card on the table, a red x showed up on the card, and there was a flash of light that dragged the senator's attention back to her. "Hey, what's going on here? Is this some kind of interrogation? Are there people watching me on the other side of those mirrors?"

Lynx surreptitiously slid the card off the table and put it in her lap. "Oh, sorry. Did you get that impression? No, I'm tasked with trying to run down some information. You know, here at Iniquus, we work to bridge the chasms between the different alphabet agencies. Right now, it's like alphabet soup." She stopped and grinned like she'd made a great joke. "We have interest from the CIA, the FBI, the DCPD, the DOD... Gosh, lots of interest. Anything you can tell me that might help clear this up quickly and neatly would be great. Let's start with this. How did you meet Lily?"

Senator Billings fumbled around in his seat. He didn't seem sure if he should lean back or forward, if he should cross his knees or ankles, or leave his feet side by side. He tried three or four different positions for his hands before he folded them on the table in front of him, like a schoolboy who was in trouble with his teacher.

"You met Lily…" Lynx encouraged.

"I met Lily at a party that I attended with some friends of mine. The Leibowitz's, Ruby and Sal. All right?"

"What do they do for a living?"

"Ruby is a forensic auditor, and Sal is a lobbyist for USIPAC —the United States Pro-Israel lobby."

"Oh yes, I've heard of them. They're working to strengthen relations between the United States and Israel. Did Sal introduce you to Lily?"

"No, Ruby did. They knew each other from college. They were both studying accounting."

"As part of that introduction, Ruby told you that Lily was a CPA over at Montrim, right? I bet that made your ears perk right up. Montrim was in your crosshairs, and this woman might, through her accounting duties, be able to get some data for you. Tell me what happened after that introduction was made."

"I brought her a drink. We had a polite conversation, where I looked for points of commonality. You're right. I wanted to woo her so that I could access more data."

"Woo her. So your intentions were personal? Sexual?"

"No," he mumbled. "Political."

"But you said 'woo.' Wooing implies flirtation and sexuality. Did you find Lily sexually attractive or politically expedient?"

"I, um…"

"Were you wooing her because you wanted to spend time in her company, or did you want to convince her that was true so you could get your hands on her…books?"

"Ah…"

"Okay, let's try it this way. At what point in your relationship did you find yourself physically attracted to Lily Winters? Did you ever find yourself physically attracted to her? Or were you simply having sex to gain the power to manipulate her?"

"No, it wasn't like that. I found myself attracted to Lily as we spent time together, and that led to expanding the scope of our relationship."

"Before you 'expanded your scope,' you made a flirtatious play for Lily. You wanted to see if she could help you with your fact gathering on Montrim."

"Montrim is a—"

Lynx held up her hand. "Let's stay on the subject of Lily for right now. You were at a Jewish event to raise support for Israel. So you knew Lily Winters was Jewish from the beginning?"

"Yes."

"And did you use this to help convince Lily that she should help you over her own self-interests of keeping her job, and despite the potential of being labeled as a whistle-blower, which would preclude many companies from hiring her?"

The senator said nothing but looked thoroughly ashamed.

"Didn't you think her loyalty should lie with her company since they paid her salary? Not to mention, much of the information she disclosed to you was classified."

Billings dropped his hands between his thighs and rubbed them together as if they were cold, and he was trying to warm himself. "You're right. At first, I played on Lily's loyalty to Israel. She knew things were being developed at Montrim that would be a disaster to Israel. Later, I discovered that Lily had three brothers in the military. She grew up as a navy brat. When she went to work for Montrim, she thought she was helping keep her brothers safe by supporting the scientific work that gave the US military its edge. As she rose in the hierarchy and was given higher security access, she realized some of the projects Montrim was developing were genocidal. She was sure the American people would think Montrim's developments were horrific. But she couldn't tell anyone. When we spent time together, and I explained the thrust of my concerns, we were already on the same page. I simply gave her an avenue to help make things right."

"What did this have to do with accounting discrepancies?"

"Do you know that Montrim is working on soundwave technology that destroys animal cells? That's you and me. *We're* animals. Lily had major moral issues with the projects she was assigned to. She was happy to help me bring it to the world's attention. If she left, someone else would just take her place. If she stayed, she could keep an eye on things."

"You said that Lily was a military brat. She had this in common with Dr. Zoe Kealoha. Do you know that name?"

"Yes."

"In what context?"

"Lily was roommates with Zoe until she moved into a place on her own."

"Lily moved into a townhouse in central DC—that's big bucks. Not really possible on a CPA's salary. But there's a parking garage right next door. Would you say that you helped Lily find that place so you could make your way into her house without detection?"

"I needed a safe place for us to meet."

"Who paid for this safe place?"

"USIPAC did after I told them that Lily was helping me with Montrim."

"Why would USIPAC be concerned with Montrim?"

"I'm not going to comment any further on USIPAC."

"We have a witness who says that you were over at Colonel Guthrie's house drunk Thursday night and that Colonel Guthrie knew about your affair with Lily."

"Stan is an old buddy of mine. We were out drinking one night. Our wives were at some female doings. Art center show, maybe. I got soft on scotch and told Stan that I had fallen in love with Lily. I was considering leaving my wife to be with her. I deserve happiness too."

"The colonel tried to dissuade you?"

"He thought it was political suicide. But I won my election last November. I've got six years for my constituency to forgive and forget. There's a template for true lovemaking an affair okay. They had that going on in Carolina with their governor, after all. He told everyone he was incommunicado because he was hiking the Appalachian Trail, for gosh sakes. Turns out he's down in Buenos Aires having a lovefest with his mistress. He comes back, does some *mea culpas,* and is elected to the House of Representatives. He's doing fine. I never lied to my state. I lied to my wife, but everyone understands that goes with the territory."

"The colonel thought this sounded wrong, though, you and Lily?"

"A man of my age, and let's be honest, my shape, with a pretty young twenty-something? It's a stretch, even for my imagination."

"What direction did his lack of trust lead you?"

"Stan suggested that I get the whole picture on Lily before I left my marriage. That was sound advice from a good friend looking out for my best interests. I appreciated his concern, even if I didn't believe they were founded."

"Still, you acted on his advice?"

"I hired a private investigator to follow her. See who she was interacting with, see if she was someone's asset."

"That seems like a smart move. The PIs, how did you come to hire them?"

"PI. Just one. He likes to work alone. I got his name from Stan."

"What did the investigator find? Was Lily true to you?"

"Yes. And Lily was providing me with a great deal of information."

"PIs, especially good ones, are expensive. How did you pay for this and not have it discoverable if you came under scrutiny?"

"USIPAC."

"Again? They've been very generous to you and Lily."

"I've always been pro-Israel. Always gone out of my way to help them in the Senate. I told a contact there, a higher-up, about the soundwave program. In my estimation, it's meant to take out the whole Middle Eastern Peninsula. If no one knows about that technology, it can be deployed without ramifications. There would be no way to trace it back to the United States. With everyone removed, the United States could easily go in and control the oil. They would control the world."

"Ah, so you *do* know why USIPAC was interested in helping Lily help you." Lynx picked up the remote control. "I'm going to put three photos up on the screen. Would you please tell me if you recognize any of the men pictured?"

Lynx clicked to show the first man Gage killed, then the second, then a picture of their prisoner.

"No, I don't recognize any of them."

"Did you think it was a conflict of interest that Colonel Guthrie is involved with Montrim, and you are fighting against Montrim?"

"He's not with Montrim. He's with DARPA. DARPA has contracts that involve Montrim, but he's an army man through and through. Look, he's a good guy, but he ultimately acts like a politician looking out for his own rear end."

"The irony of you saying that is spectacular. Let's go through this again, shall we? I need to drill down on this PI a bit more. I promise we're nearly through here."

"You said this had to do with Lily's death."

"Exactly. This PI concerns me. He wasn't simply following along with Lily's day, so you knew she bought orange juice at Giant supermarket before her yoga class. Your friend Stan had specific reservations that needed to be assuaged and certain shadows that needed to be searched."

"Stan thought it odd that Lily and I would get so hot and heavy so quickly. He suggested that the CIA might have planted her as a honey trap. He said they had a name for assets who slept with men to get information and blackmail power. They call them swallows. A swallow, for damned sake. Lily! Stan thought the soundwave technology and other Montrim projects were important to the CIA, so they'd try to stop me from shutting them down."

"The CIA would stop you?"

"That's what Stan suggested."

"Were you sharing any information with Lily?"

"Well, sure. We shared data back and forth. Lily knew what I had found out and tried to corroborate it with internal evidence. Stan said she might have been using black propaganda, seeding my research with fake information, so I would be completely discredited and become a laughingstock, and Montrim sailed off into the sunset."

"But you never believed it. You just went through the motions to reassure your friend. Do you think that Montrim found out that there was a whistleblower and decided to take her out of the equation?"

Billing put his head in his hands. "God."

"Let's go back to Zoe Kealoha. You said you recognized that name as Lily's old roommate, yes? But that was only a small portion of that story. I'd like you to finish it. How do you know Dr. Zoe Kealoha from Montrim Industries, and how is she tied to your friend Colonel Guthrie?"

"Now that, I have no idea about. I know that Zoe and Lily were roommates, college friends."

"Okay. What did your PI tell you about Lily's death? If he was following her, he should have details."

"All of this happened before. I didn't need any more proof. I trusted Lily. I asked him to stop."

"So, he took his last paycheck and left."

Attention moved to the door when a knock preceded the entrance of the woman Titus had called Margot. "Forgive me, Lynx, it's time."

Lynx checked her watch. "Senator, thank you so much for

speaking with me. I have a plane I need to catch. Someone will be in to attend to you in a moment." She leaned over and shook his hand.

The senator was obviously confused with this sudden shift. "Wait. You were going to—"

But Lynx was already out the door.

Prescott made a sucking sound with his teeth. "Oh, the tangled webs we weave. Are you all following this? Do you get what's going on?"

"The window is getting a little cleaner," Titus said.

The door popped open, and Margot beamed her smile at Titus. Gage tipped his head to see Titus's reaction to Margot. Titus looked the way Titus always looked. Like you'd better get the heck out of his way.

"Sir, Lynx asked me to give you this card. It's the man who did the PI work. She said that according to the senator's facial tells that it's the name of the man who was captured by the Panthers today. She's going to call you as soon as she gets in her car with more information."

"Okay, thank you. Margot, would you see that the senator is shown to the atrium to meet his driver? Tell him that we'll contact him on his private line if we have any further questions. And suggest that at some point that we will release the video, we have back to him. But make it subtle. It's a reminder for him to behave."

"Yes, sir." Margot was out the door.

Titus stood. "Let's head back to the war room and get Nutsbe going on a computer search."

THEY HAD JUST PUSHED through the Panther room door when Titus's phone buzzed on his hip. "Titus here."

"Lynx." Gage heard her answer.

"I'm putting you on speakerphone. The Panthers, Gage Harrison, and Damion Prescott are in the room."

"Hey, sorry about leaving so abruptly. I got caught up and forgot about the time. What did you do with the senator?"

"Margot shooed him out the door. I'm just now bringing the search to Nutsbe's attention. Did you pick up anything else?"

"Some leads to run down. The senator definitely knows who your prisoner is, and he felt ashamed by the association. I'm saying that's your guy, Levi Schultz, or an alias. You may want to drill that one deeper. Did you get his phone when you made the capture?"

"We did. It's on airplane mode until forensics can make sure it's not got a failsafe to wipe it."

"I'd say his contact numbers are going to be gold. I'd check for any photos of Lily, who she was with, and video or audio files. Forensics should be able to track them down if they were taken with that phone."

"Nutsbe's giving you the thumbs up," Titus said.

"Here's another thing Nutsbe should check—no, actually, two things, no, three things. Gosh, I wish I wasn't heading out of town. This is such a good puzzle."

"I'm taking notes," Titus said. What he really meant was that with Lynx on speakerphone, Brainiack was at the whiteboard taking notes.

"One. The senator said that he met Lily at a party with the Leibowitz's. I remember seeing that on the calendar pages that you sent over. It had little hearts all over the place. Before that party, I only saw Ruby or the Leibowitz's name one, maybe two other times. After that party, skip ahead a month, and you start seeing Ruby's name listed two or three times a week. The senator said that Ruby was a forensic auditor. I may be going out on a limb here, but it might be a good idea to have Ruby Leibowitz in for a little chat to see what she has to say about Lily. My bet is that Lily needed to know how to look for the information that the senator needed to make his case."

"Got it. We'll make contact," Titus said.

"Number two. Thursday morning, Lily had an appointment that was just indicated as *10 a.m. Victoria Park*. It's odd that Lily left work for an appointment in a park on a Thursday morning. And Thursday was bitter cold. My thought is to check with the DMV for Levi and get his plates. Then Nutsbe can run Levi's plates through the ALPR scanning system and see his route through the city that day. Do the same for Lily and see if those routes overlap."

"The senator said he called off his wolves. Levi shouldn't have been in the picture at that point," Titus said.

"Well, since we have him cuffed in our holding tank, I'd say he didn't understand that directive. Actually, I'd say he's probably playing double agent, and Levi was still handing information to someone."

"Nutsbe's holding up a sign that says that Lily didn't have a car."

"If you have her phone number, check her GPS routing. Maybe Special Agent Prescott can help you with that."

"Why do you think she was in the gardens?" Prescott called out from his seat across the way.

"I have a guess. But it might be one hell of a stretch."

"Okay, we'll take that under advisement," Prescott said.

"Did any of you see the news this morning?"

Titus looked around at the shaking heads. "That's a negative."

"One of their reporters was found dead in that park—a heart attack. The front page is dedicated to his twenty years of reporting. I'm not sure if there's any way to find out why he was in that park around the time Lily was there, but he was a government corruption specialist, and Lily was acting as a whistle-blower, according to Senator Billings."

"Hell of a coincidence," Gage muttered.

"I'd check out that story, and if by any chance he's connected to Lily, see if anyone has notes on what he was working on," Lynx continued.

"You think he was murdered?" Prescott asked.

"I'm not willing to speculate. I already feel like that's thin ice."

"Okay, you've got one more point," Titus said. They were all huddled around the phone like it was a campfire on a winter's night.

"I do?"

"You said three."

"Huh, hang on, let me think—oh before we leave the topic of the reporter in the park, another way you can trace that down are the recent calls that Gage took from Lily's phone at the morgue. See if any of those numbers go to the paper or this guy."

They could hear tire squeals and horns honking in the background.

"His name is Colin Bunsinger," Lynx said, her voice fading

and then growing louder. "Ah, yes, the third thing. I can't remember where I've seen the symbol on the business card and the tangos' tattooed wrists, but I've seen it somewhere. Not recently, but probably something I studied as a child. I remember looking at it in a book with my mother, so that tells me it's old, maybe ancient, and probably has something to do with art. Sorry, I can't tune that note for you, but it might give Nutsbe some parameters for his search. Okay, I'm going to be battling traffic from here to the airport. I need to focus. Margot gave me the trackers, so that ploy's a go. Good luck, everyone."

The men each called out their thanks and goodbyes to Lynx before the line went dead.

Damion Prescott sat back on the table. "She got all that from her session with Billings? I didn't get any of those connections."

Nutsbe laughed. "Yeah, she's kind of like the Iniquus magician, pulling rabbits from thin air." Nutsbe typed on his keyboard. "I sent a message for forensics to check the guy's phone to see any audio or video recorded on Thursday morning. Shall we lay bets on who's on the tape if it's there?" He tapped a button. "Are you ready for some follow up with what Lynx suggested?"

"Yeah." Prescott moved to the computer station. "What've you got?"

"Here you go." Up on the screen came side by side pictures of their prisoner and a professional photo of the same man in a suit and tie. "This is off his PI webpage."

"He looks better without the scruffy beard and broken jaw and nose," Brainiack remarked.

"I'm pulling up his DMV records. Okay, I have his license plate…and the parameters of Thursday, zero hundred hours to Friday, zero hundred hours, so we'll see where his car went in the city."

"How does Iniquus have this information?" Prescott flared his nostrils. "My understanding is that this data is under government control."

"That's right, and we contract with the government to do this kind of legwork and free up their staff. Right now, this is an FBI contracted job. Obviously, this series of events and crimes have national security ramifications. I'm sure the FBI will be appreciative of all of our efforts to keep America safe," Titus remarked.

"I'm sure they will," Prescott responded dryly.

Titus picked up his phone and pressed a number. "Margot? I need you to go by Ruby and Sal Leibowitz's house and pick up Ruby. She may need a little convincing to come along for the ride... I don't know. You're going to have to go with your gut. Tell her something about her friend, Lily Winters, leaving a package for her or something. Something plausible that Ruby would want to get her hands on... Yeah, well, if she's not there, you'll need to track her down. I need her here ASAP."

"Sir, I have more information." Nutsbe changed the pictures on the screen. On the top were the two men, whom Gage killed, wearing uniforms, sans black face paint. On the bottom were the man they held prisoner and another man no one recognized. Three of the men had red Xs on their faces. "Honey took ear photos and fingerprints of the target he neutralized at the safe house. This is his picture, bottom right, when he still had a face. Our forensics department was able to get his identification pretty quickly because they all have an association."

"Let me guess," Gage said. "They were all in the same Israeli unit, and they were all MIA, presumed dead."

"Bingo. And what's more, Levi Schulz is not the PI's real name. His birth name is actually Ido Mandel. Here's a picture of their unit shortly before the bombing that forensics just sent over." Nutsbe put up a photo on another screen.

Gage moved over to look at it. His brow drew together. "Huh, interesting."

Titus moved to stand next to him. "What are you seeing, Gage?"

"No tattoos on the left wrists."

Prescott pinched at his lower lip. "Son of a gun. You're right. So the team goes MIA, and at least four members show up years later on American soil with affiliation tattoos. And what's more, this guy's services were suggested to the senator by a DARPA director."

"It's possible Colonel Guthrie could only be aware of his work as a PI under the name Levi Schultz. He's well-established here in the DC area if you look at his website. There are court cases listed in which he gave testimony. They aren't small potatoes hearings either," Nutsbe added.

"Who does that?" Brainiack asked. "Gets a tattoo of their group's icon? Besides military, of course."

"I once saw a guy with a tat of a barcode on his wrist. He worked at a grocery store." Nutsbe kept typing as he spoke.

"And what was the barcode for?"

Nutsbe glanced up from his keyboard to catch Brainiack's gaze. "Potato chips."

"Ha." Brainiack laughed.

"I'm wondering if the CIA has any intel on this symbol." Prescott hiked his thumb at the photo. "If Lynx remembers it from a book she saw in her childhood, it's obviously not a corporate logo."

"Perhaps it was once something else, and some group jacked it for their own reasons."

"True." Prescott let his hands rest on the back of his head. "You have two CIA business cards. We could reach out to them. Keep this in the family, so to speak."

"I'd rather not," Gage said. "I didn't get a good vibe from these guys, and I don't want them involved until we know what role they're playing in all of this. Zoe can probably answer some of our questions about that role. Where is Zoe, by the way?"

"Margot said she ate, took a shower, and as soon as she laid her head down, she was passed out," Brainiack said. "We all know how that feels. Adrenaline can kick the shit out of you."

"I'll send someone to wake her up in a little bit if she doesn't get up on her own," Titus said, moving back to the table. "Then, we can have a chat with her about why she thinks she's being hunted internationally."

"You mean besides the biomarker research?" Gage asked.

"Sir," Nutsbe called. "Forensics sent me an audio file off of the PIs phone. They said that the phone was equipped with an app that allows for sound amplification. They've put the audio file through a scrubber to take out the ambient noise. Shall I play it?"

"Go ahead."

The room grew still.

A nervous girl's voice said, "Hi," from the speaker system.

"I'm Colin Bunsinger."

"Yes, I recognize you from your picture in the paper."

"And your name is?"

"I'd rather not say."

"I protect all of my sources. I would never share your name with anyone. But for the sake of our conversation, what shall I call you?"

"Nothing. You will call me nothing." The tension in the woman's voice ramped up.

"Does that sound like Lily to you?" Prescott asked Gage.

"Yeah, it sounds just like her."

"I usually don't meet with folks when they call and say they have a story for me. I'm not in the gossip business. I wouldn't be here except that I got a call right before you rang from Senator Billings, saying that he was sending someone my way. I'm assuming that's you since no one else contacted me. How do you know Senator Billings?"

"I don't know him. Well, I know he's working on a Senate hearing about Montrim Industries, and I have information from Montrim to share with you."

"How did you get it? Are you a Montrim employee?"

Silence followed, and Gage imagined Lily nodding.

"What's in this envelope? It feels pretty thin. Is this all of your evidence?"

"Three pieces of correspondence. The first one is about an apocalyptic weapons system currently being developed. It's based on a DARPA funded study into the use of soundwaves to destroy animal cells. DARPA was interested in developing a way to kill humans in a conflict area without incurring the expense of rebuilding infrastructure and not contaminating the land with toxins."

"So, the technology could be implemented one day, and the invaders could move in the very next?"

"That's my understanding."

The reporter let out a long low whistle. "The letter contains proof of your allegations?"

"The letter talks about technology and how we're in a race with China to develop the system. As a matter of fact, one of Montrim's employees, George Matthews, was implicated in sharing data with China. George disappeared a couple of months ago. I have no idea where he went. I wasn't able to find any information about him, and his house is empty and listed for sale."

"Billings knows all this?"

"I've provided the same emails to his office that I'm sharing with you."

"The sound technology is mind-blowing." There was a string of coughs. "You said two other items?"

"Yes, the next is a letter from a man with the Mossad. I think the Mossad is Israel's version of our CIA?"

"That's right," the reporter confirmed.

"The Mossad sought to purchase a copy of BIOMIST. BIOMIST is an *above* top-secret initiative. I don't have access to what it is. But I can tell you that it's a DARPA project that's been implemented and is similar to the FBI's CODIS system."

"And the Mossad want a copy. Was this a letter written to DARPA?"

"Nutsbe," Titus whispered. "Is that MIA Israeli unit Mossad?"

"No, sir, *Sayeret Matkal*, Special Forces," he replied.

"No, you can read it for yourself," Lily was saying. "Apparently, a Montrim board member brought the project to Mossad's attention and offered to sell them a copy of our data for forty-million dollars. They will update the data bi-monthly for an additional million dollars per update."

"Montrim initiated the sale of DARPA project data to Israel?"

"That's what it says," the woman whispered.

"And the last piece of information?"

"The CIA offered Montrim a contract to get data on a DARPA project and have a team of MONTRIM micro-robotic engineers re-engineer the project for immediate field use by the CIA."

"How would Montrim get ahold of DARPA project plans?"

"The scientist working on the project rents laboratory space at Montrim and uses the encrypted computer systems there. Much of the information there is top secret and above. The computer system passes DARPA security standards. Montrim is not supposed to have access, but when they built their computer system, they built a back door so the board could access all of the scientists' information, whether they worked for Montrim or DARPA. I have that information there for you too."

"What is the project that the CIA wants to take over?"

"RoboSphecius. The documents are in this folder. I'm not a scientist. These things don't make sense to me. But the letters should give you the information you need."

"You have no idea what the RoboSphecius project is about?"

"WASPs," she said.

"Wasps?"

"I'm really uncomfortable talking to you about this in public. I need to go. The documents are in the envelope."

"Look, I just—"

"Sorry," her voice called out. "I can't do any more."

The room sat quietly.

"I think we need to have a conversation with this PI guy," Prescott said. "Where is he right now?"

Nutsbe punched a button and brought up the image of the prisoner sitting in a well-lit white room complete with a white table and white chairs. The man sat with his cuffs attached to the tabletop. His feet were visibly shackled to the floor. "We put him on ice for a while, sir. It seems to help to give them some time to reevaluate their life choices. Makes them more talkative."

Gage looked over at the whiteboard that listed the name of the top-secret project that the CIA wanted to get their hands on. BIOMIST. That sounded ominous as hell. "Titus, Lily said her project was similar to the FBI's CODIS."

"CODIS stands for Combined DNA Index System. BIOMIST could be Blood Marker Indexing System or Biomedical Indexing System."

Gage nodded. "Makes sense to me."

"And wasps?" Titus tapped the board beside the word. "We've heard that one before."

There was a ping at Nutsbe's computer. "Sir, Zoe's on her way in."

Titus turned toward the door. "Good. Now maybe we can get some context for all of this."

*From the same flower, the bee extracts honey
and the wasp*

— ITALIAN PROVERB

ZOE FOLLOWED HER GUIDE TO THE PANTHER WAR ROOM. SHE still felt a little bit like she had been sucked into a virtual reality game and was looking for the eject button. The meal had helped. There had been a nap room with sleeping pods. She felt human again—even though she felt like she was plopped into some weird new dimension. She gave the men a wave as she entered the room.

Gage moved toward her, his eyes a turbulent blue with only a few specks of green. "We were hoping you'd come."

She let her gaze move around the room, taking it in. This was obviously a space where strategizing was done. There were three screens along a focal wall. One contained the faces of four men, three with Xs on their faces, and one displayed a photo that looked like a military unit in the desert. A photo like those her dad used to send home to her and her mom. Nutsb—er—Tad was sitting at the computer console. Titus was glowering, as usual. Prescott looked at her like she was some kind of bacterium on a petri dish.

"Are you doing okay?" Gage put his hand on her arm, pulling her attention back to him.

Zoe gave him a little smile and a slight nod.

"Why don't you come and sit down. We're making some strides in figuring things out. Is it okay if I ask you some questions? We're to the point where we need more information from you. Then I can catch you up on what we've learned."

"Sure, that's fine." She moved to a seat and laced her fingers and crossed her ankles, compressing her body into a tight package.

"Do you know the term BIOMIST?"

"Yes, that's the name of the indexing system I was telling you and Titus about."

"Who owns BIOMIST?" Prescott asked.

Zoe pulled at her fingers nervously. "I own the intellectual property of how the biomarkers work to create unique profiles. I also own the software that analyzes the data. DARPA owns the software that stores the data and makes it searchable since this application was their brainchild. Montrim is the collection and housing unit for the data."

"We know how DARPA became involved. How did Montrim get on board?" Gage asked.

"My understanding is that the United States military didn't think it would be successful in getting foreign citizens to cooperate with the project. The best way to do that was to go in as a charitable medical group. The goal was to include every human in a particular area. They dipped each person's finger in dye to indicate that they had gone through the process and gave them gifts at the end."

"Gifts?"

"I heard something in passing. I was told that it depended on the village. In some cases, for example, if the chieftain was over forty and had several wives, they would offer him Viagra in return for his people's participation. Sometimes they rewarded participation with things like chocolate bars or small solar lanterns."

"But despite their active participation, Montrim doesn't own and cannot, therefore, sell BIOMIST data to a foreign entity."

"No, absolutely not. Nor can I. The data was bought by the US government and is regulated through the DoD. Almost no one knows about its existence. Just the CIA, mainly."

"Sir, excuse me," Tad interrupted. "I have that information about travel routes that you asked me for. Also, I've received a file on the reporter."

"Let's have that," Titus said.

Brian moved toward the whiteboard and snapped up a marker. Zoe wondered if this information would give her a better handle on what she'd missed while she was in the sleep pod.

Tad put up an image of the DC area with a red line. "All right. We have him starting at the address that's listed on his driver's license."

Zoe shot a questioning glance at Gage. He turned toward her and leaned in to whisper in her ear, "We're talking about the prisoner we took from the exfil house this afternoon."

"He traveled to Lily's work just as she would typically be arriving there," Tad said.

"We don't have information from Lily's GPS yet?" Titus asked.

Prescott leaned forward. "I haven't heard back from my office yet."

Lily. How did Lily figure into the attack on the little house? Zoe wondered, feeling completely lost.

"He's taking his car and not following her on foot. I imagine that he had a tracker in her phone to keep him safer from detection if he worked as a one-man team."

Tad put up another picture.

Gage tapped his fingers on the tabletop. "I'm wondering about the possibility of a tracker, not only on Lily's phone and possibly in her other effects, as well. For example, her watch. And if they are, are they similar to those found on Zoe's phone and watch?"

"Can you get hold of that for us?" Titus asked Prescott.

Prescott pulled out his phone. "I'll text my colleague to jump on it."

"In the next photo I put up, we can tell from this street shot," Tad used a laser to indicate the Mercedes, "that the guy sat outside of the office park until zero nine forty hours. At that point, he went to the gardens and parked at the far north corner."

As Prescott slid his phone back in his pocket, he asked, "How many entrances are there to the garden?"

"Four," Tad replied. "Two on the east side, one on the south, and the one on the north. I would guess that Lily entered the garden at the northeastern corner because that's where the Metro line lets out. There's a large fountain toward the center that would be a good landmark for a meeting place of two strangers."

"Schultz got there at what time?" Gage asked.

"Zero nine fifty hours. Now, the audiotape between Lily and Bunsinger only lasted four and a half minutes. Schultz didn't follow Lily as she left. He stayed in place for another half-hour. When he left, he didn't go back to following Lily either. He went home, where he landed for ten minutes, then he went to his office, where he stayed for fifteen minutes. He left town, and we had to switch to satellite imagery, which indicated his next location was here." The red point of his laser wand circled a barn. "That's a farm in Maryland, and his car hasn't left since."

"What do you think he was doing hanging out in the park for so long when it's twenty degrees outside?" Prescott asked. "I'm thinking he put his sights on that envelope in the reporter's hands. Lynx said the reporter died of a heart attack. The guy could have had the attack after Lily left, and Schultz walked right up and took the envelope."

"Or he could have confronted the reporter, and the sheer threat might have put Bunsinger into cardiac arrest," Tad offered. "I'm opening the file on his death now. Give me a second to scan it."

Prescott tossed his pen in the air and caught it. "That time frame makes me believe the PI took the envelope. What he did with it is going to be the real question."

"Run with that thought," Titus said.

"He's not on Billings' payroll anymore. Is he working the case for his own benefit? Is he trying to blackmail the senator? I doubt it. His unit attacked Zoe and killed Lily just hours later. One would assume that the affair would be revealed through her death. Is Schultz totally loyal to his unit? With something that big in hand, why didn't he drive straight to his commander? Why did he make a pit stop at his apartment and his office before heading to the farm? That's where I'm assuming they were meeting up for the later events of the night."

"He could have faxed them. Scanned them into a computer," Tad offered.

"Is that how you'd handle this kind of sensitive material? What would you do, Gage?"

212 | FIONA QUINN

"Head straight to my commander and put the envelope in his hand. I wouldn't have opened it or looked at it."

"Thorn?"

"Ditto."

"Brainiack?"

"Same."

"There you have it," Prescott concluded. "My guess is this guy thought about the dollar amounts involved and started salivating. Developed an appetite for his own fat bank account. He didn't have to know exactly what he was going to do. He only needed to be tempted to keep those documents for himself. Blackmail? Extortion? He may need time to process, form a plan. But I'd bet my badge they're in his possession."

Titus held up his hand. "Agreed. We need to get our hands on that envelope." He pulled out his phone and dialed. "Titus here, wake up, sleeping beauty. Brainiack is going to text you some information—there's an apartment address I need you to shake, and if that's not successful, an office."

"Are we going in quiet?" came a crisp, male military voice that didn't sound to Zoe at all like someone who was just dragged from his bunk.

"I don't care if either space looks like it went through an earthquake when you're done. Walls, floors, ceilings, I want it thorough. I need you and the rest of the team to put the pedal down and bring us back a large manila envelope. The contents will have to do with Montrim Industries, Israel, and the CIA. This is a time-sensitive, code orange piece of intel. We'll send search warrants to the carfax as soon as they're signed."

"Roger. We're on it."

Titus ended the call. "Brainiack, send Honey and Dagger the addresses and get legal moving on the warrants. You done scanning, Nutsbe?"

"Yes, sir. Colin Bunsinger has had known heart issues for the last six years. Recently, his doctors recommended bypass surgery. He put surgery on hold because he had a cold. Bunsinger was on medical leave from his position. His family had no idea why he was at that park at that time of day."

"I bet no one thought to be at the park in that kind of cold," Zoe said quietly.

"Did they give time of death?" Prescott asked.

"A jogger running in the park over her lunch break found his body around thirteen hundred hours and called the paramedics. Bunsinger was pronounced dead on the scene. They can't specify the time of death at this point because of the temperature."

"They called the M.E. in?" Gage asked.

"The medical examiner took him back to the morgue, where he was identified by family members. Since he wore a medical alert bracelet, after speaking to the family, the family doctor signed off on the death certificate as natural causes. No autopsy."

"Prescott, can you find out if amongst the personal effects there happened to be a manila envelope?"

"Yep, I'll call from the hallway. Take notes if anything interesting comes up while I'm out there. I'll check on the GPS update too."

Zoe leaned over and asked Gage what this was about.

"Lily was passing information about BIOMIST, sound technology, and wasps to a reporter on the morning of her death. Subsequent to the meeting, the reporter died. They were being followed by Senator Billings's private investigator, though Billings wasn't working with him at that point."

Zoe's stomach dropped. "He got information about wasps and then just so happened to drop dead of a heart attack?"

"Zoe? Are you okay? What's going on?"

Gage's voice came from a long way away. The whole room

was swimming in front of her. Her system was simply not equipped for this level of intrigue. How did Gage do this day in and day out?

"Okay, you're looking a little better. You went gray on me all of a sudden. What gives?"

"I'm not sure that this man's death was natural. But there's no way to prove otherwise. It just is what it is," Zoe responded.

Titus's face loomed in front of hers. "I think we need to hear more about this."

29

———

ZOE

*The fangs of the green snake and the sting of a
wasp don't really make poison*

— CHINESE PROVERB

GAGE TURNED TO ZOE AND HELD HER GAZE FOR A LONG
moment. He believed in her. He stood with her. And his belief in
her reminded Zoe that typically, on most days, she believed in
herself too.

"Let's start here. Zoe, why were you admitted to the hospital
for exhaustion?" he asked quietly.

"I was working long days and nights on a problem that I
couldn't solve, and I guess it snowballed. I didn't realize how
taxing this all was on my health."

"This was the last month or so, right?" Gage was talking to
her like she was the only person in the room. She was speaking
just to him. No judgment.

"Yes. The DoD needed Sphecius to be operable in four months. They had a high-priority project underway. They said it meant the lives of hundreds, if not thousands of people. It's a lot of pressure, you know?" Zoe's eyes were glazed with tears. "I felt personally responsible for the outcome. If I could just get my WASP operable, people would live. Families would stay whole."

"Were you a big part of that program?" Gage asked. "Do you know what the project is all about?"

"No, I only know that there was a push to get it done."

"Who was pushing you?"

"The messages were being sent through Colonel Guthrie. He's the director of my project and liaisons with the Pentagon."

"Okay, good. Let's start with DARPA—what role do you play there?

"DARPA is headquartered in Arlington, VA. It's located near the Montrim industrial park. While I do my work *at* Montrim, I'm paid by DARPA. It's a little complicated. DARPA pays me for the use of BIOMIST, and that covers my research expenses and affords me my living wages. I'm working on a project that DARPA is interested in using. But while I lease them, the use of the end mechanism, the intellectual property remains mine—the robotics and the software.

"DARPA was put into place so that the American government, with an eye to military applications, could address challenges spanning the scientific spectrum. Colonel Guthrie is a program director. Normally, I would have a program manager I would be accountable to. But because of Colonel Guthrie's and my longstanding relationship, and his particular interest in supporting my scientific discoveries, he was allowed to serve both as my manager and my director."

"And this is outside his normal purview?"

Zoe wondered why Gage's brows knit together when he

asked that. "Right. Normally his responsibilities are developing the technical direction of study, hiring program managers, overseeing the execution of various programs, things like that. Colonel Guthrie is with the Biological Technologies Office, which is the office that started BIOMIST and with whom I later developed the applications for both the military and the FBI to field test the biomarkers." Zoe's gaze traveled the room where the men sat perfectly still and completely quiet.

Gage's steady gaze pulled her back to focus on him alone. "But that's not the project you're working on now. The project with the deadline."

"Yes and no. I'm sorry, but none of this is straightforward. You're going to have to bear with me while I go through it. DARPA asked for my biomarker field test to be extended. They're afraid that if these machines get into the hands of law enforcement, even though that was the reason for my developing them in the first place, others would reverse engineer them and figure out what was being measured. Or, if it went to court, I would be forced to reveal the biomarkers that were being measured. As my machines became public, the rest of the world would be closer to having the same technology."

The door opened, and Zoe jerked her head around to see who was coming in. Prescott moved into the room and slid into a nearby chair. He gave her a nod.

Gage touched her knee to get Zoe's attention. "And we would lose our ability to gather the blood census that we're accumulating. So what is this new project about? You mentioned wasps."

"Okay, so in undergrad, I developed the idea of blood biomarker applications. In grad school, I also studied biomedical engineering. That's when I developed the field test. *Then* I went on to get my Ph.D. in micro-robotics."

"And you developed a wasp robot?"

"Its name is WASP, which stands for Winged Analytical Surveillance Project."

"That's quite a leap from biomarkers to robotic wasps."

"It is, and it isn't. I was driven by the ethics of innocence. My original projects were meant to help keep people out of prison who didn't commit a crime so that the police were freed up to find the people who actually did break the law—a societal win-win. When I was in grad school, I saw news article after news article about how drones were being used to stalk terrorists and that whole compounds were being exploded, only to find out that the intel was old or faulty. Women, children, the elderly, and men who weren't involved with terrorism were being killed."

"And you wanted to stop that from happening."

"Of course, I did. But that's naïve, isn't it? I can't stop all of it. But if I stopped just one mistake? If I saved even one life? Then I'm protecting innocents."

"You thought that you could do this with wasps? I'm going to need you to lead me through this. My mind isn't coming up with any way for you to save innocent people with a robotic wasp."

"I took a class for fun in micro-robotics before I decided to continue my studies with a Ph.D. in the subject. I absolutely loved it. It was in that class that I developed a very crude wasp-like structure. My goal was to develop ocular enhancements so that a tiny lens could send pictures to a computer that could identify and augment what it was seeing, thereby becoming a means of intelligence gathering. It was my goal to develop the eyes. My plan was to develop it to send visual data to someone watching a long way away. I wasn't able to do that. But as I made progress, I was able to get this robot to send enough information to an external human, functioning as a pilot, to be able to navigate a room, and see basic human shapes."

"It needs an operator, like a drone does?"

"Most of the time. I was worried about the WASP being seen and swatted. Then people would discover that these types of micro robots exist. Colonel Guthrie and DARPA taught me about paranoia and secrecy. I have an override in the computer system. If the WASP believes it will be captured or destroyed, it will override the pilot and fly away like an actual wasp. Once it's safe, it hands the controls back to the pilot."

"That's pretty cool. How would the robot know it was in danger?"

"Analyzing shadows and detecting speed of movement, and since that's harder to do at night, in a worst-case scenario, if the pilot lost control, the robot's head contains acid that will melt the WASP into what looks like black, chewed-up gum. No way to tell what it was or how its systems functioned."

"All right, you got to a point where your optics could detect structure and basic human form. But you were after a different result."

"I couldn't get my optics to be adequate enough for identification. One day, I had one of those smacks myself in the head moments. What was I doing trying to develop these ocular definitions? I was on a fool's journey. You know, I got caught up in an idea, and it was like I couldn't see the nose in front of my face. The reason I developed biomarkers was because of the Innocence Project. If you'll remember, about seventy-five percent of the people that the program proved to be innocent were convicted because of faulty human memory and an inability to discriminate human faces. And DARPA wanted to develop BIOMIST because it was having trouble identifying terrorists because of similar cultural dress and facial hair. So why in blazes was I trying to develop a WASP that depended on visual discrimination? Stupid."

"But you didn't tank the project. You came up with a better identification system."

"Right, I decided to put the two projects together. A WASP is piloted via ocular apparatus to the possible target. At that point in the project, the pilot could see if the person were male or female. If they were old or young. Basic, basic. Imagine rubbing a thin layer of Vaseline on the inside of your glasses and being sent into a room to find your suspect. That's what the pilot has to contend with. The goal is to pilot the WASP to whoever they believe is the mark. The WASP lands on the suspect, and by inserting a proboscis that punctures the skin, it sucks up a blood sample. At the same time, a second proboscis is inserted into the skin to plant a tiny beacon. The beacon is about half the length of a piece of rice and about that diameter. The weight of the beacon is replaced with the weight of the blood. To the person, it feels like a sting. The WASP must be able to function very quickly and maneuver away. So once the pilot finds the mark, the computer takes over."

"What's the purpose of the beacon?" Prescott asked. His sudden introduction into the conversation made Zoe jump. He put up his hands up in a "sorry" gesture and leaned back.

"Say the WASP took a blood sample. It flies back to the pilot, who takes the blood and applies it to the test strip in the field analyzer. The pilot gets a plus sign. There's a good chance that they've got their terrorist in house. Then they send that info to the Air Force, or whoever wants this guy, and they move in with a bomb or boots. Preferably boots that can be more surgical about the outcome. How would I be sure that my intel is not already old? It was true in that moment, but the terrorist could leave. Then, not only would I have not helped to get the bad guy, but lots of people might be bombed on my faulty data. And we may think the guy is in there, see the rubble, declare him dead, and yet, he's still operational. There are still lots of opportunities for bad outcomes."

Gage tipped his head, his eyes far away as if he were imagining this in the field. "The beacon is something that the pilots can track?"

"No, it's too small. It can't put out enough power. But once the airstrike or other means of interception begins, the pilot can send the wasp to find its egg. That's what I call the beacon. And the pilot can verify the location. The wasp can travel up to two miles on each flight. It gets juiced up while the biomarkers are being run, and then can fly another two miles."

"Then what happens? It just stops?" Gage asked.

"It uses the acid to self-destruct with its last burst of energy. I can't let them fall into anyone else's hands."

"I'm sorry to interrupt. This is an absolutely mind-boggling concept, and I can think of hundreds of times when it would have made all the difference in the field," Brian said. "Do you have to destroy it? For example, if we had eyes three-sixty and no way for this guy to escape, would you have to destroy the WASP? Or could you use it again?"

"Each WASP can obtain only one blood sample, and then it can't be used again. The biomarker test is highly sensitive, and the WASP would be contaminated. A micro drop could change the outcome on subsequent blood samples. If, however, we were dealing with a known mark and a biomarker test wasn't required, then the WASP could be used to mark the subject with an egg and track that person. It would still need to be called back by the pilot to recharge."

"I'm sure they cost a freaking fortune. You'd better be right when you're piloting to the mark. I don't know that I could do that." Brian said.

"Agreed. I developed software that's supposed to help. When Gage killed the men in my apartment…" Zoe instantly regretted recalling that scene. Her body went right back into panic mode. Gage reached over and drew a steady hand from her elbow to her palm, then laced their fingers together.

"You're doing fine," he encouraged. "Take your time."

"If a photo was taken with ears or faces, those data points could be put into the system. Height really helps. Gender, of course. The wasp tries to help the pilot. There's a scale that shows up on the screen to facilitate pilot decision making. It runs red to blue. Hot to cold, like the children's game."

Titus slid forward in his seat. "Okay, I have a question for you. I'm going to leap in a different direction. How did the CIA know that you were in the hospital? How do they play into this WASP story?"

Zoe's gaze searched over the floor. If anything made her feel vulnerable, it was explaining what the CIA, she, and WASPs had in common.

**Do not kill a single wasp; for then a hundred
will come to its funeral.**

— *RUSSIAN PROVERB*

"HOW DID THE CIA KNOW ABOUT ME BEING IN THE HOSPITAL? I
don't know." Zoe's nose tingled, and she squeezed it to stop the
distraction.

"Do you know Grossman and Parker?"

Now her lips were going numb. Brian moved over and set a
bottle in front of her. It was a chocolate protein shake. Zoe
thought he'd probably hit on something. Her system was burning
through energy like she'd been running a marathon. "Thank
you," she said as she twisted off the top and took a sip. "Parker
and Grossman? Yes. I know them."

"How do you know them? Were you doing something for the
CIA?"

"Yes, the CIA activated the BIOMIST data. But Grossman and Parker weren't part of that. I refused to work for them."

"They were in your hospital room the other night and said they were on a time crunch," Gage said.

"They are, but that's not my worry."

"Can you tell us what they were asking you to work on?"

Zoe filled her cheeks with air and blew it out. "If this goes outside of these walls, I could go to prison. I'm probably breaking a bunch of espionage laws. My contracts all have non-disclosure statements and stuff about treason. Now I'm caught between giving you the information to save lives, including my own, or shutting up. I'm not a hero. I don't want to be shot full of drugs and dragged somewhere to do things against my will."

"Zoe, we deal in State secrets every day," Titus said. "Our job is America first. None of us is going to take this beyond the tightest possible circles. But you're right. There are choices to be made. And lives on the line. Yours, others. Innocent others, like Lily."

"Lily." Zoe still couldn't believe her friend was dead. Murdered. Yeah, she'd have to keep telling them about her work. She didn't really have a choice. "Parker and Grossman want my help getting to a guy in Pakistan. It's high stakes, the next Osama Bin Laden, they said. I'm okay with them using my identification processes—that could save innocent lives. That's been my goal all along. Keep innocent people out of jail, keep innocent people off death row, keep innocent civilians from being targeted by drones."

Gage's eyes darkened.

"They approached me about building a RoboSphecius because they wanted me to extend my research." Zoe took a big glug of her protein shake. She could feel the sugar working in her system.

"In which direction? Zoe. Are you okay?" Gage asked.

"I think I've used up most of my word quotient for the week." Zoe forced a little laugh.

"A little bit more, okay?" Gage's eyes were green now, soft and comforting.

"Yes, that's fine." She paused, wondering how to explain this to those outside of the scientific community. "Science is accumulative. There are no new ideas. Any idea that is sparked by anyone else's is simply a next step." She grimaced and tried to come up with an example. "Do you know how sticky notes came to be?" She looked around at the shaking heads. "Back in the late sixties, a chemist developed a "low-tack" adhesive. It was strong enough to hold the paper to a surface, but the genius of it was that it was also weak enough that it wouldn't tear the paper when it was removed. Silver worked for a good long time trying to figure out how to make this adhesive marketable, and he wasn't able to. One day, a colleague uses it in his choir book because he thought it would make a great bookmarker. Ta-da. Sticky notes were born. Having something already, and changing it slightly to meet a need, that's the basic story of Parker and Grossman and me."

Gage said nothing. Waited.

Zoe considered how every word out of her mouth made the circle of people who had the information wider, and she felt that the mere concepts were potentially lethal. Already had been lethal. Lily, three men that the Panthers called "tangos," and maybe, possibly, the reporter. She pulled her hand away from Gage's. She wished she had time to consider her actions further. But inaction at this point seemed dangerous too. "Parker and Grossman were on the trail of Osama Bin Laden. They were accessing BIOMIST to try to track down Bin Laden's children.

226 | FIONA QUINN

Recently they discovered my WASP project. They never told me how that got leaked to them."

"Who knows about it besides Montrim?" Titus asked.

"Montrim doesn't know what I'm working on. They just rent my lab space to DARPA."

"Weird," Brian said.

Zoe saw the men passing looks around and wondered what they were telegraphing to each other.

"As for who knows at DARPA? I'm not sure. Colonel Guthrie is my contact," Zoe finished.

"No one else? No bookkeepers or another staff at Montrim?"

"This is supposed to be above top secret—I don't know how they deal with that in terms of their accounting."

"Lily wouldn't know?"

Zoe searched the men's faces again. They were focused hard on her. This point meant something to them. "I don't know how Lily would come across the scope of my work."

"But somehow, the CIA did. Did you tell Guthrie the CIA knew?"

"Yes, I told him right away that they wanted me to change the trajectory of my research. I was worried that they'd pile that on my lap, too, because I was already on the tight deadline Guthrie had set for me. And I wasn't willing to do what they wanted anyway. Colonel Guthrie seemed pretty pissed about it. He told them to stand down that I was working on a military contract. I was there and heard his side of the phone conversation."

"But Parker and Grossman pushed you anyway. What were they pushing you to do?" Gage asked.

"Back in the 1970s, the CIA had a secret weapon used for assassinations. A dart was used to shoot a small amount of poison into their target. The dart would dissolve almost instantly, leaving the tiniest of red dots. The substance would cause a heart attack that, at that time, couldn't be thwarted. I'm not sure how that poison would stand up to modern medical interventions now. But at the time, it was very effective. It also had a short half-life, meaning any traces found in post-mortem exams would come up as naturally causative. This is why, if this reporter had documentation that brought a CIA SNAFU to light, then I'm not sure, and no one will ever be sure if Bunsinger's heart attack was a natural event or if it was triggered by the CIA's use of this poison."

"I've seen videos of those old Senate hearings, and everything Zoe's saying is true. But that initiative was nixed. They put that program aside," Prescott said.

Zoe shook her head, and the men turned to look at her. Their concern was growing palpable, and Zoe dearly wanted to leave. "The person who is hit by the dart may not feel anything at all or possibly just a bug bite or sting. Sound familiar? The CIA wanted me to develop a RoboSphecius with the capacity to detect a beacon implant and to, via proboscis, sting the person, administering a lethal dose of poison. The poison from the seventies. They have it in hand. That I can tell you with certitude."

"Did you take on the project at any point?" Prescott asked.

"No, of course not!"

"Can I ask why not?" he pushed back.

"Imagine the ramifications. Anything we have in terms of science is just leading the race, but eventually, all dedicated runners cross the finish line. Everyone would have this technology, especially if it was already functional, and the "other" got hold of the wasps or my designs and software. They could reverse engineer the thing, send the poison to their chemists. Can you imagine the ease with which our government could be taken down? How could anyone prevent senators from being stung as they exited the Capitol? I'm not having any part of that. I'm okay with identifying the players to separate the innocent from the culpable to the extent that it's possible. But my science will not be used to actually kill people."

"But the CIA won't take no for an answer." Titus's voice was a low growl.

"No. They won't leave me alone."

Prescott held up his finger. "I just got a text from the morgue. Colin Bunsinger had a phone, a wallet, and a set of car keys in his pocket, but there was no envelope on his person when his body was transported. They still have Lily Winters. They're expecting the funeral home to transport her body later today. My team has signed chain of custody paperwork and is bringing her purse and her watch here to Iniquus. I hope that's okay." He turned to Titus. "We didn't discuss it, but I think this will be the most efficient route. Of course, they'll need to maintain that chain of custody, so they'll need to remain in your forensics department with the potential evidence."

To Zoe, it seemed not quite a challenge. It was almost like Prescott wanted eyes on the inner sanctum, and this was his play. Iniquus was Zoe's protector, and she didn't like that the FBI was snooping around. Zoe thought that her aversion was probably due to her interaction with the CIA. She didn't dislike Prescott. But at this moment, she didn't like him either.

"That happens all the time. We're set up to accommodate you," Titus said evenly. He wasn't ruffled. Probably Zoe shouldn't be either.

Prescott tapped a response into his phone.

"Zoe." Brian moved to sit next to Gage. "Your work on the

WASPs is amazing. I love sci-fi. It's all I read and most of what I watch on screen. I see how these things are possible in the future. But right here and now, you're describing things that can be of so much help, and you're right. They have so much potential for harm. I like hearing you talking about the ethics of your research. It never occurred to me that scientists would be put in such difficult places. In the military, Gage and I make decisions like that on a minor scale. You're making them with a wider scope. Do you have someone you can talk to, to debate these issues as you make your decisions? Is there someone's advice you seek out? Perhaps that's how this information is getting out."

"The only person I'm allowed to discuss this with is Colonel Guthrie. None of this can get out to the wider scientific world. Mostly I try to be true to my own inner voice. Sometimes I follow through with the colonel, sometimes not. Colonel Guthrie told me to keep my head down and get the WASPs ready for intelligence, and then we'd talk about what happens next with RoboSphecius. On this, though, I'm not swayable. I could see our president being stung. I won't have any hand in that."

"But have you seen some good in your work? Do you feel uplifted by what you've accomplished?" Gage asked.

"I don't often get to know how my work is being used. I told you about the failed attempt to use it to find Osama Bin Laden. I was able to help with the Paris attacks, though, and yeah, that felt good. A few stories have siphoned back to me and really touched me, gave me courage, kept me working toward future advancements."

Brian asked, "Was this with your WASPs?"

"No, BIOMIST."

Brian went quiet, and Zoe could see him thinking hard. He shook his head. "I can't put it together. Can you explain how

BIOMIST helped in the Paris attacks? Would it breach security to share?"

Zoe opened her arms wide. "Everything I've said to you has breached security. I can't see how one more item will make that much difference. After the Paris attacks, the president told the CIA that they were to do everything in their power to help Interpol. There was a shortlist of people the CIA thought might be involved. They ran the blood samples found on scene through BIOMIST."

"What? But you said they were gathering the census markers in Iraq, Afghanistan, and Syria."

"Montrim, under CIA direction, expanded its humanitarian efforts when Europe started to be overwhelmed by refugees fleeing the war zone. Montrim's humanitarian arm set up medical stations at refugee centers to try to document everyone coming in from the Middle East and Northern Africa. Once Montrim was in the field, gathering data in the Middle East, they thought there was a glitch in my protocol because different names were coming up as matches. It turned out the patients were changing the names they were telling the relief workers. Montrim added a fingerprint identification screen to the intake. When the patients are processed, before the blood sample is taken, the finger is rolled on the digital pad, and it's stored as a name and a fingerprint with a unique number sequence. That change happened fairly early on.

"Of course, they're not Montrim in the field. They have several other names they use, like WorldMed International and WorldCares. In an attempt to get the biomarkers, people are being given basic medical interventions. That's a wonderful thing. Another good thing is that the software I wrote groups people into families—families in this instance are defined as parents and their children. A grandparent won't lead to a grandchild. But a brother can lead to a sister. A father can lead to a child. If a child came in without supervision—the adult died in passage, for example—the medical workers would flag it. They've told me that dozens of families were reunited this way. I think that's pretty cool. I had to sign off on that use for a set period of time. Montrim is giving the data to the field workers, who then do the leg work. It's their charitable outreach, and they receive a great deal of goodwill in the communities for doing this kind of thing. The whole hearts and minds initiative. They say it's name recognition software, putting people together."

"Wow." Brian sat back in his chair. "Wow," he said again, then scrubbed a hand over his short military cut. "That must be an amazing feeling."

Zoe offered up what Gage called her Mona Lisa smile. Yeah, it did feel good. It made her proud to know she was helping to make the world a better place. Then she sighed. "And now my science is responsible for four, maybe five deaths. I don't know if one side of the scale balances the other." She rubbed her hands together.

"I'm sorry, but I'm still stuck on the Paris attacks. How did your research help?" Gage asked.

"At first, the authorities had a blood sample they found at the scene where one of the terrorists exploded himself, and that's how they found the name of Brahim Abdeslam in BIOMIST. Then the authorities worked to find his family. They also found a fingerprint that pinpointed Salah. The CIA, of course, didn't identify the means by which they made the identification. And they even tried to stay off the radar as the entity that identified him."

"But the Abdeslam family was from Brussels," Prescott pointed out.

"Brahim Abdeslam traveled to Turkey, intending to go to

Syria, but Turkish authorities deported him back to Brussels. That's when the sample was taken. Authorities had him pass through one of the Montrim sites for a health check. I really have very little information on the subject—there was an addendum to the contract I needed to sign so that the CIA could give the information to Interpol. That's the only reason I have this much. I'm sure that their media briefings disguised the true facts because my index isn't supposed to exist. As soon as it's a known entity, our government will no longer have the freedom it has now to expand the database."

"Have you ever considered selling a copy of BIOMIST to Israel?" Prescott asked.

"No, absolutely not. Once this becomes known, the program is done. It's just now getting populated to the point that it can be helpful."

"Montrim never approached you about making a sale to Israel?" Titus asked.

"No." Zoe was thoroughly confused. She looked at the men's photos on the screen. The two attackers from her condo had spoken another language. It could have been Hebrew. Was Israel trying to kidnap her?

"Is there any way that Montrim can access your data without your consent?"

"It's protected. I have a hacker friend who helped me write the code for the firewalls. But nothing's foolproof. DARPA has its own firewalls in place. All we can do is hold people off. My best defense for the database is that Montrim likes the money they get for gathering the data. DARPA needs this mission to be a secret. No one should be looking for it."

"Montrim has some of the best minds in the world working for them on their military software applications. They could have put someone on the task of hacking you."

"Why would they? That's cutting off their nose to spite their face, right?"

Silence.

"*Right?*"

Gage had his warrior face on again. "We're trying to figure all of this out."

If I be waspish, best beware my sting

— WILLIAM SHAKESPEARE, THE TAMING OF
THE SHREW

ZOE STOOD AND WALKED TO THE CORNER TO GET SOME AIR. NO one stopped her. Twenty-four hours ago, she was eating Chinese take-out and reading a book in peace. In less than a day, someone had tried to kidnap her, she lost a dear friend, she was hidden, tracked, shot at, and chased some more. And now she realized that she was at the center of international intrigue, playing with people who didn't have any rules. She pressed her forehead against the polished wood wall and tried to be still.

"Zoe." Gage's warm voice came from a good distance away. He sounded like he wanted permission to approach, and she very much appreciated that he was trying to honor her space.

When she turned, he took two steps forward. "We'll figure this out. Okay?"

"In the wrong hands...the wrong mindset... Just think. Can you imagine what would happen if I developed a RoboSphecius to kill? When the CIA brought the project to me, I could see how simple it would be to make the change. It's simply a matter of up-taking poison instead of blood and secreting poison into the skin instead of onto a test strip. Depending on the weight and viscosity of the poison, it's probably just a matter of making a few changes to the software, and bam, it's a killing machine. I could probably rig something together in less than a day. And what if this went open source? Or there was a mole? Our enemies could kill any leader not liked by someone with a RoboSphecius. Imagine if they could build as many RoboSphecius as they wanted? Soldiers could send the micro-robots into the camps. Sting. Pilot them back, refill, sting again, and again. They could sting an entire army, and they'd all drop dead in the blink of an eye. Marines like you." A picture of Gage laying in the desert, clutching at his chest, gasping for his last breath, with no way to protect himself against this assault, came vividly to mind, and it felt like she was being stabbed.

"Hey." Gage reached out and covered her hand with his. "I agree with you. I think you made the right choice."

"Zoe and Gage, sorry to interrupt." Tad walked toward them. "Forensics called to let me know that they've been monitoring your phones. Colonel Guthrie made three calls to Zoe and two calls to you, Gage. The timing is getting closer and closer, so we can assume he's agitated. Zoe, your phone needs to be tossed in the trash. It's too corrupted for forensics to guarantee they got it completely clean. Yours passed their tests, Gage, and you can use that one to make the call. They're bringing it down now. Be careful, though, don't reveal any new information since you last saw him, including your present location, or any of the intelligence we've compiled."

"Roger that."

Tad went to answer a knock at the Panther War Room door. Zoe assumed it was the forensics guy bringing down Gage's phone.

Gage turned to Zoe. "Do you want to call, or should I?"

"I really don't want to talk to him. I'm not good at subterfuge, and he knows me too well. I think he'd press less with you."

"Agreed." Gage took the phone from Tad. He pulled up recent missed calls and pressed the number for Colonel Guthrie. As it rang, Gage laced his fingers with hers and leaned in so she could hear.

"Gage? Thank you so much for calling," the colonel said. "My blood pressure's been inching up all day. I called the hospital. They said Zoe was discharged. I tried her number. I hope I'm not bothering you, but it worries me that I'm going right to voicemail."

"She's fine. She just woke up from a long nap. We'll be headed out to dinner here in a couple of minutes."

"Good, good. Is she with you? Can I chat with her for a second?"

"Sorry, no. Zoe's not available at the moment. Is there a message I can pass along?"

"Yeah, sure. Great. Let Zoe know that Maeve and I'd like her to come stay at our house until this is all settled. The more I think about the break-in, the more concerned I'm becoming. I should also tell you that I didn't call Zoe's parents. I thought she should be the one who decides what, if anything, she wants to say to them. She is an adult, after all."

"She'll appreciate that, sir. I'll pass the invitation on to her. I'm sure she'll want to talk to you tomorrow."

"But tonight, Gage? Does she have someplace to stay? I want her to be safe. I couldn't forgive myself if something were to happen."

"She's fine right now. We're with friends."

"She's fine," the colonel repeated. There was a long pause. "You've been great through all of this, Major. Thanks for being there for her. I'll check in tomorrow."

"Good night, Colonel."

"Incoming," Tad called and put a new image up on the screen.

"Hey, that's Ruby Goldstein." Zoe walked over to stand in front of the live picture. "She and Lily were friends in undergrad. Where is this?"

"An interview room here at Iniquus," Brian told her.

"Is she here because of Lily's death?"

"Ruby's married name is Leibowitz. Do you know her husband, Sal Leibowitz?" Titus asked.

"No. I haven't seen Ruby since…well, it's been years."

"Lily left her husband and was living with you when she went to a party for the USIPAC as a guest of the Leibowitz's. She didn't mention that to you?"

"I wasn't Lily's keeper. We didn't run our schedules by each other. We got along because we both like our boundaries."

"When did she tell you that she started dating Charlie?"

"I don't know, months ago. I never met him. He was someone I knew about peripherally. His name. That he was older. That he made her happy. It was nice to see her bloom again after that disaster of a relationship with her ex. That is seriously all I can tell you. I had my mind occupied with the DARPA push to get the WASPs actionable, and," she caught Gage's eye, "I had my own social life. I wasn't really involved in Lily's."

"We need to figure out who's the best person to talk to, Mrs. Leibowitz," Titus said.

"How did Margot get her here?" Prescott asked.

Tad smiled. "She said that they had spoken with the senator earlier about Lily, and Ruby's name had come up. Margot thought she'd like to have the information, so she was well-armed if any reporters came knocking on her door."

"Smart move." Titus folded his arms over his chest and scanned the room. "Okay, I think we send Zoe in, since Ruby and she know each other, but we also send Gage in to do the questioning because he's been in the room through all stages of information gathering. He'll know best how to get to the needed intel. Thoughts?" He looked at Prescott.

"Agreed. Gage has enough field experience. He knows what he's doing," Prescott said.

"Zoe?" Gage asked.

"I'm just there to greet her and make her feel safe? I don't have to talk to her?"

"That's right," Titus said.

Zoe didn't dislike Titus, but his hard face always made her feel like she had been caught doing something wrong. She felt unsettled and apprehensive around him, though his words and actions had done nothing but support and protect her. So why did she feel like he was sending her into the lion's den?

Don't pick a wasp out of a cream-jug

— JEWISH PROVERB

GAGE PUT HIS HAND ON THE SMALL OF HER BACK. THE ROOMFUL of people filed out the door and moved up the hallway.

In a completely different part of the building, where things looked less like a military complex and more like a resort hotel, Titus opened a door, and Zoe started to walk in.

"That's the observation room." Gage pointed to the door next to it. "We go in here. Ready?"

"Yup." Not really. But they said all she had to do was sit there. She could do that.

As they moved through the door, Margot stood, shook hands with Ruby, and slid past them.

"Hi, Ruby," Zoe said.

"Zoe, oh goodness, Lily is *dead*, can you imagine?"

Ruby stood and wrapped Zoe in an embrace. Lily was dead. Why did Zoe have so much trouble grasping that? She pulled back and shook her head. No, she couldn't imagine Lily dead, despite all of the evidence, all the things people had been telling her. It seemed more nightmare than real.

Ruby's gaze traveled between her and Gage and back to her.

"This is Gage Harrison. He knew Lily too."

"Why do they have us here? What do they need us to know? The woman who brought me in said that they had information they wanted to share with me in case the media came around asking questions. Does this have to do with Lily's affair with Senator Billings, do you think?"

"Why don't we sit down?" Zoe pulled out a chair and slid into the seat.

Gage followed suit. "I'm trying to understand what brought us together too. We were told that you introduced Lily to the senator?"

"That's right. I did. Do you think people are trying to hold me accountable for their affair? That would be…I don't want to be embroiled in this."

"None of us do. Let's see if we can't help each other figure this out," Gage said. "You and Lily weren't close friends, were you?"

"No." Ruby shook her head. "In college, yes, but she married outside of the Jewish faith, and my husband didn't like that. It caused tension. Lily and I were estranged until I learned that Lily divorced her husband. Sal thought it would be okay for us to bring her back into our lives, that maybe we could get her involved in our work with the USIPAC, and she would meet a nice man she could settle down with."

"Yet Senator Billings is a Christian," Gage said.

"That introduction was happenstance. I never thought that

Lily would have an affair with the man. He was married. He was twice her age." She leaned forward and lowered her voice. "He's not exactly in the best shape." She sat up again. "My mind never went in that direction."

"Recently, you and Lily were getting together frequently, several times a week." Gage tried to lead her in the direction they needed her to go.

Ruby's brows knit as she crossed her arms over her chest and leaned back. "Now, how exactly would you know that?"

"Did you know that Lily and I were roommates?" Zoe inquired.

"No." Ruby seemed to relax. "She didn't tell me that."

"Did Lily talk about me with you?" Zoe watched Ruby quickly look up to the right, then she shook her head. "No. No, you didn't come up."

"What *did* come up in your time with Lily? You were helping her help your friend, Senator Billings, weren't you?"

"How do you know all this?"

"Lily and I were roommates." Zoe was offering a false door for Ruby to walk through. True, Lily and Zoe had been roommates, but Lily had never mentioned anything about Ruby. By juxtaposing the statement with Ruby's question, Ruby would assume it was the answer to her question, and Zoe wouldn't need to lie. She hated to lie.

"Did Lily seek out your expertise in forensic auditing to help her find information for the senator?" Gage asked.

"Yes, she did. And I was helping. Of course, I was."

"And you talked to someone else about this, didn't you?" he asked.

Ruby went pink. Her hand slid to her throat. "What is this?" she whispered. "Why are we really here?"

Zoe reached out and took Ruby's hand. "I'm here because

I'm scared, to be honest. Lily told someone something, and it's putting lives at risk. The people here are telling me that Lily was murdered. That it wasn't an accident at all."

Ruby's eyebrows stretched toward her hairline. "The news said she committed suicide."

Zoe looked her in the eye and thought she saw fear but also guilt. "What did you do, Ruby? You told someone something. And you told them my name."

Ruby just stared at her, dumbfounded.

"People came to my condo to kidnap me." Gage gave her knee a warning squeeze. She must be disclosing too much. She was supposed to leave it to him and his field interrogation skills. But she couldn't seem to sit back and let him take over. "I can't go home. I'm terrified. Ruby, help me. Tell me what you did so I know how to be safe."

Ruby opened her mouth and shut it again. She pulled her hand from Zoe's and clutched it to her chest. "Lily was *killed*?" Her hands came up to cover her face. "You were attacked?"

Zoe reached out and pulled Ruby's hands away so she could look Ruby in the eye. "You made a mistake. You can help to correct it. Please, tell me."

"I'm sure that's not right. I didn't speak to anyone in the United States. I only spoke to my cousin because he's studying the same thing you are."

"What am I studying?" Zoe asked. "What did you tell him?"

"That you developed a means of identification through blood that's more useful than DNA because it's a quick and dirty, yes or no kind of test, and that you had developed a system like CODIS to index your findings. He's trying to do this—has been working on this for decades. I thought he could come and speak to you and get a direction for his work. Maybe you could collaborate."

"Lily told you that's what I do?"

"Your name is on the files that she was able to find to give to the senator."

"You said you spoke to no one in the United States. Where does your cousin live?" Gage asked.

"Jerusalem."

Zoe could feel his tension rising. "And when was this phone call?"

"This past Wednesday, late afternoon, is when I spoke with him."

"Wednesday, you're sure? Not earlier than that?"

"I promise you, that's when I called. See?" She pulled her phone from her purse and showed Gage the number. She'd called at 16:39, almost midnight in Israel.

"Thank you, Ruby. This is helpful to our timeline. Is there anything else you told your cousin besides the information about the biomarkers?"

"He asked if the program was already being implemented, and I said yes, for years now, and he wondered what new project Zoe was working on."

"And what did you tell him?" Gage asked.

Zoe was astonished that Gage had kept his face so placid like he didn't really know what was going on. He, like Zoe, was a friend of Lily's who'd got caught up in something scary. She needed to think later about the ease with which he slid into this role and how simple he seemed to find it to maintain. But not now. Now she needed to know how her secrets were being shared.

Ruby's voice was so low that both she and Gage had to lean in until they were almost head to head to hear her. "I told him you were working on a new program for the CIA. With your new weapon, you can remotely pinpoint people for assassination. I told him that was the technology that he should be developing."

"Wait." Zoe sat straight up. "That's not true. That's not what I do. Why would you tell him that?"

"It *is* what you do. It was in one of the files that Lily shared with me when we were trying to follow the money trail for the Senate hearings. The CIA had come to an agreement on the price they would pay Montrim to have you develop your micro-robotics in this direction."

Zoe felt a noose tightening around her neck. Her voice could hardly squeak through. "And you told all this to your cousin?"

"Yes, but Zoe…" This time it was Ruby who was reaching out with placating hands, petting arms, clutching at her fingers. "He is very circumspect. He would never tell anyone. I just thought it might be interesting for him to come and see what you were doing. I thought Lily wouldn't mind introducing you two and that it might be a good project for him to be involved with. We are, after all, allies. Friends. But then Lily…" Her voice drifted off, and her eyes filled with tears.

"The Israelis think that I'm building a remote killing machine?"

Ruby swiped her wrist across her eyelids and sniffed loudly. "Aren't you?"

"No. I am most certainly *not*. I'm not developing anything with the CIA."

"Well, what are you working on?" Ruby looked thoroughly confused.

"Field forensics analysis of bloodstains."

"Oh. Well, that is very different." Ruby glanced around, tears streaming down her face. Her gaze landed on a box of tissues.

Gage followed her line of sight and went to retrieve the box for her. "Why did you think that Zoe would share a project like that with the Israeli government?"

"Not the government. I was only thinking of my cousin, the researcher."

"Still."

"Well, the Israelis are furious with the Americans over the new Iran agreement, and of course, the billion and a half dollars given to the Iranian government."

"It's Iranian money, not American money," Gage said.

"That's completely irrelevant. Now the Iranians have over a billion dollars to use against Israel, and a goodwill gesture from the US might help. Who knows? I put a toe in the water to see."

Zoe looked at Gage, who had the same incredulous look on his face as what she felt. This was a stunning revelation. Were the Israeli's responsible for killing Lily and trying to kidnap her? Were they going to take her out of the United States to Israel? Away from any kind of support or help? How could Zoe stuff that cat back in the bag and convince people that she wasn't making a remote killing machine?

33

THE MORE GAGE HEARD, THE DEEPER HE SAW THE HOLE THAT Zoe had fallen into. Releasing her name, releasing her research, of course, she was going to be the focus of international intrigue. He was only glad that they were dealing with the possibility of an ally being embroiled in all this. What if a different government figured out Zoe's ability with possibly lethal microrobots? A country where they had little leverage, like Iran or Russia?

Gage's mind flashed back to Thursday evening as he was getting in from field training. It had been a shit kind of day. The team he was working to build wasn't gelling. They were nowhere near ready to be sent out on missions, but their training was coming to an end. Stressed out, the text from Zoe had instantly brightened his day. Sure, he could provide her with "a little stress relief." He'd enjoy some of that too. He had been grinning broadly when he used the key Zoe had offered him once Lily moved out. It felt like coming home, to slide *his* key into the lock, to hear the click, to know there was a beautiful woman in her bed waiting for him.

Then the scream. He'd been stumbling around mostly blind

ever since. Learning things about Zoe, learning things about himself, and how deeply he was aligned with her. How much he needed to keep her safe. How *personally* threatening this all seemed. To know someone was training their sights on Zoe gave him the same feeling he had on the battlefield when he knew he was caught in someone's crosshairs.

"Do you have any copies of what Lily found at Montrim?" Gage pulled himself together enough to ask Ruby the question.

"No. Nothing. She showed me and took it all away with her when she left. It was mostly us trying to follow the money trails. Accounting ledgers. The information I shared with my cousin is a tiny portion of a much bigger picture."

"Speaking of pictures, I have one I'd like you to look at." Gage reached over to the seat beside him and pulled out an eight by ten color photo of a tattoo. Gage watched Ruby's face carefully as he placed the image in front of her.

She pulled it over and frowned, wiping away the last of her tears, the clutching at her Kleenex. "Someone tattooed that on themselves?"

"You recognize it then?" Gage asked.

"This is based on a form of the Sephirot. It comes from the divine tradition of the Kabbalah that is associated with an esoteric group back around the time of the Crusades. It has to do with the Knights Templar, which some say was a group actually formed by Jews to protect priceless treasures."

Gage lifted a brow, silently asking for more information.

"Some historians believe that there was a group of European royalty who were descendants of Jewish Elders who had fled the Holy Land before the first century of the Common Era when the area was invaded by the Romans."

"What kinds of treasure?" Zoe asked.

"Oh, not what you'd think. Not chests of gold and jewels.

They were priceless Kabbalistic and Essene scrolls that had been secretly stored around various regions of the Holy Land to guard them against being plundered as spoils of war by the Roman invader Titus."

"Titus?" Zoe glanced toward the wall of two-way mirrors where Titus was listening.

"Yes, that's right. When the Elders fled Titus, they married into the European continents' noble families. According to lore, twenty-four men would eventually become the leaders known as the *Rex Deus* or sometimes called the Star families." She tapped the picture where the design had a definite star shape. "They formed into the Knights Templar, not to be crusaders in the common sense of the word, but to retrieve the treasures. The legend says that those who survived through the crusades continued using the name *Rex Deus,* becoming the Jewish Illuminati, and their descendants secretly rule the world."

"Does this group really exist? The *Rex Deus*?" Gage asked.

"No. It's the stuff of conspiracy theories and wild imaginations. It's a way to tell people that the Jews have a secret international banking system that rules the world and other scary things that make people suspect Jewish people of great malevolence. With Sal's and my work with USIPAC, we're trying to fight stereotypes." She tapped the photo again. "This upsets me. I don't like to think that people are playing with the concept of *Rex Deus.*" She stopped and looked from him to Zoe. "Now that I've told you what I know, what do you know? Who has this tattoo? How did you get this picture?"

Ruby was looking at Zoe, but of course, Zoe had no clue. She batted her long eyelashes at Ruby, looking like a doe in the headlights.

"It was on a man's arm who was recently taken prisoner," Gage said. "It ties back to Lily, and we'd like to know-how.

Could your cousin have anything to do with this group?" He pushed the photo closer to her.

"Isaac? Oh no, he isn't involved in anything but his laboratory. His head in a book. His eye to a microscope. Nothing else exists for him."

They all stared at each other. Zoe looked like she was in shock. Gage didn't know what else to wring out of this woman. The silence was becoming embarrassing when a knock sounded on the door.

"Hello," Margot said with her big smile. "I have word that your car has been driven around by the valet. It's outside the atrium." She held out her hand toward Ruby.

"Aren't they coming?" Ruby stood and gathered her purse.

"They'll be done soon," Margot said, holding the door and gesturing Ruby out.

As Ruby moved into the hallway, she glanced over her shoulder with deep concern in her eyes.

Zoe didn't move as Margot shut the door. She didn't say anything. She sat, staring at the wall. Gage knew that she'd gone inside her head, wrestling with this new information. But the thought that Ruby's cousin was out there with high-level, beyond top secret information, possibly putting the BIOMIST program at risk, spiked adrenaline through his system. They needed to jump on that and jump on it now.

Gage moved to the door and opened it a crack to peek into the hallway. "Okay, Zoe." He held out his hand. "Let's go next door and see what they think."

In the observation room, the men stood in a loose circle. Titus was on the phone in the corner.

"The *Rex Deus*? Descendants of the Knights *freaking* Templar? Is this going to get any more nuts?" Brainiack asked.

"Who's he on the phone with?" Gage lifted his chin toward Titus.

"The CIA," Prescott said in a voice that said what they all knew. This had started out bad and kept getting worse. "Titus needs to give them a heads up to go sit on this cousin. We can't have Zoe's name out there, and we can't let him spread the word about BIOMIST or the RoboSphecius."

"Right. But this cousin..." Gage scrubbed a hand over his forehead. "Shit! I didn't get his name."

"Yeah, you did." Brainiack leaned back in the captain's chair. "You held the phone under our optics, and we got a screenshot of the number. Nutsbe traced it. We've got all his vital stats, and they're being passed to the right people. Things'll be fine."

"You guys sure do work fast," Zoe said.

Brainiack turned to her. "We don't have the luxury of slow, ma'am."

"The cousin isn't responsible for the ops group coming after Zoe." Gage paced the small confines of the room. "He didn't have time to find the right contact, bring it to their attention."

Titus tucked his phone back in its holster and joined them. "Agreed," he said to Gage before he turned to Zoe. "The CIA is going to squash that bug, Zoe. They'll keep this quiet."

She nodded her head vigorously.

"We need to look elsewhere for the group that came after Lily and Zoe. Who needed Lily dead? And who needs Zoe off-grid?"

"Montrim is under fire from the Senate committee. They could lose their federal paycheck. That would basically put them out of business," Prescott said. "It's not a stretch to think they'd kill Lily. It certainly doesn't explain Zoe."

"Zoe, do you remember earlier you were telling us a story about Lily and you having dinner when she was in DC to interview for a job." Titus had added a worry line to his scowl. "And you also mentioned WASPs."

"Lily asked for an update over dinner. I started on the WASPs in grad school. They had no military tie at the time, so I wasn't keeping my research on them a secret."

Titus pressed her, "But they became secret. They became above top secret, right?"

"Where are you going with this?" she asked.

"What was your answer to her about the WASPs."

"That I was under DARPA contract and couldn't discuss it."

Titus put his knuckles on the table and leaned in. "And you were working on that at Montrim, in rented research space, but Montrim had no connection to your research, so they had no idea what you were working on."

"That's right." Zoe looked at him, baffled.

Gage saw where Titus was going. "Did you eat dinner with Lily before her job interview or after?"

"Before." She scrunched her brows together. "Do you think Lily used her connection with me to land her job?"

"What if she knew the secret of what was behind door number one, and she shared it with Montrim? They had to learn about what you were doing somehow."

"Why do you think they know about the WASPs?" Zoe asked.

"They were negotiating with the CIA. They were supposed to gain access to your work, and then the Montrim micro-roboticists would rework your designs to meet the CIA parameters of use," Gage told her.

Zoe looked like she might puke. Gage pulled a chair around and pressed her into it.

"Wait. Do we know which direction that came from?" Brainiack asked. "Did the CIA approach Montrim? Or did

Montrim approach the CIA? I'd love to have been a fly on the wall for that discussion." Brainiack turned red around the ears and turned to Zoe. "Sorry, ma'am, I didn't mean to joke. It was a figure of speech."

Zoe sent him a smile, but her face was still pale. Brainiack noticed, too, because he turned and poured a glass of water from one of the bottles on the buffet and pressed it into her hand.

"Lily told the reporter that Billings had copies of what she was handing to the reporter," Brainiack said. "Maybe we can find out more in that direction."

"Asked and answered," Titus told them. "Margot tried to get him to share the information Lily gathered when she was taking him down to his car. Billings is claiming they can't release copies to us because we aren't officially read into the CIA program, and we shouldn't know anything that's going on in a sealed Senate chamber."

"And yet he wanted Lily to hand the evidence to a reporter and made the call to facilitate that." Gage wished he was back in a room alone with the senator. He'd help the guy see reason.

"It makes sense," Prescott said. "Billings couldn't release this himself, so he needed a whistleblower to do it in order to keep his hands clean from any sign of sharing State secrets."

Everyone stilled as Titus's phone buzzed. "Titus here. What have you got, Honey? I'm putting you on speakerphone." He held the phone in the flat of his palm.

"We had *carte blanche* with our search warrants." There was a decided grin in the man's resonant voice. His team had obviously had fun with the shake. "You asked us to put the apartment on the Richter scale, sir. If we shook it any harder, the whole building would have collapsed."

"You cover your tracks?"

"We went in as a renovation team. If you can believe renovators would be pulling down drywall this time on a Friday evening, then we're covered." His booming laugh filled the room.

"And?" Titus cut him off.

"Negative, sir," Honey snapped back to military precision. "There was no manila envelope of any kind in either location. As a matter of fact, there wasn't even much in the way of paper in either locale. The apartment looked like it was all window dressing. He kept it as depersonalized as a motel room. His office is paper-free. There's not even a computer system in there. He must carry a laptop with him. We're guessing the envelope is in his car."

"Nutsbe." Titus raised his voice. "The guy went home, to his office, and then directly to the farm?"

Nutsbe responded over a speaker system. "Yes, sir."

"Let's pull that farm up on satellite and see what we've got going there. All right, I need Panther Force in battle rattle, pronto. We can't leave that envelope in the wind. It's fucking dangerous."

"I'm in," Gage said, knowing it was a long shot that he'd be allowed.

"You haven't signed the contract, Gage. You're a liability. You stay here with Zoe. Have some dinner, try to relax."

The thought of relaxing while that envelope was in Israeli hands didn't sit well. Not being part of the team didn't either. "What if I signed?"

"It's bad to make life choices based on adrenaline and momentary goals," Titus said.

Gage knew Titus was right, was giving him good counsel. But Gage had been on the fence for weeks. And now, seeing Iniquus in operation, seeing the team in play? Yeah. He was in.

"I've been making up my mind ever since you showed up at the hospital. If this is what you do, I'm your man."

Titus considered him, then, with a nod, said, "Margot, facilitate Major Harrison's Iniquus contracts and get him fitted out in tactical gear. Double time."

"Sir." She caught Gage's eye and headed toward the door. Gage gave Zoe's shoulder a squeeze, dropped a kiss into her hair, and whispered, "I'll see you in a little bit. Please get some more rest." Then he followed after Margot, glad to know he'd be boots on the ground.

As he moved toward the door, he heard Titus ask, "Prescott, you in or you out?"

"You get warrants in hand, and I'm in."

"Nutsbe, you on that?" Titus asked.

"On it." Nutsbe's disembodied voice came through the speaker.

Prescott was right behind him as Gage moved through the door. "I think I'd like to interrogate Schultz, now," Prescott said. "Wring out some intel. See what we're headed into."

34

GAGE

"GAGE? HEY, MAN, I'M HONEY." THE MAN TO HIS RIGHT STOOD almost seven feet tall and was built for the gridiron. He held up his fist, and Gage tapped it with his. They were doing weapons checks in the Panther war room.

The man next to him raised a fist as well. "Dude, your glow is blinding me. You'll want to kick some dust on them shiny new boots."

Gage bumped his fist.

"I'm Thorn," the man continued. "We're a man down at the moment, glad to have you mix it up with the team. Give us a chance to see the newbie in action. Welcome aboard."

"Special Agent Prescott's going to be riding shotgun tonight, so Sunday manners," Titus said. "He's finishing up his intel roundup with our prisoner. Here's the deal, we aren't looking for any blood tonight. We just need to get our hands on the Mercedes. That car is the only thing covered in our search warrant. We will not be entering the residence."

Nutsbe put up a graphic. "We need to go in now rather than later. It's a matter of satellite coverage with the weather pattern that's moving in. Besides, no one wants the possibility of a gunfight in a sleet storm. That's the bad news. The good news is, it's a new moon, and we have a thick cloud cover. It's going to be as black as ink, boys."

Titus moved to the graphic. "We're staging a tow truck down here around this bend. The plan is to roll the car over, hook it up, drive it out. One of our easier nights. But that doesn't mean complacence. This group is Israeli Special Forces trained. Granted, they've been MIA for about a decade. They've got some age on their bodies and maybe not the same level of training they had back in their military days. But let's not think we're wrestling with Grandpa. We've had three bodies to look over, and they're all hard as rocks. Maybe even put you princesses to shame."

Titus moved over to the picture of the Israeli unit. "If this team stayed intact, we've kicked the hornets' nest by taking out four members. Gage went hand-to-hand with the first two, and Brainiack sniped the other. Levi Schultz is in our tank on his blind date with Prescott."

"That leaves possibly eight left," Brainiack said.

"Seems fair. There are seven of us who'll be boots on the ground, too, counting Prescott and Gage." Thorn yawned. "I like a little challenge."

"Let's not get cocky. They were trained to be some of the most lethal Special Ops in the world. This is their hidey-hole. Imagine what we'd do to make our home safe. And gentlemen, we don't have the luxury of time or intel." Titus put his knuckles on the table and made sure he caught each and every one of them in his glare.

Panther Force was comprised of elite military operators. He and Titus were trained Marine Raiders. The others all Special Forces from various branches—Army, Navy, Air Force, and Marines. Their Ranger was out on loan to Strike Force, a fraternal Iniquus unit. Hence, one man down. They were the best of the best, and Gage was honored to be invited to join. Gage knew that though they were messing around, keeping things light, so they were in good mental shape when they were under the gun, each and every one of them had lost brothers out on the battlefield to hidden threats. It went part and parcel with the job. But it meant that this easy camaraderie would be swapped for battle faces once they were in place.

Thorn grinned broadly. "One thing we do have, though, is a set of Mercedes GLC SUV keys that the guy kept in his wall safe." He fished them out of his pocket. "That should take care of the alarm system and shifting it into neutral."

"Careful, these guys are big into booby traps. It's all fun and games until someone loses an eye," Nutsbe said.

"Thanks, Mom." Thorn slapped him on the shoulder and reached for a banana from the buffet filled with food.

The men were wolfing down burgers and power shakes, making sure they had the fuel for whatever lay ahead. Margot had taken Zoe down to the cafeteria. They were going to go back to Margot's apartment in the women's dorm and hang out there until the team got back. That was as far as their planning had gone. If nothing else, at least he knew Zoe'd be safe here on the Iniquus campus.

Prescott moved into the room. "Well, the guy's a brick wall. His SERE training—survival, evasion, resistance, escape—was in full swing. I got his alias repeated back at me about a hundred times. We talked about how he could resist his little heart out, but he was heading down the CIA hole, and the only chance for better treatment was timely information."

"And?" Titus asked.

"I learned he can spit like a camel."

"Nice. Anything else?"

"We had him hooked up to a polygraph. I concluded that he hasn't handed over the envelope. We played twenty questions for a while." Prescott grabbed a burger from the platter and took a bite. "I think the smell of steak on the grill and fresh-baked bread you had wafting in was a nice touch. Made me hungry as a horse, and the sound of the guy's stomach gurgling was echoing off the walls." Prescott moved to the map. "I'm guessing from the polygraph that we're facing seven members of his unit." He stopped and took another bite of his burger. Speaking between chews, he said, "They're all housed in the same place. Arms? They're loaded. They've got flashbang, grenades, rifles sidearms, and dogs."

The men threw their hands in the air.

Brainiack gave voice to men's thoughts. "Shit, man, are you kidding me? I hate when they have dogs."

"Steaks and tranqs," Nutsbe said.

"And time. All that takes time," Thorn added.

Gage was focused on Prescott. "Did you ask about booby traps?"

"That one, I couldn't tell. Either they had them, and he wanted to hide it bad, or they didn't have them, and he wanted me to think they did. That's a crapshoot. I'd assume we'll be tiptoeing through a minefield, ladies."

THE TOW TRUCK was already in place around the bend. Honey got the short straw and was twiddling his thumbs behind the wheel. The rest of the team lay on their bellies in the brittle weeds. The December cold seeped through their battle gear and into their bones. They did a comms check. Gage's transmitter wrapped around his throat, his receiver was dropped into his ear canal. He was hands-free as he whispered, "Gage, check."

Thorn was apparently the team's dog whisperer. He had laid piles of steak, carefully seasoned with a sedative that would kick in after twenty minutes, and a powder that would disarm their sense of smell immediately and make them dizzy as hell in the process. Now Thorn was off in the trees. The wind carried the slight tinny note of a dog whistle along with the smell of raw beef toward the house.

As a beautiful German shepherd pushed his way past the man holding the door, Gage was glad that their treats were in no way lethal. It would merely buy the team some time and ensure safety for the dogs as well as for the men.

Through the binoculars on his night vision apparatus, Gage watched the man dressed in jeans and a sweatshirt cast his gaze over the field. The guy's arm hugged tightly to his chest in a sling, and Gage could see the corner of a large dressing sticking out of his shirt's neck hole. Gage guessed that this was the man he'd shot earlier. Gage hoped the guy was loopy on pain meds and had lost his observation skills and some of the sixth sense that warriors developed over time in hostile surroundings. Would the guy go in and announce their presence, or were they still under the radar? Thorn was smart to put the meat on the other side of the rise where the man couldn't follow the line of sight.

A second dog pushed past the man, a third, and a fourth. Then he shut the door. Gage watched to see if there was any change to the farmhouse. Lights that suddenly snapped on or off. Movement at the curtains. He thought they'd probably gotten away with the ruse. The guy didn't attempt to call the dogs in. The evening was still but for the last of the brown leaves rustling in the wind.

Thorn, from his location, reported over the comms. "Beta

One. The dogs are all high as loons. I put on the harnesses and have them chained in the woods. Even if things take longer than expected, the most they can do is raise hell with their barking. But most likely, they'll just sleep it off."

"Base. Panther Force, be aware cloud cover's giving us satellite problems. I'm getting intermittent visual. I've got your locations from your tracking units on screen. Everyone is in position."

"Panther actual. Copy," Titus whispered over the comms. "Alpha team, go."

Gage was Alpha One, and Brainiack was Alpha Two. They had drawn the long straws and got to go after the car. The others were at vantage points with their eyes on the windows and doors. Nutsbe was back in the war room with his bird's eye view up on the screen.

Gage had a pistol in his side holster and another at his ankle. If things got bad, they could and would defend themselves. But Titus and Prescott wanted anyone who got in their way captured, not killed. To that end, he'd been handed a stun rifle. He'd never seen, let alone used one before. He knew that the Marines had asked for the development of this weapon for room-clearing operations and to be able to take potential threats into custody using non-lethal means. Gage would have liked to have used it at least once on a firing range before trying it in the field. The shell for the twelve-gauge shotgun had a range of only a hundred feet. That was damned close if he was going up against an MP5.

"Alpha team, move."

"Alpha One, moving," Gage whispered back as he belly crawled toward the side of the barn. Brainiack repeated the answer, and they both squirmed from their observation points toward the Mercedes.

Brainiack had the fob and would push and steer from the

front as Gage shoved from the rear. The Mercedes was parked at the top of a gravel-lined drive, and while the decline made pushing easier, the gravel was a definite deficit. There was no way to move the car silently. The trees lining the drive meant there was no space to maneuver the car onto dirt or grass. "Come on, wind. This would be a good time to pick up the noise level," Gage muttered under his breath.

Brainiack hit the key fob, somehow timing it with a flash of lightning, hiding the chirrup behind a boom of thunder. Brainiack quickly popped open the driver's side door and slammed the light switch off.

The farmhouse door banged open. Gage threw himself flat, squirming under the edge of the fender where the dim house light created a shadow. From his position, he could see the same man who had let the dogs out before. His good hand wrapped around the collar of a massive Rottweiler. The dog was barking and lunging, his fangs gnashing at the air. The man whistled. Waited. Whistled again. Then he let the dog go, and he banged the door shut. They were made.

"Go. Go. Go," he whisper-yelled to Brainiack. Brainiack had one hand on the door frame and the other on the steering wheel. Gage came up into a lunge, pushing with all his weight into the back of the car to get it rolling down the hill, falling forward as he did. Through his night-vision goggles, Gage saw the dog at the corner of the barn, staring at him. The Rottweiler's massive muscles vibrated. His mouth frothed with saliva. Gage could feel the growls in his bones as they rumbled through the air, low and threatening. Gage knew he had one shot at not getting mauled. With a twist of his torso, he grabbed for the rifle, pulled it to his shoulder, and fired off an electrical shell as the dog leaped toward his throat. The device hit the dog's thigh and was quickly shaken off. The Rottweiler took off in the opposite direction, whimpering his surprise and pain. Gage was relieved that he didn't have to use a bullet to save himself.

The slow crunch of gravel in the distance told Gage that Brainiack was making good progress.

"Beta one. I've got the dog," Thorn's voice came over his comms. "I'm chaining him up with his buddies. He's going to get a steak and sleeping pill reward for coming right over to me when I called."

Relief was short-lived.

Flashbang exploded where the Mercedes had once been. Gage had been scanning the area with his night-vision goggles when his optic nerves exploded into an inferno. All he could hear was the squeal of his ears ringing. A thick blanket of smoke choked him. Blindly he rolled toward the barn, hoping for something sturdy at his back while his system fought the overwhelming stimulus.

He was on his knees, gagging up the toxic sludge that he had breathed in when the sound of firepower seeped through the cacophony. The terse communications of his teammates resonated in his ear, but he couldn't make out the words. He staggered up to crouching position then snaked his way along the length of the old barn. Gage put the stun rifle to his shoulder before rounding the corner, thinking what a piece of shit this damned thing was with its hundred-foot range when that strafe of bullets being laid down was coming from a submachine gun. Gage yanked the rifle strap, so the weapon swung to his back. He pulled his pistol from his side holster.

Gage's aim was the tree line and some concealment while he got himself back to operational. He blew the stress from his lungs, and with his pistol squeezed between his palms, his finger ready to pull the trigger, he rounded the corner to find himself nose to nose with a figure. Gage's momentum was already swinging right, so he extended and continued the gesture, bringing the butt of his pistol into someone's temple. The guy toppled into the barn wall and used it for leverage to spring back at Gage, knocking the gun from his hand.

The night was pitch black. His eyes were still burning. Gage couldn't get a visual of who was on top of him. What weapons were on hand, what was nearby. Someone slammed their fist into his cheekbone. He rolled and could feel the second punch hit the ground where his head had just been. From the feel of the man's clothing, Gage knew he wasn't going hand to hand with a friendly. This person wasn't wearing the Iniquus uniform. Gage locked his legs around the guy and flipped him over, crawled up his body until he was sitting on the tango's chest. Gage pinned the man's shoulders under his knees. With the advantage of space and height, Gage pummeled the guy until his target stopped writhing beneath him. He rolled the unconscious man onto his stomach and pulled out a pair of flexi-cuffs.

Flexi-cuffs, Gage reasoned, would do little against a seasoned special ops guy. He'd just jump up and run to the nearest sharp object. Gage grabbed the man by the collar and dragged him into the woods. Gage stretched the man's arms over his head with a sizable tree between them and locked him in place lying on his back. Gage scrambled down and did the same with the man's legs. This combatant was trussed and ready for Prescott to pick him up.

"Alpha team, sitrep." Gage heard Titus's voice in his ear, still garbled but at least understandable.

"Alpha One. I've taken custody of one tango. Over."

"Alpha Two. The car is loaded on the flatbed, moving. Over."

"Beta team, sitrep," Titus called.

Prescott answered first. "Beta Two. I have custody of one

male with an earlier bullet wound. He's sustained another. Medic required. Over."

"Beta One," Thorn said. "Dogs secured and sleeping. I have a bead on a guy who's sneaking around the right side of the house."

"Nutsbe. Beta Two, be advised that has him rounding on you."

The angry sound of electrical sparks filled the air, along with the garbled screams of a man.

"Beta Two. Taking the guy into custody now. I'm liking these stun rifles," Prescott said.

"Panther actual." Titus came over the comms. "I'm moving toward you to take hold of your captures. Since you have the badge, Prescott, I'm going to let you take lead on the house search. Now that we've been fired upon, I'd say we have probable cause for securing the place. I'll lock the prisoners down, then we'll stack up and finish this mission."

35

GAGE STOOD IN THE INFIRMARY WHILE THE MEDIC GAVE HIM THE required once over. He had a pretty good bruise on his cheekbone, but the tango he'd wrestled had lost four teeth. Gage would take that for an outcome most days of the week. The good news was that they had all three tangos alive and kicking their shackles, each in their own interrogation rooms. Turned out, the guy who took his second bullet in less than twenty-four hours was just grazed. The medics stitched him up, gave him some antibiotics, and called it a day. His wound from the exfil house looked like homegrown surgery. If he hadn't chosen to go to the hospital for that, no reason why they should force the guy to go now.

Thorn had crated the dogs and transported them to the Iniquus' Cerberus K9 kennels for a vet check and housing. Prescott was elsewhere, applying his interrogation magic. His FBI team was fine-tooth combing the farmhouse. Brainiack and Honey were doing the same with the Mercedes in the Iniquus garage. Hopefully, the teams would have news soon. Solid information about what was going on and where the five other soldiers from the unit were located now.

Gage and Titus left together and walked to the women's barracks where Zoe was waiting for them. The women's dorm was designed to look like a McMansion on the

"Gage and Titus came to get you," Margot said softly. Potomac River. They took the front steps two at a time and knocked on the door. Margot opened it, and without a word, turned to get Zoe. The men weren't allowed in—women only. Gage could see Margot shaking Zoe awake, where she was curled under a throw blanket at the end of the sofa.

A few moments later, Zoe was at the door. Her eyes widened at the sight of the bruise and scratches on his face. When she locked her eyes on his, she seemed to find the answers to her unspoken questions. She nodded and accepted his wounds. There was none of the hysteria he'd experienced with past women in his life—no babying and sympathy. And Gage appreciated being treated like a man instead of a boy who needed mothering.

Titus left the porch as Zoe and Gage thanked Margot, then they moved as a unit to Titus's SUV, heading to the new safe house.

"No food at the house, so we need to run by the grocery store to get something for tonight and breakfast in the morning. We can fill the fridge tomorrow. Zoe, this might end up being your home for a while."

"Thank you," Zoe said, still looking out the side window.

"Did you have dinner? Are you hungry?" Titus asked. "It's late, but I'm sure I can find some fast food if you can't wait for Gage and me to cook."

"I'm not hungry, but thank you." Her voice was too soft.

Gage remembered her trembling under the metallic rescue blanket. He didn't want them to be making another emergency run to the hospital. It was too hard to secure her there.

"When we get to the store, I'll just run in real quick. Is that okay, Titus?"

"You can do the shopping." He pulled into an all-night grocery store. "We all need to get out here, though. We're changing cars. We'll go in this door." He pointed to the far door near where they had parked in the shadows. "And out the pharmacy door on the other side of the building. I'll escort Zoe. Gage, when you come out, you'll see a blue sedan, lots of rust, looks like a piece of shit, but that's just its cover. It's a good machine."

As they walked through the automatic doors, Gage turned to Zoe and asked, "What do you want to eat?"

"Anything is fine." Zoe's eyes were scanning the walls.

Gage wanted a straight answer. He was too damned tired to be playing games. "Zoe, I don't want to go get eggs and bacon and bring it back and have you pout because you didn't want eggs and bacon. Just answer me."

The look she sent him showed confusion. "Who are you talking to right now?"

"You!" His voice boomed louder than he'd expected.

"No, you're not. I've never pouted over the food you've brought me. This isn't some kind of test. I'm not playing games. If you brought me a jar of pickles, I'd eat them. I. Don't. Care."

That was Zoe, clearly and rationally pointing out the facts. Of course, she was right. She didn't set traps for him to fall into.

"I'm going to the ladies' room." She pointed to their left and walked away.

"Gage, you've found yourself one hell of a woman," Titus

said as he and Gage followed her. "She doesn't say much, but what she says is what she means. Who wouldn't love that?"

Some Neanderthal instinct roused in Gage the need to stake his claim. This was *his* woman. Ha. Zoe was her own woman. He was along for the ride. Gage worked to squash the feelings, knowing that he'd been on his own adrenaline rollercoaster with no sleep, and it was affecting him like it would anyone else on the team. This was not the time to tick off his new boss.

"But take my advice," Titus was saying. "Get her something other than a jar of pickles."

Gage loped off.

"Oh, and pick up some beer," Titus called after him.

TITUS TURNED the piece of shit car into the long drive. A little yellow house sat in the middle of a wide field, positioned like a postage stamp on an envelope. On three sides, there was a thick copse of trees, shielding the house from its neighbors. It was the very last house on the street that had a cul-de-sac for people who mistakenly arrived at the dead end. It was a great set up, Gage thought. Easily defended.

The driveway curved around the back of the house, and Titus pressed a button near his mirror to power up the garage door. A gunmetal grey Iniquus SUV was parked inside.

"Gage, why don't you sit tight? I'm going to go give the house a quick run-through, and once I've determined it's safe, you can park next to the Tahoe." The implication being that if it wasn't safe, he should take Zoe and get the hell gone.

Gage moved to the driver's seat and repositioned the car, so he had the option of backing into the garage or speeding forward.

Zoe was back in Zoe-land, and he drummed his fingers on the steering wheel, thinking back to the grocery store conversation.

Zoe? While she was as tantalizing and sexy as the sway of a hula dancer's hips, she was also self-contained. Yeah, there was something undeniably... He couldn't pull out the right word. She didn't fit a form or pattern. He bet that freaked guys out—that they weren't able to mold and manipulate her into something more recognizable, something that they had a better handle on. That wasn't Zoe. She didn't need translating into his language. He needed to learn hers, just as she learned his.

He thought about the Skype calls she'd had in her living room while she thought he was asleep—how free she was, gabbing with her friends. How goofy and funny. Laughter in every word. He wanted to have that with her. Sometimes. Not all the time. He liked how she looked up at the ceiling with that little frown between her eyes as she worked out some conundrum. She could sit that way for hours. Now he knew what kinds of thoughts filled her head. When he'd realized what she did for a living, Gage couldn't say he was surprised. It was like a puzzle piece falling into place.

He was proud of how fiercely she defended innocent people. How she put her amazing brain to work every day to keep them safe. Yeah. Zoe being Zoe, in all of her facets, he wanted to be the guy who got to stand next to her and watch her shine. He rubbed his hands over his thighs and looked up to see Titus waving them in. *Shit, I've got it bad.*

After scooping up the grocery bags, Gage followed Zoe through the garage and into a small hallway. Bathroom to the right. Laundry to the left. Then a great room with living, dining, and kitchen.

"I'll cook," he said, moving into the kitchen and putting the ingredients for dinner on the counter and the ingredients for breakfast in the fridge. He found a cutting board and knife and switched on the oven to warm the loaf of bread he'd purchased.

In the living room, Titus moved to the flat-screen TV and turned it on. "Let's see what the news is saying about the events of the day." He moved to the couch and sat.

To Gage's surprise, Zoe didn't go up the stairs to look around but went to sit on the other end of the couch.

The newscaster was concluding his remarks on Senator Billings's very bad day and the Montrim Industries inquiry.

"The senator is going after Montrim. Are you worried about that?" Titus asked Zoe.

Zoe curled herself up with her knees under her chin. "I don't work for Montrim. I work out of their laboratory because it's secure. I think the Senate probably should go after them. Montrim's got some things going on there that are pretty horrific."

"Like what?" Titus asked.

Gage was paying close attention to the conversation while he chopped onions.

"The soundwave technology that takes out entire cities but leaves the infrastructure and flora intact—that you know about now. That, to me, needs to be stopped."

"Were you read into that program?"

"No. I eat in the cafeteria. I can hear people talking around me."

"Are they allowed to do that? Just chat about top-secret studies in front of others?"

Zoe tipped her head. "Folks there all have high clearance levels, at least the ones who eat in the same cafeteria I do. Montrim has this social psychology interior design. The public spaces are developed to encourage people to bump into each other and communicate. Montrim wants projects to cross-pollinate. I told you about the sticky notes. Someone says something that's an ah-ha moment for someone else."

"And that works?"

Zoe shrugged. "As much as it can in a room full of unsocial science geeks. Synchronicity happens."

"What else have you overheard?"

Gage tried to move around the kitchen as softly as possible to hear as he pulled out a skillet and flipped on the burner.

"Montrim Labs are developing things that can easily be seen as destabilizing in the wrong hands—or even the right hands. It's scary stuff." Zoe got up and headed for the stairs.

"I guess she's done." Titus moved to the kitchen.

"Yup." Gage followed her progress with his gaze until she rounded the corner.

Titus opened the fridge and pulled out two beers, handing one to Gage. "Do you need to go check on her?"

"Are you serious?" Gage accepted it, twisting off the top and taking a swig. "No. She wants her thoughts to herself. And we probably want that to happen, too, so she can churn through what's happening. She's the genius, after all."

Titus looked up the staircase where Zoe had disappeared. "I can't envision a mean thought in her head. Do you think she'll be able to figure out how criminals think?"

"Nope. That's why she needs us. She knows it, or she would have walked out the front door and not through the bedroom door."

Beware of a man's shadow and a bee's sting.

— BURMESE PROVERB

TITUS HAD HEADED HOME IN THE INIQUUS SUV, LEAVING THEM with the sedan. That felt okay to Zoe. She felt comfortable being in this little yellow house, especially after the car ruse at the grocery store. She stood at the sink, pouring liquid soap under the hot water faucet so she and Gage could clean up the dishes.

Gage scraped the plates and put the stack next to the sink. "Do you want to wash or dry?"

"Wash," Zoe said and watched Gage pull a couple of dish towels from the cupboard. She liked that he was as neat about his environment as she was and that he pitched in equally to keep things up without being asked. She grabbed the glasses and slid them into the water.

"Today is our half-year anniversary. We started dating on June fourteenth."

Zoe pushed a cloth into the glass and swirled it around while sending Gage a smile. "That's romantic of you to realize." She rinsed it and handed it over to Gage to dry.

"You know, most girls I've gone out with talk about wedding plans and kids' names by week three. We're at six months. Obviously, honeymoon destinations aren't on your list of topics to think about."

"Nope." Zoe pulled out another glass and gave it a swish.

"You don't think I'm a catch?"

Zoe loved it when Gage got that teasing lilt in his voice. She thought it was sexy as all get out. "A *catch*? Oh my God, this is a cheesy conversation." She handed him the glass. "I'm not sure how you'd define a catch."

He smiled at her, accepting the glass but not defining his parameters. Instead, he asked, "I'm wondering what you see when you look into the future, Zoe. Are you married to your job? If you are, I get that." He dipped his head as he studiously dried the glass. "Or maybe you see a husband and children?"

Zoe picked up a plate, confused by the switch in tone. "Sure, I have an idea of what I'd like my life to look like. A husband, yes. Eventually adopting some kids, eight years old or so."

"I'm sure there's exhaustive reasoning for that particular age." Now he was grinning.

She studied his face and decided there was nothing malicious there. Not even amusement, really. It was kind of like joy. Now that was really perplexing. She handed him the clean plate. "Not everyone has to want the same thing. Science is my thing. Alpha-dogging is your thing."

"Alpha-dogging? That isn't the title on my contract."

"Did you know that societies are balanced?" She clattered

the silverware into the suds. "China is having a real problem with that right now. Most families get one child, and they thought for a long time that boy babies were more desirable than girl babies, aborting female fetuses, putting girl babies up for adoption. The same thing is happening in India, where they have like forty-three million more men than women. They've thrown their culture off balance. Too many males without a similar ratio of females create disturbing outcomes."

"Too much testosterone and not enough estrogen? Is this something to do with Alpha dogs?"

"Not really. I was just thinking about the fight you were in tonight." She focused on the multicolored bruise, stretching across his cheekbone. "You said that you had seven good guys, and you expected about the same number of bad guys. That's how things work in our populations. One percent of our population is made up of psychopaths—people who can kill with no moral barometer. One percent is what I'm calling Alpha-dogs—people who can kill *because* of their moral barometer. It's a balancing act."

"That's pretty interesting." Gage pulled out the cutlery drawer, dropping the knives and forks into place as he dried them. "What else works that way?"

Zoe let the water out and leaned against the counter. "Artistic brains and mathematical brains, extroverts, and introverts. I'm oversimplifying to make the point. One of my friends in undergrad said I should find the markers for that in blood. She said that the phrase 'It runs in my blood' is true."

"Do you think that's right? Do you think that someone's profession is something that they're physiologically predestined to do?" Gage placed the dishes up into the cabinets.

"I'm not willing to study it."

"Because?"

"The ramifications of such a test could be pretty awful."

"I don't know," Gage said, shutting the doors as Zoe cleaned out the sink. "There are a lot of people who search their whole lives to find the thing that's right for them. And if we blood tested them in third grade—"

Zoe followed Gage out of the kitchen. "And said, you will be a musician whether you like it or not?" she asked.

"It wouldn't be like that." Gage caught her around the waist and pulled her hips tight to his.

"It's been that way. I have an older friend who escaped from Hungary when it was still a communist country. She was designated a musician and was given a flute—Here is your future, they said. What does she do now? She plays the flute."

"See?" Gage kissed her lightly.

"No. She didn't want to be told. She wanted free will. Do you see the difference between choice and no choice?"

"Well, maybe it could be a privately-run venture where people who have no idea what they should be doing could go and pay to have the blood test done."

"Maybe not knowing what to do is exactly what they're supposed to do. Maybe in this lifetime, they were sent here to quest."

"This lifetime? Do you believe in reincarnation?" he asked.

"I don't *not* believe in it. I believe that seekers are an important component in our social chemical solution. All of the substances in that solution are added in the right proportions, or our grand human experiment wouldn't work. That's my hypothesis, anyway. But it's an experiment that I think is unethical to undertake."

"You'd be a millionaire," he crooned.

Zoe caught the playfulness in his eye. This wasn't a serious philosophical discussion. She didn't know what this was. She was grateful, though, that they weren't rehashing the day. She'd had quite enough of the day. "If I were interested in being a millionaire, I would have asked the government to compensate me correctly for the ongoing use of my intellectual property for the biomarker database."

Gage's brow furrowed. "They don't?"

"No, I only ask them for enough money to run my lab and pay my bills. I don't need the distractions that come with wealth. I want to focus on my projects."

"I can understand that." He dropped a kiss on her forehead and reached down for her hand. She could see the fatigue in his eyes. "Come on, Zoe, I need to take a shower. I want you to shower with me."

Water sluiced over Gage's skin. Zoe stood back while he gave himself a quick wash. He didn't want her pressed up against the filth he'd been rolling in. As he scrubbed himself down, he was thinking about Zoe and her biomarker tests that she refused to perform to see if certain traits ran in someone's blood. He wondered if Zoe could find the familial biomarkers that would predict the outcome of their relationship. Was serial philandering part of his paternal genetic code? He'd never considered cheating in a relationship before. But it could lie there, latently waiting. What about maternal alcoholism and suicidal tendencies? Was that what he was bringing to a relation-ship with Zoe? At least he'd found a strong woman, someone who wanted to remain separate and whole. Someone who could leave him and save herself if he turned out anything like his parents. That made him feel safer about broaching the idea of a future, especially one with kids in it.

When Gage was less contaminated, he reached for Zoe's hand and pulled her under the water.

With her round bottom pressed against his abdomen, he

reached around, rubbing suds over her belly. He let his finger graze over her ribs so she'd giggle and squirm.

"Stop, Gage, that tickles!" She was laughing, and his cock stood at attention. When she tried to pull away, he held her tight until she stilled.

"Well, at least I got a smile out of you." He poured shampoo onto his palm, then rubbed it into her hair. "You know how you laugh and kid with your old dance company friends? I'd like you to feel that comfortable with me," he said as he rubbed bubbles into her scalp and down the long strands. "To feel that level of—"

"Immaturity?" She laughed as she put a hand on the shower wall to steady herself and kept her hips pinned to his, using her other hand to move his hard-on between her warm thighs.

"I was thinking, *abandon*." He leaned down and kissed her shoulder. "Where you let yourself be playful without using brakes."

She leaned her head back as he massaged the suds into her hair. He felt her body stiffen under his hands. That was the opposite reaction to what he wanted.

"That's an interesting way of perceiving that relationship. For me, talking with my childhood friends, I have that childlike relationship with them. You know? The jokes we're laughing at are private jokes from many, many years ago." She turned her head for a kiss, then put her hands back on the wall, relaxing again.

He massaged the bubbles down her back, being extremely gentle over the three angry looking bruises from the rounds she took to her bulletproof vest.

"I can't have that with you because even if we have private jokes, I'm not filtering them through a middle school mindset. I have no desire to be that person again." She paused for a second, then asked in a smaller voice, "Is that who you're waiting for in our relationship?"

"Nope." He tilted her head back so he could rinse the shampoo out. "I guess what I'm waiting for is the level of comfort and trust I hear in your voice when you're having fun with them."

Zoe stepped forward, turning and running her hand up and down his dick before she sandwiched it between their bodies. She looked up for a kiss. "I trust you." And another kiss. "And I appreciate you." Then she laid her head on his shoulder.

Gage turned so the water would run down her back and keep her warm.

"Because you seem to get me and don't try to make me something I'm not," Zoe said. "I didn't misread that, did I, Gage?" She leaned back so they were eye to eye. "Were you waiting for me to morph into a different person over time?"

Gage could lose himself in Zoe's eyes. The honesty. The depth. "No, Zoe." He sent her a smile. "It's impossible for a flower to change her petals." He held her chin so she wouldn't look away when he said, "And you are the most beautiful orchid."

Zoe's eyes filled with bashful curiosity.

Gage turned her again, so her back was against him, and he reached for the soap to play with her breasts. Her nipples pebbled under his fingers, and she reached between his legs to massage his cock, then guided it inside of her. As she undulated her hips to move up and down his shaft, he drew a long breath between his teeth. After a day like today, his emotions were on edge. His orgasm was right there. A few more strokes and he'd be done. Gage forced the sensations down and pushed his thoughts to his rational mind so he could wait for her to catch up.

"Orchids look delicate, but they are incredibly hardy," he whispered into her ear. "The plant blooms for weeks, if not months on end, where other flowers blossom and fade in just days."

Zoe arched her back with a moan as his hands moved over her breasts, her belly, her ass. He rocked his hips to move in and out of her. He took another breath and tried to focus on words, not sensations. "Where other flowers need to be watered constantly, you are satisfied with very little—in fact, giving you the same amount of water as I would a different flower would be harmful."

Zoe pushed against him.

"Orchids like diffused light. If the light is too intense, they don't do well. They need just the right touch." He reached between her legs to drag the rough pad of his thumb over her clitoris. With one arm holding her tight against him and the other hand rubbing her clit, he stroked gently in and out of her. "Orchids are graceful flowers. Oh-so beautiful to look at. But I'd never pick one and take it home to put in a vase. Orchids have to be left alone."

She made little mewling noises as she steadied herself on the wall, then pushed her bottom back into him, her signal that she wanted it harder. Deeper.

Thank God. Gage wrapped his hands around her hips, happy to comply.

GAGE'S LEGS were rubbery underneath him. He couldn't remember ever having an orgasm that wild. Every nerve in his body lit up as heat spread through him like wildfire. He wrapped Zoe in his arm and held both of them up with his other hand on the toiletry shelf. She was like a rag doll draped over him, reaching one arm up to hook around his neck.

When he bent to kiss her, her eyes were shut, and her mouth

was bowed into a perfect pink smile of satisfaction. Gage couldn't have loved her more than he did at that moment. With that thought, his dick hardened again. Gage wasn't sure he could survive another orgasm like that. He moved them out of the tub, wrapped Zoe in a towel, and together they made their way to the bedroom to collapse on the king-sized bed.

"I love you, Zoe," Gage said for the very first time.

She didn't answer.

He looked down to see her smile fall away and her eyes flash open. Her breath went shallow. What did that mean? Didn't she feel the same? That would be a hell of a thing. "I'm crazy about you." He pushed the wet hair from her face.

She shook her head.

Gage flipped onto his side and propped his head on his bent arm, resting his other hand on her stomach. "You don't feel the same?"

"That's not what our relationship's been about." She pulled the towel tighter. "We agreed that we were going to enjoy each other's company. Have sex. We talked about no commitments. You were very clear about no commitments. You could be sent off at any time. Attachments could be problematic. Let's enjoy the here and now. Does this sound familiar?"

"Yes." That was exactly what he'd said. He'd laid out his parameters from the start. It was his go-to beginning of a relationship discussion. "I've moved on from there," Gage said.

She flipped on her side, mirroring his position. Once again, tucking the towel tightly around her like a shield. "What does that look like to you?"

What did that look like to him? If she was this shocked with an 'I love you,' he wasn't willing to test the waters with the rest of it. Gage combed his fingers through the damp ropes of her hair.

"A committed relationship?" she asked, refocusing him on her words.

Gage was silent, trying to weigh what he wanted to say. A life. A family. Those seemed too big of an ask—too much of a leap. "Yes, actually," was what he finally offered.

She blinked like he had blown dust into her eyes, and she was trying to clear her vision. "What does committed look like to you?" She put her hand on her chest as if she felt pain. "Moving in together? Marriage?"

"Well, yes. Both," Gage said softly.

"Gage, no." She rolled off the bed and moved to her suitcase. "I'm sorry. But no."

Gage tensed his muscles like she was delivering body blows. *No.* He felt like he'd been kicked in the guts, his lungs deflated. He held perfectly still, praying the feeling would go away.

With the towel as a screen, she pulled on a pair of panties and then the oversized t-shirt she slept in. Dressed, she turned back to look at him. "I grew up as a military brat." Her voice was whisper-soft, and she looked like a praying angel as she hugged the towel to her chest. "Every time my roots took hold, my parents yanked me up and stuck me in some new plot of earth. I'm over that lifestyle. I've established a career and friendships. I learned from my mom's experience that not only do I need to stand strong on my own, I also have to live my own life, not dictated to by the whims of my husband's employer. I'm not marrying into the military. I'm not falling in love with a Marine. I won't let it happen."

Gage swallowed. "But it has, just a little bit, hasn't it?" The words caught in his throat, and he had to clear them before he could say, "You love me at least a little." As soon as the words slipped past his lips, Gage knew it was a mistake. Zoe completely slammed the doors down and turned her face to the wall.

"What if I weren't in the military? Would you feel differently then?"

"I don't do hypotheticals with relationships," she told the wall.

"You might have missed it in all of the hullabaloo today, but I signed a contract to work with Iniquus. I won't be re-upping with the Marines. Iniquus, they're headquartered right here in Washington D.C. I'll have overseas assignments, but D.C. would always be my jumping off block."

She turned turbulent eyes on him and pursed her lips as she studied him. "I hope that that didn't have anything to do with me. I'm not getting involved in your career. Don't add me and our relationship to any scale you're using to weigh your decisions."

"That's kinda cold, Zoe." Gage moved to the top of the bed, where he sat completely naked with his back to the headboard.

Zoe came and sat on the corner of the bed, facing him. "You have to be you. You have to be your own tree with your own root system."

"Hah! I know where you got that from."

Zoe canted her head.

"Kahlil—"

"Gibran, right. I think it's one of the wisest things I've ever read when it comes to relationships."

"Agreed. We're of the same mind on that." That they both knew the same poem, and both used it as a means of defining a perfect relationship only served to deepen Gage's trust in their connection. They belonged together. "So here are the facts. As soon as my contract is up with Uncle Sam next month, I'll be the newest member of Panther Force. I'll be working under Titus

Kane. These next few weeks, I'll still be at Quantico." He paused. "Now that the military change of address is off the table…"

Zoe pursed her lips and let her breath out slowly.

Gage stopped. She hadn't said no. She didn't say yes. But that gave him room to try. "What are you thinking, Zoe?"

She did it again, a deep breath in, then the slow release through her beautiful pink lips. All he wanted to do was grab her up and kiss her. Hard.

She held up her hand. "You threw me off balance with that one, Gage. I need some time to process. Can we please take one crisis at a time?"

"Our relationship is a crisis?" For some reason, that amused him, and he offered up a grin.

"No. No." She crawled up the bed and scooted under the covers, rolling until she was resting in his arms. "I didn't mean that. I simply meant that I need brain space to process what you're saying, and right now, my brain is busy."

"Gotcha." He bent to kiss her and moved Zoe so he could better hold her. "So first, we save you and the world as we know it." He reached back to click off the light. "And once the apocalypse is averted, we can figure out who we are to each other."

38

THE SMELL OF COFFEE PULLED HIM TO A SITTING POSITION. GAGE rubbed his eyes and reached out to yank open the blackout curtains that hid the morning light. The clock read zero eight hundred hours. He could probably sleep a few more hours and be the better for it.

Zoe, of course, wasn't in bed. He reached over, and the warmth was gone from her side. She must have been up for a while. Gage decided to shower and brush his teeth before he went down to see her. The noise would give her time to adjust to someone else being around, interrupting her thoughts. He scratched his hand through his two-day-old beard. He'd probably feel better after a shave too.

Titus had brought in Zoe's overnight bag, and he had a sports bag for Gage. When Gage opened it, he found an Iniquus uniform, a new set of socks and briefs, and a Dopp Kit with all he needed toiletries. That would do. He brought them with him into the bathroom for a quick clean up.

Now revived, he was ready for a cup of joe. He headed down the steps to find Zoe sitting at the breakfast bar with papers spread in front of her and her hands wrapped around an oversized, green coffee mug.

He moved toward her. "Did you sleep at all last night?" He dropped a kiss onto her forehead as he wandered into the kitchen.

"No." She sighed. "My brain was on overdrive."

Gage picked up one of the papers scattered across the counter. One was covered in doodles and had his name framed in squiggly lines. The other looked like a math formula on steroids. At the bottom, it said Colonel Guthrie, and that too was surrounded by squiggly lines. "What's this all about?" He laid the papers back in front of her.

"Two different ways of thinking things through. This is my emotional thought process and nonlinear thinking." She put her finger on the page with his name. "And these are my logic formulas."

"You can take the girl out of the lab," he said, snagging a coffee mug from the shelf. "But you can't take the lab out of the girl." He moved back and pointed to the doodle page. "Obviously, this is the one that interests me the most." He poured the coffee and moved to the stool next to Zoe's. "What do these squiggles around my name represent?"

"Conclusion drawn."

His heart stumbled, then raced forward. He scanned over the page to see if he could pull any information from it. Was this a conclusion that was in his favor or not? "An ice cream cone. That's when we met?"

"Yes." Zoe wasn't giving anything up for free. Her eyes looked troubled, angst-filled.

He looked at the upper right-hand corner that took up a sizable portion of the page. "And this symbol? Is that a bomb going off?"

"It's an explosion."

Gage had felt this way one other time in his life. He'd been doing field training. Coming under simulated firepower, he dove headfirst into the icy Mississippi River. Pain flooded his system as he immersed himself. He had to battle his inner demons as much as the current to get his boots safely underneath him.

She rolled her lips in and looked into her mug, then her lashes flew up as she caught him with her gaze. "It represents our sex life."

Maybe that was the solid footing he needed. "That's good, then?"

"It's excellent. Don't you think?" Her brows went up.

He held her gaze for a long moment. He saw that really was a question. She wasn't being flip. She never was. He hadn't quite gotten used to the fact that Zoe spoke in facts, not sarcasm. He shouldn't layer in the times from his past when he'd had relationship conversations with other women and had to be wary of all the trip wires laid across the path. Zoe was Zoe, and different. "Yeah, I think."

He stared at the paper and started recognizing symbols of things they had done together, the canoe trip, the book fair, the lecture on Zika, for chrissake. Not what he normally thought of as dating scene stuff. Interesting stuff, though. He'd liked it, anyway. "And here at the bottom, these leaves?"

"The oak and the cypress."

"Kahlil Gibran's poem. What conclusion did you come to, Zoe?"

She pulled the paper in front of her. "That I fell in love with you here." Zoe put her finger on the ice cream cone. Then she traced her finger over the other images. "And all of these things are reasons that that love became solid."

"That huge suitcase is baggage, though?" Gage asked. "Yours or mine?"

"Not baggage, per se. It's the reason that I wouldn't allow myself to do anything but hold you at arm's-length. To protect my heart, because eventually, you'd be at a new base—back at Lejeune, or wherever—and I'd be saying goodbye to you…to us."

Gage wouldn't consider that last sentence. That wasn't something he was prepared to do, say goodbye, and never see Zoe again. He turned his attention to something more hopeful. "These, then?" He pointed to the bottom of the page under his name.

"The leaves are the reason I would be willing to dedicate my heart to you. I know you'll appreciate me for who I am and not try to make me into something I'm not because it suits you better. Not that I'm not willing to bend. If we're together, the gales that blow against you will be the same winds that buffet me."

Something inside him grew big and broad. Fierce. Zoe wasn't playing coy. She was simply unfolding her thought process for him. But he felt like storming the barricade and capturing the flag. He wanted his yes. "I need a clearer answer than that."

She looked straight into his eyes, then tilted her head. "I think committing myself to our relationship is what I want to do."

"You think, or you *know*?" Gage asked. She still sounded like the answer was a maybe. And that wasn't good enough. He needed that solid ground under him. He needed to know where he stood. "Because I *know*. If these last few days have taught me anything, it's how deeply I love you and how much I want you in my life, always."

"Please don't say that." She reached out and wrapped her hands around his forearm, the look in her eyes a little wild. "Crisis emotions are temporary."

Gage realized he was combat-focused. His face and his body had taken on a hard-muscled stance. He was in self-protection mode, and that was the wrong place for his head to be right now. He stepped even closer to her and gently lifted her chin to look her in the eye. He kissed her softly and rested his forehead against hers until he felt himself letting down his guard. Only then did he say, "No, Zoe, I thought those thoughts on the drive to your place before any of this started."

He stood up and reached for her hands and pulled them to his heart. "I got your text after a shit day, and everything was suddenly better. I'm happy when I'm with you." He watched her eyes to gauge her reaction. "I look forward to your smile. I look forward to you in my arms. I look forward to us talking about life's complexities and your unique way of seeing simple beauty." There, that was what he was hoping to see shine back at him. Belief. "You are the bright spot in my life. I've loved you since you leaned under the hood of that car. And I want to love you that way for the rest of my life."

This was the time he wanted to pull a ring from his pocket and take a knee. But the pockets he was wearing belonged to Iniquus. Besides, he wanted to make that moment special for both of them. Not a conversation on the run from the devil, hiding in a safe house.

Zoe heaved a sigh.

He needed to lighten this for her. This shouldn't feel so heavy. "You know, Zoe, when I look into the depths of your eyes, I can actually see the machinations of your brain, like a giant clock with the gears moving."

"Robot-like?"

296 | FIONA QUINN

"Mmm. As a member of the US military's elite forces, I think maybe I'd better give you a thorough once-over to make sure you're human in nature."

"Once-over?"

"You sound disappointed."

"Well, twice might be more fun."

"I could definitely use that right now." But he knew this was banter, and they weren't headed back up the stairs.

As if she could read his thoughts, she said, "This is important. We're important, and I want to be able to focus on that conversation. Right now, I'm distracted. My thoughts are cluttered. I'm conflicted—not about you. Not about us. About this mess, I'm in." She glanced down at a page of formulas. "I can't see a way out of it. The "us" discussion needs to wait until there's some kind of conclusion. If they end up putting me in some kind of protective program, then those life choices may not work for you. And if you say, 'I don't care. I'll follow you anywhere,' then I know that you're not an oak, and I'm not a cypress. I'll know you've bent your life to mine. So don't."

He shook his head. Of course, he could find a way to make his life work, no matter where she went. But he'd never seen her eyes so fierce. This meant everything to them—that Zoe was Zoe and that he stood strong as an individual too.

He forced his gaze onto the other piece of paper. "Tell me about these formulas."

She twisted around on her stool until she faced the counter. "Once I realized that I wanted our relationship to evolve into being your life partner—"

"Wife," Gage corrected with no wiggle room.

"Once I decided that I wanted to be your *wife*, I needed to resolve the problem that is keeping us from moving forward in our lives."

"And the conclusion was Colonel Guthrie? You think he's the answer to our problem? That he can do something to help?"

"I think he *is* our problem."

"What?" Gage sat on the stool beside Zoe.

"I was thinking about what you said. The solution is a formula, the chemicals, and their combination. If I could figure out the formula of how this came to be, then I could reverse engineer the end result, me in a safe house and Lily dead."

Gage leaned against the backrest and crossed his arms over his chest. His brow knit with concentration. And he waited.

"The colonel is the common denominator. He's the one who asked me to work for DARPA. He's the one who suggested that Montrim do the data collection with a humanitarian front. He's the one who brought BIOMIST to the CIA's attention to help find Osama. He's the one who sent me to set up my labs on the Montrim campus after I got my doctorate."

"He's the one who knew that Billings was going after Montrim long before it became public," Gage said. "He's the one who said Lily might be a spy, either for the CIA or Montrim. He's the one who suggested she be followed and gave the senator the card for the private investigator, Levi Schultz, who is really an Israeli former special op on the run."

"Exactly." Zoe nodded her head vigorously.

"Colonel Guthrie's the one who we assume planted one of the trackers on me in the hospital. And most likely the one who called Christopher Bilik."

"There are other ways Bilik could have known." Zoe tucked her hair behind her ears.

"Maybe. But at the hospital, Bilik said Colonel Guthrie called him," Gage noted.

"You said there was a deal between Israel and Montrim for

forty million. I can see Montrim getting through my computer firewalls. But they couldn't get through DARPAs."

Gage picked up the pen and pointed to Guthrie's name on the paper. "What if this was a private deal between Bilik, Guthrie, and the Mossad? Guthrie had access."

"Absolutely. And you put my phone on airplane mode in my apartment. Guthrie could have determined that after you left his house. He became worried that the phone was off or lost or—"

"No. This doesn't fit neatly together. I don't think Guthrie knew about the break-in at your apartment. He seemed genuinely upset when I went by his house to tell him. And he was also surprised that Lily was dead when Senator Billings showed up at his house drunk."

"I think that that's where the chemistry analogy went wrong. I think it's more like a Venn Diagram. There are some holes. Who needed to stop the hearing? Who would benefit the most?"

"Montrim," Gage said without any doubt.

"What if Guthrie and Bilik decided to guard Montrim to protect a private deal they were doing with Israel. A forty-million-dollar deal couldn't be hidden. I don't know how they could do that as a corporate entity and keep that hidden from the US military." Zoe paused, thinking. "Say it's just Bilik and Guthrie in on that deal. They really needed to save Montrim Industries."

"Save them for two reasons that we know about—there's an Israeli deal on the table and a CIA deal on the table. If the Federal government severed ties, whoever was orchestrating those deals would lose access to the data for both deals."

"My thoughts exactly." Zoe nodded. "Okay, now Guthrie tells Bilik. Bilik, by the way, is a big-time donor to USIPAC, and that would give him the connections to approach Israel with the database information. It could very well have been Bilik who handed over the card for the PI, told Guthrie to convince Billings to have Lily followed, and arranged for USIPAC to both move Lily to her own place and pay for the PIs bill. You said that the PI kept following Lily after Billings said to stop. If the guy was working for USIPAC, he'd still be working the case, right?"

"Yeah, I don't know about that," Gage said. "Why would USIPAC do that? Why wouldn't they put a PI on Lily and not triangulate with Billings? For that matter, why wouldn't Bilik fire Lily?"

"I wouldn't fire her," Zoe said. "It's like that Montrim scientist, George Matthews, who was spying on the soundwave technology studies and selling the updates to China. What did the investigators do? The scuttlebutt is that Montrim hired agents in to watch him to see who all was involved and how the operation worked. Only when they had all the pieces of the puzzle did the guy disappear. I would guess the FBI is dealing with him."

"That makes sense," Gage agreed. Montrim, or maybe Bilik and Guthrie, wanted to learn from Lily what the senator knew and how he was going to go about taking down Montrim. They would have discussed this at Lily's house, provided by USIPAC, which I'd guess was fully wired for audiovisual. Gage pulled a fresh piece of paper over and started scrawling notes. "If nothing else, that would give them blackmail material." Now he realized why Zoe had filled so many pages. This wasn't a straight line. This was the convergence of variables. "Prescott needs to go check for bugs, though whoever planted them probably pulled them out again."

"The PI was associated with this group of Israeli special ops," Zoe said. "Who else is a player here?"

Gage thought back to his pocket full of business cards, and two of them were from "The CIA."

"Is it possible that the CIA could have rewarded the Israeli special ops guys for some action, some piece of intel, with a viable cover story of their deaths, and then brought the unit to the US under new names? They can do that, can't they?"

"They can." Gage dragged out the words, thinking that was more stuff of movies than reality. "They do. But it would be one hell of a reward."

"If anyone could warrant that reward, it would be these guys. Let's say they had CIA operatives in danger's way, and these guys had the wherewithal to get them out. That might be an even exchange. Right?"

"Yes." *Shit, they might have made that kind of deal.*

"The CIA may use these guys from time to time to do things that they couldn't get away with on US soil. There may be some reason that they got those tattoos and kept up their training. I put the CIA in that loop for keeping Montrim viable, not because they know about the sale of BIOMIST data, but because they really want the killer wasp, RoboSphecius, in play." Zoe pointed to some of her symbolic math that meant zero to Gage. "What if the CIA ordered Lily to be killed to protect Montrim—she could no longer testify, and the affair would discredit Senator Billings. And what if that same night they also send two of their guys to capture me? In that case, the CIA killed Lily to keep Montrim viable because they wanted their RoboSphecius. And they could have tried to kidnap me to force me to make it for them. And as I say it out loud, I find all of this ludicrously outside the realm of actual reality. But if there's even a hair of truth to that tale, the CIA could only know about the WASP from one direction, and that's—"

"Guthrie," Gage growled.

"Guthrie may not have known about the hit on Lily or that I was to be captured. He may have thought that I was safe in all of this. He could actually be completely innocent of any wrongdoing and only passed DARPA intel to the CIA as his position required. I want to believe that. He's been friends with Senator Billings for a very long time. And he's been a friend of my dad's even longer. Colonel Guthrie is like family to me. But his innocence doesn't mean that he had no hand in this outcome. It seems to me he was the engine that drove this bus. I believe that. I think if we bring this to the attention of Iniquus and the FBI, that they will be able to find the proof that Guthrie inadvertently created this fiasco with Bilik and the CIA. Guthrie was duped. He was a pawn, I'm sure. But he's the connector. I bet he can help us figure out what's happening."

"We need to get back to Iniquus, Zoe. They need to hear this. Now."

Zoe piled into the car beside Gage, putting her purse on the floor near her feet, and pulling her safety belt into place. The interior of the car was as beat to hell as the exterior, but the engine hummed, the tires were first-rate, and it maneuvered like a sports car.

Gage pressed the button on the dash, and the garage door closed behind them. He pushed the button to the right.

"Communications," came the man's voice.

"Gage Harrison, Panther Force, Zoe Kealoha, and I are heading to Iniquus Headquarters. Our ETA is forty-five minutes."

"Copy. We have you on satellite. Be advised there is a road crew ahead. Traffic is being detoured. We estimate an additional ten minutes to your drive time."

"Roger. Out." He tapped the button again.

"That's handy," Zoe said.

They drove in silence down the country road. They were the only ones around. Gage enjoyed the quiet and the stark beauty of the winter landscape. But his head was still on a swivel. It was illegal for the CIA to operate, for the most part, in the United States, but that didn't mean much, especially in this case. Zoe's research put her square in the sphere of CIA intelligence gathering. And they were the masters when it came to technology. They could be following their progress down this lonely road the same way Iniquus was. Their only real safety was in the anonymity they gained through the grocery store car switch.

Gage was glad that he had a heads up from Iniquus that there was construction up ahead. He was ready for it when he saw a flagman. Iniquus had said it was a detour, though. That's not what was happening here. This guy held a stop sign. Gage slowed to a roll. There were ditches on either side, and this Olds had a low-slung body. He pushed the comms button.

"Communications."

"Gage here. Heads up, we're at the construction crew. There's a flagman. I'm inching up on a stop sign."

"Copy."

Gage could see men with their backs to him in the road and dirt that looked freshly dug.

"There's another flagman ahead, holding back two cars," the comms guy said.

The workers moved out of the road. The flagman spoke into his radio. He spun the sign to "slow" and waved them through.

Gage tapped the gas to pick up speed as he maneuvered left to go around the digger. As they moved over the dirt, four pops sounded like rifle fire. Gage's right hand shot out and dragged Zoe's head down to her lap. He stomped the gas pedal to the ground, and the car moved forward on the hard edges of his run flat tires. He'd hit a spike strip.

Two cars, one in the left lane, one in the right, barreled toward them. Gage slammed his foot on the brake until they jerked to a stop. He threw the car in reverse, burning rubber a he tried to backtrack out of this ambush. All the while, Gage was calling the play by play to the communication tech, hoping they had some Iniquus guys somewhere nearby.

The digger moved across the road before Gage could make it past. They were trapped.

"Zoe, sit up and put your hands in the air," Gage said with as much steadiness as he could muster.

"Communications. Listening in silence. Iniquus support is mobilized to your location. We have you locked on satellite. We can see everything," the man said.

"Look, Zoe, they've pulled ski masks over their faces. That means they don't want to be identified. They aren't here to kill you. They're going to take you, prisoner." They turned to each other. "Zoe, I need you to be strong. Give them whatever they want. Do whatever they want. We'll figure out how to undo that later. Don't try to be a hero."

Zoe never missed a thing. "You said they'll take *me* prisoner. What will they do to you?"

The butts of a pair of rifles smashed through their windows, showering them with safety glass. Men dressed in tactical gear stepped up with pistols in their hands.

"Colonel Guthrie," Zoe's shocked voice called out as darts pierced their necks.

Gage felt the medication flowing into his artery.

Zoe spun back to look at him with bewilderment and fear, yanking the dart from her skin. "Gage, oh my God. I'm so sorry."

Women are like wasps in their anger

— ENGLISH PROVERB

"IF YOU DIDN'T WANT TO HELP THE CIA AND OUR MILITARY, why the hell did you sign a contract with DARPA, Zoe?"

Zoe swallowed. She was seated on a folding metal chair in the middle of a room painted pink, with circus animals dancing around the border paper. She had pulled herself out of her stupor about an hour ago. But she was still a little wobbly. She stuck her feet out on either side of her like a bicycle kickstand to hold herself upright.

There was a table with a computer, it was pointed at her, and Zoe imagined that this conversation was being recorded.

She had recognized Colonel Guthrie at the side of the car, despite his face mask. Now that they were inside, he'd pulled his disguise off and stood red-faced and seething in front of her. She had never seen him look like this before. Zoe was afraid. Afraid for herself. Afraid for Gage. She wondered if he was still alive.

"How did you find me?" Zoe demanded. Anger boiled under her skin.

"Grossman and Parker need the WASP functioning. They got a heads-up from the CIA that you were at Iniquus. With CIA technology, the rest isn't rocket science. And speaking of science," Guthrie kicked the leg of her chair, "why'd you sign a DARPA contract if you didn't want to help your country?"

Zoe grabbed the seat lest she go flying. "I watched a YouTube video about 9-11. Not about the towers coming down, but about the greatest maritime rescue effort in human history. A half-million people were plucked off Manhattan Island by the men and women who worked on boats in the area. The Coast Guard put out a call, 'if you can, come help.' The boats converged. At the beginning of the video, they posted the Romain Rolland quote, 'A hero is a man who does what he can.'"

Colonel Guthrie reached out to swipe a tear that brightened the corner of Zoe's lashes. "Are you crying?"

She smacked his hand away. She wondered where her glasses were. She'd feel much better if she could see clearly. "I can do biomedical engineering and micro-robotics. If my inventions mean saving lives, then that's what I stepped up to do. And it's not just for military applications. My inventions, once they're out of prototype, can have an impact on making our law enforce-ment more effective."

"Again, I'm asking you why you signed up. It's because you want to help your country. You're a patriot, aren't you, Zoe?"

"I love my country. I want what's best for my country."

"Your country needs you. The CIA needs you. We need, for the best future of America, to have the RoboSphecius in play. The CIA needs them to function in a little over four months. That should be enough time for you to get them flying, so to speak."

Zoe's brows came together. "That's the timeline you gave me for the WASPs to function for military intelligence."

Colonel Guthrie shook his head with a sigh. "We need both. A WASP to identify and monitor the mark, and a RoboSphecius to find your beacon and sting the target. Once you have one that's actionable, the second is easy. It's the same damned mechanism with a different fluid. Getting the WASP to identify the right person. That's the big deal."

"All along, I've been developing a CIA project."

"Of course. I can't understand why this is a problem for you. You want to save lives. This is a no-brainer. When your WASP identifies a subject, instead of bombing the compound, we can take out the single culprit. How many lives could you save, Zoe? How many innocents?"

"Colonel, that argument is myopic, simplistic, illogical, and completely beside the point."

"Do tell."

"I will never develop a means of killing. Identification? Yes. Killing? *No*. I will not be responsible for anyone else's death. Period. My developing a means of identification is meant to prevent bombs from being used in error. I am not responsible for the decisions that come after. For example, the military could choose to track that person until they are in seclusion and then take them out. They can send in a sniper. If others decide to take out a complex, that's on them. Once my micro-robotics and software are functional, they become part of the human experience. That means other scientists can and will do the same. I will not provide the world with a new weapons system by adding to the knowledge scaffolding. Scientific knowledge is accumulative, and we don't know where this could lead."

"Enough. You are far too naïve to weigh the ethics of your recalcitrance." Colonel Guthrie leaned his hips into the table with the laptop. As he bumped it, the screen filled with an image.

Zoe squinted at the screen, not sure what she was seeing. Guthrie pulled her purse toward him and handed her her glasses.

Now the image was crystal clear. Gage sat in a chair. His face was bloody. His clothes were ripped. He looked dazed. His hands were cuffed in place. His feet were shackled.

Zoe jumped from her chair.

"Sit your ass down!" Colonel Guthrie yelled at her. "Gage is our incentive. He's going to stay with us for a while. Right there in that chair." He pointed at the video. "You want him to eat? You behave. You want him to drink? You behave. You want him to get up and use the bathroom instead of pissing down his leg and sitting in his own filth? You behave."

Zoe gasped. "Are you going to kill me? Kill Gage?"

"With a brain like yours? Why would I do that? You're an asset. Kill Gage? That depends. You will do whatever I tell you to do. Sign whatever I tell you to sign."

"Of course," she said. She looked around the child's room again. "How am I to work here?"

"Not here. You need your laboratory, obviously. You will go home. You will go to work. You will make progress. You won't try any cute tricks to make things self-destruct or tell me that you need more time. Gage Harrison's life is on a time clock. March fifteenth—three months from today—if we don't have the *two* kinds of wasps operationally ready, I will personally electrocute Gage in front of you with a low enough voltage that it will be a excruciatingly slow and painful death."

Zoe started vibrating. She shook so hard; she could hardly keep herself planted on the seat.

"And that's when I call your parents. I'll tell them you've gone missing, and they need to come to DC right away, stay at my house. And we will start again. And if they die, then we will go after your friends. I will be relentless. I will be heartless. I will be the devil himself. I will have these wasps." Colonel Guthrie moved over and leaned in until their noses touched. "Do I make myself clear?" he spat out, his eyes demonic. Everything about this man made Zoe recoil.

"And if you think you can find a way to get a message to Iniquus or your buddy Damion Prescott, be aware that you will have a shadow six inches from your elbow until I am satisfied. You won't eat alone. You won't sleep alone. You won't bathe or pee alone. There will always be one of my men six inches away. And let me tell you, they have lost seven of their unit members to this FUBAR op already. They aren't feeling magnanimous when it comes to you. I'd tread carefully where they're concerned."

Zoe went numb. Her mouth fell open. Her brain failed her completely. She loved her brain. It was her superpower. But when she needed it, it let her down. Nothing came to her. No stories to help her find a way clear. No clever ideas. She was nothing but an autonomic nervous system, exchanging oxygen for carbon dioxide.

"Are you doubting me? Do you doubt the integrity of my team?" Colonel Guthrie sneered. "Lily died by my command. People don't go around falling onto Metro rails just as the subway is powering toward them." He reached over tapped the screen, bringing up a picture of a car that had slammed into the side of a cement mixer. The next picture he scrolled to was a close up of the driver who was obviously dead, crushed under the steering wheel. "This is what happened to Ruby Leibowitz on her drive home from Iniquus. Poor thing. I couldn't let her go to USIPAC with her information. And now I have Gage." He waited while this seeped into her consciousness.

"How many people do you want to see dead, Zoe? Should I call your folks in Hawaii? Pay your friends Sydney and Holland a visit? Jurnee? She lives nearby, doesn't she? In central Virginia? That's only a few hours from here. A nice drive."

He seemed to be waiting for a response, but Zoe wasn't in her body. Besides the ability to see and hear, she was little else. She was floating. Weightless.

"There are people you love that can suffer greatly for your heroics. But in the end, you know you're a patriot and want to help your country. There is nothing intrinsically bad about what you're developing in terms of safety for the American people."

"And what do you get out of this? A gigantic paycheck. One from the CIA and the other between you and Bilik from the Mossad."

Colonel Guthrie squeezed her jaw until she thought it would pop. "Who else knows that?"

"I do."

"Who else?"

"No one else. I figured it out last night when I was thinking it all through. I'm right, aren't I?"

The colonel threw her off the chair. She splayed across the floor. She had gotten her answer.

"Really, I shouldn't need to twist your arm to get you to comply. But I can certainly twist his." Guthrie flipped back to Gage's picture.

He needs medical help. "Is Gage here? Can I tell him that I'll be following your directives to the T?"

"I'm not stupid enough to put you in the same location."

Zoe stood and caught at the back of the chair as she wobbled. "Well, I guess you'd better drive me to Montrim so I can get going in my lab."

"That's my girl." Colonel Guthrie took her elbow in an iron clasp, snagged her purse, and steered her out the door.

A wasp stings the crying face

— **Japanese Proverb**

Zoe put the RoboSphecius down on its petri dish. Her hands were shaking to the point of being ineffectual. She turned her microscope off. Instead of moving forward, she was destroying what she already had in hand. As much as she hated the idea of taking a break while Gage was tied to that chair, she needed to eat. She needed a big fat sleeping pill. She needed to black out like she had at the hospital. She needed to wrangle control of her nervous system.

The man who was tasked to be her shadow was taking his assignment too literally. He hadn't been six inches from her side since she got out of the car at Montrim. His breath had been hot on her neck for the last two hours. She was a tall woman, but this guy was a behemoth. He'd even make Gage seem small in comparison. So far, she hadn't tested out Colonel Guthrie's threat that he'd even be six inches from her while she used the bathroom.

"Do you have a car? I need to go home." She stood.

The man followed her to the lab door and waited while she entered her codes to lock up. Without speaking to her, he took her elbow, just as Colonel Guthrie had, and steered her down the hall. They wound their way through the labyrinth of Montrim's campus, out the side door, through the courtyard, through another door down the hallway, and up some stairs to come out in a back parking lot that Zoe didn't even know existed.

The man was speaking into his cuff in a foreign language. He pressed her up against an air conditioning unit, and they waited. The wind blew. The cold got into her lungs. She coughed to expel it, which reminded her that she'd been holding her bladder all day long.

A car came around the corner and stopped. With an iron claw gripping her elbow, the behemoth thrust her forward. A door popped open on the sedan. Zoe heard a bang. Suddenly, her guard leaned over her, making guttural noises and twitching. He grasped at her convulsively. A ball-like object flew past her into the open car door. There was an explosion that lit her auricular nerves on fire. She stuck her fingers in her ears and collapsed under the guard's weight. She tried to push him off and saw that the car had filled with billowing smoke. The air became acidic. Zoe breathed into the fabric, covering her elbow.

The driver tried to take off driving, but the smoke was too thick to see through. He ran straight into the cooling unit, not two feet from where she and her captor lay. Zoe screamed and flung her arms out, making the guard drop off of her. Two men fast roped down the side of the portico roof. One grabbed her and jerked her back inside of Montrim.

Zoe fought with everything she had. But the man had wrapped her in his arms and had a hand over her mouth, stoppering her screams.

"Zoe. Calm."

She bit his finger hard, and he flung her out away from him but kept a good grip on her wrist.

"Zoe. Calm. It's Titus."

Zoe panted. Relief and danger fought for dominance. "No, you *can't* save me. I need... They have Gage!"

"Zoe. Shhh. *We* have Gage. He's at the Iniquus infirmary." He held up his cellphone with a picture of Gage lying on a cot. The wounds she had seen earlier were cleaned and dressed in pristine white bandages.

"You saved him? How?" Zoe was completely confused. "You saved *me*? How?"

"We're good at what we do." He held out his hand. "Come on."

"But the CIA is good at what they do too. They have the same capability as you do. More."

Titus touched the comms that wrapped his neck. "Panther actual. Roger that. I'm exiting with our precious cargo." He pushed the door open and took her by the hand. "We weren't up against the CIA, just Guthrie. Guthrie had a friend at NSA who was helping him with satellite images. We have friends there too."

"But Colonel Guthrie said—"

"Let's get you back with Gage, and we'll tell you what we found out."

Zoe moved out into the diffused light of a gray winter's day. Red Christmas bells, hanging on the parking lot lights, swung in the wind cheerily. Special Agent Prescott was hefting her captor to his feet. He was in cuffs. Prescott looked over at

Titus. "I'm loving these stun rifles, man. So much less paperwork."

Brian had another man bent over the hood of his car, cuffing him, as well. Smoke billowed around them.

Zoe was escorted to Titus's SUV. He helped her in, then scooted around to his side. She was too stunned to speak.

"You'll feel better once you see Gage," Titus predicted. He did her the great kindness of not talking again until she was in Gage's arms.

ZOE SAT as close as she could get to Gage without actually crawling into his lap. Touching him helped her remember that he was safe, not being beaten and bound, with his life on the line for her ethics. He reached up to stroke his hand over her hair and planted a kiss on her temple.

After she had gone to the infirmary to see Gage, the female doctor had taken her off to make sure that she hadn't been sexually attacked during her captivity. Zoe hadn't even considered the possibility. It was, though. Possible. And she remembered again how Colonel Guthrie had said these men would be within six inches of her when she slept and peed and bathed. She was fine. Thank God, both she and Gage were fine. Lily was not. Ruby was not. What a horrible string of events.

She and Gage had eaten, and now they were back in the Panther war room, waiting for Special Agent Prescott to come and debrief them.

"Can you tell me what they found in the Mercedes?" Gage asked, lacing his fingers with Zoe's. Zoe grasped his hand with both of hers and pulled it up against her belly.

"Yeah, sure," Brian said. "We stripped it down. The envelope was taped up under the rear seat. It had Colin Bunsinger's name on it. The envelope was still sealed when we handed it over to Prescott."

"They charged the men at the farmhouse? They're still in custody?" Gage asked.

"Yeah, we have eleven of the twelve up here, counting both hot and cold bodies. We have one who was picked up in Miami," Brian said.

"Lynx's ploy dragged one of their guys down there?" Gage grinned.

"Looks like it. He was caught trying to sneak onto the cruise ship. Either he was on his way to the Panama Canal on vacation, or he was falling into her trap. Strike Force kept an eye on the cabin for us. They're the ones who nabbed him. FBI took control of the guy and is shipping him back here."

Gage was laughing and held up a hand for a high five.

Zoe decided to ask Gage about the story of Lynx and the cruise ship later. Right now, she wanted to be very still and very quiet. Gage seemed to answer that thought with the kiss he brushed into her hair.

The Panthers rose respectfully as Special Agent Prescott moved through the door. Gage went to stand as well, but Prescott caught his eye and waved him back into his seat. Zoe sat up straight as the mood shifted from hanging out to official debrief.

Prescott stood at the front of the room. "I want to tell Panther Force how appreciative my unit is and how grateful I am for your help on this case. Nine men from the Israeli Special Forces are in custody, and three of them were killed while committing their crimes. We haven't yet learned how they came to be in America. This case will continue to unfold." He reached up to scratch his brow. "The CIA has been apprised and will be working with the FBI on the best way to handle the situation from this point forward."

There was a general groan that went up with the Panthers. Prescott acknowledged this with a calming hand gesture. "I know that's a stretch of the imagination, but in this case, it is in America's best interests that these criminals be kept under wraps. We can't let the public know in any way, shape, or form about the BIOMIST program. You're right, Zoe." Prescott opened his hand toward her. "This database has been of immense help to our intelligence community. On that, there is no disagreement between the FBI and CIA."

Prescott focused on Gage, and Zoe could feel Gage's muscles stiffening. "I have spoken directly with the Director of the CIA and apprised him of the actions and pressures that were put on Dr. Kealoha as well as the illegal contract they had developed with Montrim's board member, Christopher Bilik."

"Only Bilik?" Titus asked.

"From the papers that the team brought in that were meant to be disclosed to Colin Bunsinger, the funds were to go into two offshore accounts, both in shell companies' names. Bilik, of course, needed someone of Guthrie's stature at DARPA to gain access to the designs that Zoe was developing. It's being investigated. Guthrie is being held on two counts of kidnapping, and one count of torture, and a list of accompanying crimes. He won't be free from prison in this lifetime."

"What's the CIA's position on my research?" Zoe asked.

"The CIA's unofficial position is that their need was great. They were forced by circumstances to use whatever means they had at their disposal, bribery being one of the tools they have in their toolbox."

"They were okay with the plan to steal Zoe's intellectual property?" Brian asked.

"That's what the CIA does. That's their job. You'd under-stand that better if you made Zoe a stranger. Pull the personal out of the equation," Prescott said. "And again, that's unofficial. Officially? Grossman and Parker are being reprimanded for their actions and for reckless behavior that put lives at risk, ultimately leading to two deaths."

"Wait. The CIA wasn't running the Israelis?" Gage asked.

"As far as we can tell, in this set of circumstances, they were not. They did know that the project was in danger because Lily was helping Senator Billings. They're the ones who put the spyware on both Lily and Zoe's phones."

"And in their watches?"

"We haven't figured that out yet. The CIA says it's not them, and they've been forthright with the rest of the information."

"Colonel Guthrie said that he had ordered Lily's and Ruby's deaths." Zoe felt the full weight of the betrayal resting on her chest. She had trusted the colonel. He'd been an uncle to her her whole life.

"We were apprised that she was in a car accident."

"She hit a cement mixer. I think it was the same one that chased us."

"We can pin that down through license plate recognition," Nutsbe said as he tapped his keyboard.

"At this point, we know Guthrie is a key player in all of this. We believe that Bilik is complicit in the BIOMIST scheme as well," Prescott said. "We have a warrant out for his arrest based on the correspondence between him and the Mossad."

"What was going on with the tattoos and the Rex Deus?" Titus asked.

"The men all say that it was a pledge of brotherhood they made to each other. They claim it has no implications beyond that. We are, of course, at the beginning of the investigation," Prescott said.

Gage leaned forward, propping his elbows on his knees. "And Bilik's not in custody yet?"

Prescott checked his watch. "There's a team on it now. As soon as we have him in pocket, you should be safe again, Zoe."

"Thank you." Zoe's eyes filled with the tears that had been turning off and on like a water faucet since Thursday evening. She scanned the faces of all the men, including them in her gratitude.

Titus crossed his arms over his chest. "Zoe, Mr. Spencer, one of the Iniquus owners, also let the Director of the CIA know about Grossman's and Parker's connection with everything that's happened. At that time, Spencer made it clear that you, Zoe, are under Iniquus's protective wing. We don't allow bad things to happen to one of our own." He gave her a nod that punctuated the statement.

"This is part of the FBI contract?" Zoe asked, confused.

"No," Titus said. "It's part of Gage's contract. He listed you as his fiancée. Like I said, we take care of the Iniquus family. By contract, that means you."

Titus walked up to shake Prescott's hand, and they moved toward the computer system when Nutsbe flagged them over.

Zoe and Gage moved to the corner to talk privately. They wrapped their arms around each other.

Zoe tipped her head up. Gage's eyes were turquoise green. The shade they turned when he was very happy.

"You didn't ask me yet—we hadn't decided on marriage when you signed those contracts with Iniquus," she whispered.

Gage canted his head and sent Zoe a sexy grin. "You didn't ask me yet either when you signed my name to your advance hospital directive, giving me the right to make life or death health decisions for you."

"My Montrim contract required me to put two local names."

"Funny." He planted a kiss on the tip of her nose. "My contract only asked for one. Aren't you glad I picked you?

"Yes." Zoe came up on her tiptoes to give Gage a gentle kiss. "As a matter of fact, I am."

The end

Thank you for reading about Zoe and Gage.
In Gulf Lynx, you'll hear a bit about Zoe's work and her wedding plans.
In Protective Instinct, you'll learn more about the legal case.

Keep reading for a sneak peek at the next book in the Iniquus chronology, *In Too Deep*!

Readers, I hope you enjoyed getting to know Gage and Zoe. If you had fun reading WASP, I'd appreciate it if you'd help others enjoy it too.

Recommend it: Just a few words to your friends, your book groups, and your social networks would be wonderful.

Review it: Please tell your fellow readers what you liked about my book by reviewing WASP on Amazon and Goodreads. If you do write a review, please send me a note at hello@fionaquinn-books.com. I'd like to thank you with a personal e-mail. Or stop by my website, FionaQuinnBooks.com, to keep up with my news and chat through my contact form.

IN TOO DEEP

In a world where everything isn't black and white, survival depends on trust...

Lacey Stewart was a normal woman with a mundane job at a D.C. art gallery. But that was before. Before a man was stabbed in front of her. Before someone tried to kill her. Now, Lacey needs help. She just never expected that help to come from the only man she's ever truly loved. The man she can't have…

Retired Marine Special Operator Deep Del Toro knew the men who had Lacey in their sights were professionals. He also knew the cops and the FBI couldn't keep her safe. What he didn't know was just how far he'd go to protect the woman he loved. And as it turned out, there wasn't anything he wouldn't do for her.

Before Lacey and Deep can claim their happily ever after, they'll need to unravel an international web of interconnected crimes in a world where right and wrong so often overlap. It won't be easy. But they're in far too deep to back out now...

In Too Deep is an action-adventure, military romance, mystery thriller suspense filled with spies, conspiracies, and international terror. Grab your copy and join the fight for survival.

1

THURSDAY NIGHT

LACEY STUART'S muscles tightened as irritation prickled through her nervous system. She gave her phone yet another check—no new messages. A swirl of frustration blew past her lips as she pushed the phone farther back on the bar. It didn't look like Steve was going to show. Emergencies popped up, she thought, trying to be generous. But really, what could have stopped him from sending a quick text? She slid her thigh farther up her crossed legs, trying not to skate off the ultra-modern, ultra-awkward bar stool made for someone much taller than she. Lacey caught the server's eye and tapped the rim of her empty Cosmo glass, signaling that another one was in order. She decided to take a Lyft back to her apartment after she finished this drink – with or without Steve.

She should probably be worried about Steve. It wasn't like him to stand her up. But honestly, the only thing she felt was aggravation. It had been a long, miserable day at work. All Lacey wanted was to be back in her apartment, curled up with a cup of hot tea and her book. Lacey glanced down at the winter coat she'd thrown across the stool beside hers to save a place for Steve — a good thirty minutes ago. She couldn't understand why he'd been so insistent on meeting her here and then not been courteous enough to give her a heads-up that he was running late.

As the server set a fresh drink in front of her, Lacey caught scotch-on-the-rocks guy staring at her mouth. Again. She wondered if he had a thing for bright red lipstick or if she had a strand of spinach from her afternoon snack caught in her teeth. Lacey held her hand over her mouth, lowering her head to stare at her lap while her tongue foraged in the crevices and along the gum line, hoping to excavate any residue.

As she raised her eyes, they caught on a man by the door. He was staring at her as if he knew her and was trying to make a decision. She didn't recognize him, but his attention made a tingle of apprehension skitter across her scalp. Lacey hated living with this pervasive paranoia. Fear and hypervigilance had made her find demons in the shadows. After everything that had happened to her last fall, she no longer trusted her ability to tell the difference between some guy checking her out and some guy who meant to hurt her. *I need to find a therapist*, she told herself. Lacey reached out to touch the base of the pink girly drink in front of her. An anchor. A reason for her to be sitting alone at the bar. Her shaking fingers encircled the delicate stem, and she lifted the glass for a sip.

Out of the corner of her eye, Lacey watched the man by the door take another step forward into the room. As his interest pulled her focus back over to him, he tipped his head as if asking her a question. The stranger's eyes didn't move from hers, even as he eased his shoulder against the wall, letting a boisterous girl-group push past him in a cloud of perfume and shiny fabrics.

The man was tall; his sports jacket looked tailored to his athletic body. He bunched his brow into a wrinkled knot as they looked at each other. His face might have been handsome in a rugged Marlboro-man kind of way in his earlier years, but now he was weathered and balding, and there was something vicious about the slash of his mouth and the way he held his shoulders.

Lacey stopped breathing. Vulnerability swept up from her stomach and stuck in her throat. She forced her eyes away from his and scanned the screen on her phone. No, Steve still hadn't texted with a reason for not showing or a time he'd arrive. She tapped the app to call a car. She glanced at scotch-on-the rocks guy, who dangled his glass from his fingertips in such a way as to hide his attention. But his gaze was firmly on her mouth. Lacey felt threats everywhere. She worked at being reasonable. She was a woman alone in a bar. Of course, she had attracted attention. Though neither of these men was giving off the usual bar signals – there was no hoping-for-a-hook-up vibe. These guys seemed a different kind of predatory. And she felt trapped. Panicked.

Lacey leaned into the bar. "Hey there, I think I'm going to take my check, please." She pushed her almost-full glass away from her to signal that she was finished.

As the bartender slid her tab into a leather folder and placed it in front of her, Lacey jerked her credit card from her phone case. She wished she could ask the manager to let her slip out the back door of the kitchen rather than make her skitter past the guy spooking her at the front. While she signed the bottom of the receipt, Lacey peeked past the long layers of her hair over to the man at the entrance. He was fishing in his pocket, then pulled something out.

Lacey jolted as a crack of thunder erupted violently, causing a wave of gasps and startled giggles from around the room. The lights flickered, and Lacey slid off her stool to leave. As her feet touched the ground, the doors crashed open, and a group of festively dressed couples surged in, laughing and shaking off the sudden rain. With the noise and commotion as a backdrop, the man made his move. In an instant, he towered in front of her, blocking Lacey's retreat.

"Danika?" he said quietly.

Even though the room was loud, Lacey could hear him clearly. When she heard that name, her joints solidified, and she couldn't move or speak. Her dark brown eyes, heavy with mascara, pulled wide as they filled with shock. Another clap of thunder worked its way across the sky; the sound held Lacey in place, sucking the oxygen from her lungs.

The man bent his head closer to her ear. "Danika, you're in danger." His last word became a sharp sucking sound as he arched backward. His fingers curled into the pewter satin of Lacey's blouse. He pulled her sideways, reeling to the left, hitting the floor first with his shoulder, then with his head, taking her with him.

Lacey tried to scramble up, to pull her skirt back down below her hips, to regain some decorum now that she had flashed the bar with her pink silk panties. But the stranger tightened his grip and locked her to him with a tight fist. "They know who you are. Trust no one. Run." His words bubbled out with red spittle, and the visual made Lacey's mind go numb. She worked hard at processing what was happening, but her brain snagged on the red froth at the corners of his lips, and she couldn't think past it.

As the man exhaled the word "run," he unwound his right hand from the fabric of her blouse. He shoved something cold and hard down into her bra. Lacey tried to pull free. She dropped her jaw to scream, but Lacey couldn't make any air pass by her vocal cords, so her mouth hung open and empty.

Someone gripped Lacey's upper arms, lifted her, questioned her, was she all right?

All right? Lacey stared down at the stranger, trying to process the fact that he had called her Danika. That he was there to warn her. And now, a red puddle pooled from under his shoulders.

The bartender rolled the man onto his stomach as the well-clad patrons fished out their phones. Lacey prayed that someone was calling 911. But the bright strobe of flashes meant that most were grabbing pictures to post on Instagram and Snapchat to show what dangerous and exciting lives they led. The flashing lights turned the scene into an impressionist's painting where the eye only took in and defined certain aspects, the outline of a leg, the hem of a skirt, the swirl of burgundy leaching across the floor.

Lacey pinned her focus on the knife handle protruding from the man's herringbone jacket. Someone had stabbed into his lungs, and now he was gasping like a trout lugged from the river. *That doesn't belong there*, was all Lacey's shocked mind could manage. She reached down and yanked the blade from the stranger's back. Blood dripped from the sharp edge. Lacey dropped the weapon to the ground in disgust. She held her hands wide and let the wine-colored droplets trickle from the webbing of her fingers.

Hands now pulled Lacey backward, away from the stranger's flailing legs. A linen napkin rubbed over her fingers. Lacey twisted to see over her shoulder where she found scotch-on-the-rocks guy.

"I'm so sorry," he said, dropping the napkin to the floor. "He's a good friend of yours?" His voice was kind and solicitous. With a solid grip, he moved Lacey away from the dying man, around the back of the fascinated crowd, and toward the front door.

It wasn't until she was propelled out of the bar and a shot of cold, wet air hit her face that Lacey registered the dying man's warning. "Trust no one. Run." She hadn't a clue what he could have meant. All she knew was that Scotch-on-the-rocks had tightened his grip and was herding her toward a black car with its back door gaping open.

Lacey set her high heels into the mortar of the rain-slicked brick sidewalk. She snaked her body and protested, but she made no progress in freeing herself. Without forethought, Lacey's knee slammed into the man's groin. He collapsed with a grunt. As he hit the ground, he stretched out a hand, shackling her ankle with an iron grasp. Lacey freaked.

She kicked at his face with her free foot, yelling for help. Swinging her head, she searched the crowd for a hero. She spotted two men clambering from the black sedan and knew she had seconds to get herself free. Lacey aimed her stiletto at her captor's chest. He blocked it with his free arm. Releasing her ankle, he reached into his jacket. Lacey felt sure he was going for a gun.

Her scream should have cut through the bar patrons' glee at tonight's horrific adventure, should have brought someone to her rescue. But the scream was masked by an EMS truck, speeding up the street, sirens wailing. Lacey reeled back into the bar and ran as fast as her high heels and tight skirt would allow, pushing people out of the way, clambering past chairs. She had to find another way out–a back exit–some way to escape.

Lacey burst out of the kitchen door, stumbling headlong into a pile of black trash bags lining the alleyway. The downpour stung her upturned face as headlights caught her in their abrupt illumination. Car doors popped open.

Pushing herself up—her shoes left behind—Lacey sprinted down the alley, down the road, down the Metro stairs, and into the late-evening crowd. Away from the men's angry shouting.

SOPPING WET AND GARBAGE STREAKED, Lacey slid behind a Metro System's construction curtain. She panted behind the yellow plastic fabric, replaying the scene of her alley escape from the second car of scary men.

Lacey was sure she had heard a man bark, "Secret Service." But the dead man had said, "Trust no one."

Was he dead? Lacey had never seen anyone blow blood bubbles before and couldn't imagine coming back from that. It was the stuff of horror flicks and midnight campfire stories – the kind of imagery that ruined sleep for nights, maybe even for years, to come. Lacey lifted her hands, crusty with flaked blood where she had squeezed her fists as she pumped her arms and fled. She rubbed her palms together in disbelief.

It was possible that the man was alive, she tried to reason. Surely someone had gotten to him with medical help in time. If he lived, Lacey would like to talk to him and find out what was going on. And while she wanted the information, she also never wanted to be near that guy again. Ever. But still. . . Lacey's head danced with questions like pointillist dots on a canvas, all blending together to paint a picture of absolute terror. Lacey was terrified. This was what the word meant. She had used the word so many times when it was just silly – rollercoasters and exam grades. Lacey pushed the strands of her damp hair back off her face and bit at her lip to stop its trembling.

Did the man really mean trust no one? Lacey sat on an over-turned bucket, propping her elbows on her knees and holding her head, trying hard to calm her shaking. Secret Service seemed like reasonable people to trust. Maybe the police? "They know who you are." Suddenly, Lacey wondered why scary people would know who she was. Her mind slipped to her great uncle, Bartholomew Winslow, who owned the art gallery she managed. He was hiding out at his home in Bali and wouldn't be coming back to the United States until things settled down – until the arrest warrant went away. Did this have something to do with him and his affiliation with the Assembly? She reached into her blouse to retrieve what the dying man had thrust into her bra.

A flash drive.

She sat there, staring at it.

Finish reading In Too DEEP by downloading your copy.

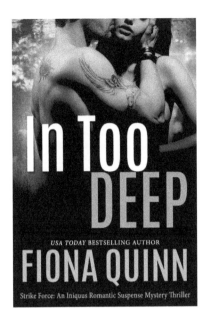

Turn the page to find a chronological list of the stories in the world of Iniquus.

THE WORLD of INIQUUS

Chronological Order

Ubicumque, Quoties. Quidquid

Weakest Lynx (Lynx Series)

Missing Lynx (Lynx Series)

Chain Lynx (Lynx Series)

Cuff Lynx (Lynx Series)

WASP (Uncommon Enemies)

In Too DEEP (Strike Force)

Relic (Uncommon Enemies)

Mine (Kate Hamilton Mystery)

Jack Be Quick (Strike Force)

Deadlock (Uncommon Enemies)

Instigator (Strike Force)

Yours (Kate Hamilton Mystery)

Gulf Lynx (Lynx Series)

Open Secret (FBI Joint Task Force)

Thorn (Uncommon Enemies)
Ours (Kate Hamilton Mysteries)
Cold Red (FBI Joint Task Force)
Even Odds (FBI Joint Task Force)
Survival Instinct - (Cerberus Tactical K9)
Protective Instinct - (Cerberus Tactical K9)
Defender's Instinct - (Cerberus Tactical K9)
Danger Signs - (Delta Force Echo)
Hyper Lynx - (Lynx Series)
Danger Zone - (Delta Force Echo)
Danger Close - (Delta Force Echo)
Fear the REAPER – (Strike Force)
Cerberus Tactical K9 Team Bravo

Coming soon, more great stories from the ex-special forces security team members who live, work, and love in a tightly knit family.

FOR MORE INFORMATION VISIT
WWW.FIONAQUINNBOOKS.COM

ACKNOWLEDGMENTS

My great appreciation ~

   To my editor, Kathleen Payne

   To my publicist, Margaret Daly

   To my cover artist, Melody Simmons

   To my Beta Force, who are always honest and kind at the same time, especially M. Carlon and E. Hordon

   To my Street Force, who support me and my writing with such enthusiasm. If you're interested in joining this group, please send me an email. **Hello@FionaQuinnBooks.com**

   Thank you to the real-world military and CIA who serve to protect us.

   To all the wonderful professionals whom I called on to get the details right. Please note: This is a work of fiction, and while I always try my best to get all the details correct, there are times when it serves the story to go slightly to the left or right of perfection. Please understand that any mistakes or discrepancies are my authorial decision making alone and sit squarely on my shoulders.

   Thank you to my family.

I send my love to my husband, and my great appreciation. T, you are my happily ever after. You are my encouragement and my adventure. Thank you.

And of course, thank *YOU* for reading my stories. I'm smiling joyfully as I type this. I so appreciate you!

ABOUT THE AUTHOR

Fiona Quinn is a six-time USA Today bestselling author, a Kindle Scout winner, and an Amazon All-Star.

Quinn writes action-adventure in her Iniquus World of books, including Lynx, Strike Force, Uncommon Enemies, Kate Hamilton Mysteries, FBI Joint Task Force, Cerberus Tactical K9, and Delta Force Echo series.

She writes urban fantasy as Fiona Angelica Quinn for her Elemental Witches Series.

And, just for fun, she writes the Badge Bunny Booze Mystery Collection with her dear friend, Tina Glasneck.

Quinn is rooted in the Old Dominion, where she lives with her husband. There, she pops chocolates, devours books, and taps continuously on her laptop.

Visit www.FionaQuinnBooks.com

©2017 Fiona Quinn
All Rights Reserved
ISBN: 978-1-946661-29-6
Chesterfield, VA
Library of Congress Control Number: 2021912623

Cover Design by Melody Simmons from eBookindlecovers
Fonts with permission from Microsoft
Publisher's Note:

Lightning Source UK Ltd.
Milton Keynes UK
UKHW042046101122
412007UK00004B/22

9 781946 661296